DEATH
OF A PATRIOT

DEATH
OF A PATRIOT

A Novel
by
R. E. Harrington

G. P. Putnam's Sons
New York

First American Edition

Copyright © 1979 by R. E. Harrington

Library of Congress Cataloging in Publication Data

Harrington, R. E.
    Death of a patriot.

    I. Title.
PZ4.H31115De   1979   [PS3558.A6295]   813'.5'4   78-27809
ISBN 0-399-12187-0

Printed in the United States of America

For My Parents

PROLOGUE

Vernon Dooley sat hunched in the chair like an old man. Halladay stared impassively across his desk at him. Dooley lit a cigarette and was racked with a cough.

"You should cut out those cigarettes, Vern," Halladay said.

Dooley wiped his mouth with a handkerchief. He hadn't yet been able to bring himself to look at Halladay sitting behind the desk that only a few days before had been his own.

"How was your weekend?" Halladay asked.

"Two days with interrogation is always fun," Dooley replied. His eyes were still dilated from the drugs he'd been given.

"I thought we should discuss your future."

"I'm surprised you think I have one."

"Not with the CIA, perhaps." Halladay smiled. "You're barred from government employment for life."

Dooley didn't reply. He stared at his hands clasped in his lap.

Halladay picked up a file folder from the desk. "We thought it would be a nice touch if you closed the file—signed the reports, identified the body—"

Dooley raised his eyes to Halladay's face. "What?"

"He had no living relatives. He worked for you. We thought you might like to wrap up the case as your last official act."

Dooley's face was rigid with anger. He leaned forward in his chair and stared at Halladay. "Do I have to tell you what you can do with your file?"

Halladay's eyes were cold. "I'll let you tell that to interrogation."

Dooley continued to stare at Halladay for a moment and then slumped back in the chair. He shielded his eyes with a hand. "Where is he?"

"He's here—in the morgue." Halladay opened the folder. "This should amuse you. It's been decided that he will be a hero. Posthumous citation in the file."

Dooley didn't look up. "You don't miss a trick, do you?"

"I wish I'd thought of it, but the idea came from the top. It was decided he'd be given credit for the capture of Clawson and Fisher. You know the form. Two dangerous Russian agents. Our hero giving his life for his country."

"And if I sign the reports, everyone's off the hook in case that little scenario collapses."

Halladay shrugged. "I didn't get you into this situation, Vern. You did it to yourself."

Dooley got to his feet. His posture was erect. Years seemed to fall away from him. He leaned on his fists on the desk. "I'll do it. And it won't bother me a goddamn bit."

Halladay smiled. "Good for you."

Dooley stared into Halladay's eyes. "Years ago I should have sent you on a one-way assignment."

Halladay's smile broadened. "Your mistake, Vern."

* * *

8

Dooley went to a vacant office to complete the forms in the file. As he opened the folder, the name Peevey seemed to leap off the page at him. Dooley stared at the page. *Horace Peevey.* Dooley hit the desk with his fist. That old fool! Dooley massaged his forehead. If he hadn't decided to have Peevey put away, none of this would've happened. He would have still been head of the branch. If he had just not let his compulsion to cover every detail, to think of every eventuality, carry him away. If. If. Dooley shuddered in self-disgust and picked up a pen.

After he had completed the forms, Dooley got a fingerprint kit from the identification section and went down to the morgue. He presented his authorization to the white-coated attendant in the anteroom. The man led Dooley into the vault area. The room was cold and smelled of formaldehyde. The attendant ran his finger down a tier of vaults. He pressed a black button beside one of the doors. The door slid down, and a slab shot silently into the room. On it was a naked body.

"There you are," the attendant said. "Thomas Hobbes."

Dooley bent over the body.

ONE

Thomas Hobbes had the girl under surveillance the day they took Commander Peevey away. He had been following her for the entire weekend, since he had discovered her at the Washington Downtown Athletic Club.

He'd been sitting on the lower terrace of the club on a sweltering Saturday morning, drinking Pernod and coffee. He was at a table near the stone balustrade overlooking Pennsylvania Avenue and the campus of George Washington University across the way. He was idly watching the weekend athletes—the tennis players, the handball players, the squash players—limp onto the terrace after their games, their faces glowing with a false light of health. They had towels around their necks, their badges of fraternity, and they swaggered a little to hide their limping. They took tables, and laughed and ordered drinks, and wiped the sweat from their faces with their towels.

Thomas Hobbes had joined the Downtown Athletic Club when he first came to Washington. He didn't play the games the club offered. He joined because he liked to belong to clubs. He liked the opportunity they afforded to sit quietly and watch. He liked to carry the membership cards in the calfskin pocket secretary in his hip pocket. He also belonged to the Helix Drinking Club, a group that met on Friday nights to drink and debate Great Issues; the South Side Duplicate Bridge Club; The Society of Federal Employees; and the Compatible Singles Club, which held dances. He didn't debate, play bridge or dance. He sat and watched. No one had ever approached him at a club and asked him why he didn't participate. As far as he could tell, no one had ever noticed him. Sometimes, when he was alone in his room at the Lincoln Hotel late at night, he would take the calfskin secretary from its nighttime drawer and run his finger down the membership cards in their leather slots. He did it the way some men counted their money.

He recognized her the moment she came onto the terrace. He felt the chill in his spine that always told him before his brain had time to register it that he had a surveillance coming up. She was with an older woman, and they both were dressed for the street. She had a flowing, loose walk that she had the habit of punctuating at times with a toss of her head. She reminded Hobbes of a free-spirited animal—a young colt or perhaps a deer—yet at the same time the movements were uniquely her own.

The women sat at a table and ordered drinks. He watched them casually, so it would appear his interest was general and indifferent.

The women finished their drinks and signaled for the check. Hobbes removed his calfskin wallet, took bills from it, and dropped them on the table. The women were making their way through the tables toward the street exit. When Hobbes came out onto the street, they were at the corner waiting for the light to change. Hobbes stood beside them and studied the girl from the corners of his eyes. She had thick dark hair. Her profile was finely mod-

12

eled, her forehead high, her nose straight and rather long for the rest of her face. As he watched her, he could see the faint beat of her pulse in the delicate flesh of her temple.

The women walked north. Hobbes followed half a block behind. He enjoyed watching the girl walk with her fluid rhythm. He enjoyed seeing her toss her head in that free way she had. For the first time on a surveillance he felt a strange sense of regret at what he was doing.

By the time he had gone three blocks Hobbes' back and armpits were seething with sweat. He took off his gray raincoat and carried it across his arm. He took a handkerchief from his pocket and mopped his neck with it. The women walked for more than a mile and then entered the Washington Zoological Gardens. He discovered them near the entrance buying soft drinks from a vendor's cart. After they had strolled on, he bought a drink and followed. They went to the monkey island and fed peanuts to the monkeys. He sat on a bench and watched. The girl's laugh was low in her throat, and when he heard it, it made Hobbes' face feel flushed. He followed them to the cages of the big cats, where lions lolled on the ledges cut from the native stone, their yellow eyes burning with cunning. He followed them through the aviary. He sat several tables away and ate a hot dog while the women had lunch at an outdoor concession. After lunch they left the gardens, caught a cab, and Hobbes caught one right behind them. He showed the driver his CIA card and told him to follow the women's cab.

They stopped in front of a condominium apartment complex in Georgetown. Hobbes had his driver stop a block back. The girl got out of the cab alone and waved as it drove away. Hobbes paid his driver and walked past the apartments. He saw the girl unlocking the door of an apartment.

After she went in her apartment, Hobbes made a reconnaissance of the buildings. The condominiums were

13

made of wood and glass cubes stacked together in a studied randomness. In their center was a small courtyard. Her apartment was accessible from a ramp that led up from the courtyard to a small porch at the front door. Opposite was another ramp that led to a walled-off area of garbage containers at the rear of the buildings. He carefully noted the layout and then went home.

The next morning, the Sunday they came and took Commander Peevey away, Hobbes was up early and across the street when the girl came out of her apartment. He followed her to church. After services he followed her to a small, fragrant park. It was eleven o'clock when they entered the park. At that very moment, although of course, Hobbes didn't know it then, they had come to take Commander Peevey away. The girl sat on a bench in the park and opened a book. Hobbes found a bench further down. He took out his notebook. At that very moment, as Hobbes would later reconstruct events in his mind, they were subduing Commander Peevey. Hobbes imagined in the reconstruction that there were three of them: two in white uniforms, with short sleeves showing their muscled smooth arms and a man in a suit with a black medical bag. The struggle, Hobbes knew, would have been fierce. Commander Peevey was old; but he was also very large, and fear and desperation would have returned to him the strength of his younger days. Later that day, as Hobbes stood in Commander Peevey's shabby empty room, he saw vividly the old man's arms flailing at the smooth-muscled young men. He saw one of them catch the old man from behind and pin him around the chest. He saw the other young man with an armlock on Commander Peevey, exposing the shrunken veins behind his elbow to the needle of the man in the suit. He imagined for a moment that the smell of the alcohol used to disinfect the needle puncture lingered in the room.

But while this was going on, Hobbes sat in the park and

looked at the girl. He made many notes about her. He even tried to sketch her in his notebook; but his drawing abilities were poor, and he wadded up the sketch and dropped it into a trash container. Normally he would've been bored. He liked his subjects to move around, so he could feel the excitement of going to unknown destinations. But watching the girl in repose had a strangely calming effect on him.

The girl closed the book, stood, and walked from the park. Hobbes followed her back to her apartment. He loitered on the street outside the building, reluctant to leave. Finally, he went through the small courtyard and up the service ramp. He found that by standing at the rear of the ramp, he could see the window of her living room without being observed. The drapes were open, and he could see her moving about in the living room. Later, in his reconstruction, he would think that this was the time that the ambulance arrived with Commander Peevey. He would imagine the two men in white uniforms unloading the stretcher from the back of the ambulance. He would see in his mind Commander Peevey's great white head rolling from side to side as they lifted the stretcher and put it down on the drive. He would see the two men stooping over, one at each end of the stretcher, as they moved it through glass doors into a reception area while the man in the suit walked beside it, carrying his medical bag.

The girl disappeared from the living room. Hobbes waited for nearly an hour for her to reappear. Then a tall man in a light tan suit walked through the courtyard. The man had crisp black hair that curled over his brow. He was deeply tanned and walked with an air of animal self-assurance. Hobbes knew him.

Hobbes drew back against the wall and watched the man go up the ramp and stop in front of the girl's door. The door opened, and he went in. For a long moment nothing happened. Then, with an abruptness that star-

15

tled Hobbes, the drapes in the living room were closed. A strip of glass not more than a foot wide remained exposed. Through it, the man's back appeared. He was naked. He held out his arms. Slim white arms encircled the man's waist. The girl's face appeared over his shoulder. Her eyes were closed, her mouth moist and parted. Hobbes went down the ramp, through the courtyard, and out onto the street. He found he still had his note pad open in one hand, and he stared uncomprehendingly at his handwriting for a moment. Then he put the note pad away and went home to the Lincoln Hotel.

TWO

When Thomas Hobbes returned late that afternoon to the Lincoln Hotel, he found Sophie Crump, the manager of the hotel, in the lobby. Sophie told Hobbes Commander Peevey had been taken away to the Veteran's Hospital. She took Hobbes to see Peevey's room, as though she expected him to provide some explanation for what had happened. But the room looked as it always had: The lumpy, overstuffed chair placed by the window so Peevey could get the east light in the morning to read his *New Yorker;* the high bed with the sheet of plywood between mattress and springs for the sake of his arthritic back; the oak highboy in the corner with the huge old Peevey family Bible resting on top. The closet was empty, the suitcase that had been on its shelf gone. Thomas Hobbes stood in the room and imagined what had happened there a few hours before. It was then that he imagined he detected the lingering smell of alcohol.

Sophie Crump squeezed the ends of her gnarled fingers and peered up at Hobbes. Sophie was seventy-six years old. She had been manager of the Lincoln Hotel for twelve years. Her pay consisted of a free room behind the desk in the lobby. She received a widow's pension of one hundred and twenty-five dollars a month from Social Security. That was all she had. Dr. Marshall, the retired chiropractor who lived in 3ll, said that Sophie Crump was undernourished. He said a lot of old people were starving in this land of plenty. That was the way Dr. Marshall talked. He was seventy-eight and skinny as a reed himself.

Thomas Hobbes told Sophie he would see what he could find out about Commander Peevey on Monday. Sophie locked the door after them with trembling fingers.

Hobbes went to his room. He hung his gray raincoat in his closet. He removed his shoes and sat on his bed with his shoulders propped against the headboard. He opened a drawer in the bedside table that supported a lamp with a blue shade and, between plain metal bookends, his collection of paperback suspense novels. He took from the drawer a pack of Rothman cigarettes and a gold Dunhill lighter. He lit a cigarette and thought about Peevey.

Two years before, when Hobbes had first come to Washington to work for the CIA, Peevey had met him at the airport. Hobbes immediately picked him out of a crowd waiting for passengers disembarking from the flight from California. Hobbes' father had often described to him Peevey's massive size and commanding presence, the white head thrust above the crowd on broad shoulders could have belonged to no other.

Although already in his seventies, Peevey had only recently retired from the CIA when Hobbes came to Washington, having stayed on past the mandatory age through the influence of powerful old friends on Capitol Hill.

Peevey's blue eyes stared piercingly at Hobbes from the moment he first took Hobbes' hand in the airport waiting room through the taxi ride to downtown Washington. Finally even Hobbes' ingrained diffidence couldn't prevent his asking the reason for the strange look.

"Sorry," Peevey rumbled. "But dammit, you bear a remarkable resemblance to a man who works for me. Or," he corrected himself, "did work for me." He paused and added, "I'm retired," choking on the last word as though it had stuck sideways in his throat.

It gave Hobbes an unexpected odd feeling of displacement to think about the man who resembled him, as though the new beginning he had imagined for himself at Langley had somehow been preempted. But Peevey didn't mention the man again, and the looks stopped, and by the time the cab arrived in front of the Lincoln Hotel the strange feeling had dissipated.

Peevey had reserved a room at the hotel for Hobbes, expecting it would be a temporary arrangement while Hobbes looked for permanent quarters more suitable for a man of twenty-seven. Peevey himself had moved to the Lincoln a few months before retiring. It was a residential hotel, in a run-down neighborhood of Southeast Washington, populated exclusively by old people living on pensions. Peevey had moved there in anticipation of retirement because the hotel was conveniently situated and the rent was cheap and included maid service.

Peevey saw Hobbes settled in his room and then stood at the door and cleared his throat. "I was sorry to hear about your father."

"Yes," Hobbes said.

"Vince was one of the best who ever drew pay at Langley," Peevey said.

Hobbes nodded, embarrassed. "I—I didn't get there in time. He was gone when I got there. I was at school—"

"I remember," Peevey continued, as though Hobbes hadn't spoken. "It was in the fifties. Vince and I were in Tokyo when that Red pilot defected with a MIG. We were assigned to interrogate the pilot in a safe house in

19

the country. Vince spoke Chinese like a native—four or five dialects. A couple of North Korean thugs tried to blast the pilot out of the safe house. It was a hell of a row. Vince was magnificent. Saved my life—"

Hobbes had heard the story many times. He stood awkwardly, not knowing what to say. But Peevey was in another place, his eyes unfocused and staring beyond the room into a bullet-riddled house in the past. He brought himself back with a visible effort. "You need anything," he said, "you let me know." Hobbes mumbled his thanks.

"It's a damn fine thing to see Vince's son carrying on," Peevey said. "I know he'd be pleased."

Through a kind of attrition of will Hobbes had ended up staying on at the Lincoln Hotel. For four days he was administered a battery of tests at Langley to determine what job his aptitudes suited him for. He returned to the hotel each night too emotionally drained to think about finding another place to live. By the time the test results were evaluated and he'd been assigned a job he was too depressed to move on, so he stayed.

While the tests were going on, Peevey seemed as anxious about the results as Hobbes was. "Give 'em what they want," he advised. "Be tough! Remember—you're Vincent Hobbes' son."

The day Hobbes got his job assignment Peevey was waiting when he returned to the hotel. "Well?" Peevey demanded, chewing on a cigar, his red-rimmed eyes glaring. "Did you get Operations Branch?"

Hobbes avoided his gaze. "Something like that."

Peevey winked broadly. "I get it!" He slapped Hobbes on the shoulder. "I know how it works. You can't tell me." He chuckled heartily. "But congratulations anyway." Hobbes gave him a pale smile.

After weeks had passed, Peevey asked, "Isn't your training over?"

"It's over."

"Damn," Peevey fumed. "I thought they'd be giving you a field assignment, Vincent Hobbes' son, and all."

"I—I'm going to be doing some things at Langley for a while."

"Well," Peevey had said gruffly, "don't be too disappointed. The field can come later. Langley's where the power is. Keep your eyes and ears open. They're probably saving you for a special assignment." And he'd grinned and added in a husky whisper, "At least you're in the right branch, eh?"

Now a rhomboid of afternoon sunlight slanted through the window beside his bed and grazed Hobbes' leg. He blew smoke into the light and studied its gray swirls while he thought of Peevey's words to him nearly two years before: "saving you for a special assignment."

Hobbes let out a short, bitter laugh. He stubbed out the cigarette in an ashtray, stood, and went to a cheap foot locker in a corner under a shelf that held his hot plate. He knelt on the floor, took a ring of keys from his pocket, unlocked a brass padlock, and raised the lid of the locker. On a tray at one end of the locker was a row of manila folders labeled in Hobbes' neat printing with names and dates. At the other end of the locker was a packet of letters bound by a rubber band and a gun, wrapped in a chamois cloth, that had belonged to Hobbes' father.

The gun and the letters rested on a plastic clothes bag that covered the bottom of the locker and that contained the dress uniform of an army colonel. This, too, had belonged to Hobbes' father. Before his illustrious work as a CIA agent, Vincent Hobbes had had a famous career in the army.

Hobbes removed a sheet of paper from one of the manila folders. It was a photocopy of an article from the Washington *Post*. Dr. Marshall, the retired chiropractor, had given the article to Hobbes months before. He had cau-

21

tioned Hobbes not to mention it to Peevey, who didn't like to talk about his naval career.

The article was one of a series about World War II heroes and what had happened to them since. It contained a short biography of Peevey: He'd graduated from Annapolis in 1925; married a Grace Hotchkiss in 1931 and she had died in 1953; they had had no children; Peevey had retired from the navy after his wife's death and gone with the CIA.

During the war Peevey had gained the distinction of being reprimanded and decorated for the same action. At the Battle of Savo Island in the Pacific Peevey had been in command of a destroyer. The Japanese had bottled up the American ships in a bay and battered them with murderous salvos. Peevey had been ordered to flee with his ship for the open sea. Instead, he had made a run on the nearest Japanese cruiser and, with the aid of an American submarine, had sunk it. He was wounded. After the battle he was given the Navy Cross and a reprimand for disobeying orders. The article said nothing of his CIA career, but Hobbes knew from his father that it had been distinguished. Hobbes put the article back in its folder and sighed. He remembered Sophie Crump's face as she had shown him Peevey's empty room, the beseeching look that seemed to say that Hobbes held all the answers and had the power to restore Peevey to his rightful place. Hobbes, the mysterious agent of the government with hidden strings to pull, seedy little bureaucrats at his beck to manipulate. Hobbes gave another bitter laugh of self-disgust.

He opened his notebook and tore out the notes he had made over the past two days while he had followed the girl. He selected an unused folder, printed "Victoria Prentice" and the dates he had followed her on it, and dropped the notes into the folder. He sat back on his heels, the folder in his hand, and stared at the name as if he had never heard or seen it before. Then another name came creeping from somewhere in his mind and wiped away the strange feeling. *Darrin Semple.*

Hobbes put the folder in with the others. He riffled them idly with his thumb, calculating all the hours he had spent in the past months on surveillances. He picked up the packet of letters and weighed them in his hand. He didn't need to open them to remember what they said. They were all from his father, received while Hobbes had been away at college in California and his father had been living quietly on a little acreage in Wyoming, unaware that certain cells in his pancreas were already going crazy. The last letter had been written only a few months before Hobbes came to Washington. It had brought the news that Vincent Hobbes had pulled strings and got him a job after graduation with the CIA. Hobbes knew it made up in some large degree for the disappointment his father had felt when Hobbes hadn't got the appointment to West Point.

Hobbes' mother had died of a brain tumor when he was only three. In one of the file folders was a yellowed clipping, powdery with age, that was her obituary. Even though his father had given him the clipping when he was seven, Hobbes was nevertheless haunted for a long period in his teens with the irrational thought that his father might have violently murdered his mother. During that time he had a recurring dream in which his father hacked the woman in the faded newspaper photo to death with a hatchet. In the dream his father's face wore a maniacal, twisted expression that Hobbes had never seen on it in life. In his last letter, only a week before he died so swiftly, Hobbes' father had said that he knew his son would distinguish himself in the service of his country. The phrase stuck in Hobbes' mind. Kneeling now on the worn carpet, holding the letters in his hand, he wondered if his father had ever held any expectation of his only child that had been fulfilled. Hobbes tried to remember one thing, anything. He couldn't.

23

THREE

When Hobbes awoke one Monday morning, it was raining. Gusts of wind drummed large drops against the windows. There was a dark, close smell in the room.

He showered and shaved and ate a package of dried apricots. He dressed in the cleaner of his two gray suits. He put on a dark blue tie. He put on the gray raincoat and buttoned it to his chin.

Dr. Marshall and Sophie Crump were in the lobby when Hobbes got out of the elevator. Dr. Marshall stood behind Sophie Crump's chair, his muscular hands working on her neck and shoulders. Sophie's eyes were closed, and there was a furrow of pleasure in her forehead. Dr. Marshall stopped working on Sophie when he saw Hobbes.

"You'll see him today, Mr. Hobbes?" Dr. Marshall asked, peering up at Hobbes.

"I'll try," Hobbes said. "I'll run over on my lunch hour."

"Good," Dr. Marshall replied.

24

Sophie put her hand on Hobbes' arm. It felt like a bird's claw, trembling and of no substance. "Get him out of there," she said.

"Now, Mrs. Crump," Dr. Marshall said. "We mustn't expect miracles of Mr. Hobbes."

"I'll do what I can," Hobbes said.

"I'm sure you will," Dr. Marshall said soothingly.

Hobbes continued across the lobby to the door. "Get him out of there," Mrs. Crump called after him.

Outside, the wind drove the rain against him. He ran the block to the garage where he kept his car. His car was an old Lincoln, one of the four-door convertibles no longer manufactured. The top was frayed, the upholstery worn and split at the seams, and the maroon paint faded.

Hobbes got the car onto the Southwest Freeway and stayed in the right lane, droning along at fifty. The muffler made a throaty rumble that soothed him. He crossed the Potomac and got onto the Memorial Parkway, still holding at fifty. The rain pounded a gray mist out of the pavement that made the taillights of the cars ahead glow eerily. Hobbes took the pack of Rothmans from his raincoat pocket and lit one with the gold lighter. Sophie Crump's words lingered in him like an aftertaste: "Get him out of there."

The day before, Sunday, Hobbes had fallen into numbing lassitude. He tried to read the Washington *Post* that was delivered to his door each day, but he couldn't concentrate. He dressed and went down to the lobby. Most of the residents of the hotel were there. The television was on. The Washington Redskins were playing the Dallas Cowboys. A feeble cheer went up from the group around the TV as Hobbes entered the lobby. The Redskins had scored a field goal. Across the lobby Mrs. Crump, Dr. Marshall and old Mr. Darling sat at a spindly card table playing dominoes. Mr. Darling was a wizened little man in his eighties with a large, doughy nose separating black, raisin eyes. He had been born in the hills of Kentucky,

25

and his high, piercing voice still carried vestigial accents of his origins. Hobbes always saved his newspaper for Mr. Darling, who could make a day's occupation out of the Sunday edition.

Dr. Marshall rose and waved Hobbes over to the empty chair at the table. Hobbes handed his Washington *Post* to Mr. Darling and sat down. Mr. Darling examined the paper disapprovingly and began meticulously refolding the pages Hobbes had opened.

"Mr. Hobbes," Dr. Marshall said, "do you play dominoes?"

"No."

"Too bad. With Commander Peevey gone we can't play partners."

"Racehorse is best anyhow," Mr. Darling piped without looking up from his paper folding.

"You're not working tonight?" Dr. Marshall asked solicitously.

"No."

"Well, it's about time," Sophie Crump said. "I can't think what the government's come to, making a young man work all weekend."

"What is it you do on weekends anyhow?" Mr. Darling asked.

"Now, Mr. Darling," Dr. Marshall said reprovingly, "you know Mr. Hobbes' work is confidential."

"I don't mind," Hobbes replied. His weariness was having a strange effect. He felt he would answer anything anyone asked him. "I've been doing surveillances."

"Surveillances?" Dr. Marshall said. "You mean watching people?"

"Yes."

"My," Sophie Crump said.

Mr. Darling put the paper in his lap and stared at Hobbes. "Who you been watching? Spies?"

"No. Just random people."

"Random people?" Dr. Marshall said.

26

"People who interest me."

Dr. Marshall frowned. "The CIA assigns you to watch people who interest you?"

"My Jesus," Sophie Crump said. "But that's stupid. Making a young man waste his weekends that way. Get yourself a girlfriend. You got a girlfriend?"

"The CIA doesn't know about it," Hobbes said.

"I get it," Dr. Marshall said brightly. "Keeping your hand in, eh?"

Hobbes stared at his hands resting on his knees and shook his head. "No. I'm a personnel analyst. Kind of a glorified clerk. I'm not a spy at all."

"I don't get it," Mr. Darling said combatively. "Why're you wasting your time following people around? That's weird."

"Now, now," Dr. Marshall admonished Mr. Darling.

"I make notes," Hobbes said weakly. "I—I'm interested in people."

"Nothing wrong with that," Dr. Marshall said heartily. "Someday you can write a book, eh?"

"I've given it up," Hobbes said.

"Just as well," Sophie Crump said adamantly. "Young fellow like you. Get a girlfriend."

Dr. Marshall put a hand on Hobbes' shoulder. "Look. Why don't we teach you dominoes?"

Hobbes nodded.

Dr. Marshall began to shuffle the dominoes with his big white hands.

"I still say it's weird," Mr. Darling muttered.

A muffled groan went up from the television watchers. Dallas had recovered a Redskins fumble.

Hobbes parked the Lincoln in the general lot at Langley and ran through the rain to his building. The guard gave a bored look at Hobbes' plastic ID card, then at his face, and pushed the lever that opened the bulletproof glass door. Hobbes stepped into the tiled lobby and shook the

27

water from his raincoat. A stream of people passed through the lobby, going to work. No one noticed Hobbes.

He unlocked the door of his small office and went in. It was a windowless cubicle. The walls were painted pale green. A gray metal desk stood in the center of the vinyl tile floor. A gray filing cabinet with combination locks on its drawers stood against one wall. Beside it was a small table that held Hobbes' electric pot, his paraphernalia for tea, and a delicate porcelain teacup and saucer with red birds glazed into their surfaces.

He hung his raincoat on the coat-tree behind his desk, went to the table, and plugged in the water. He rubbed his hands over the pot for a moment and shuddered. It was always too cold or too hot in his office.

He sat at his desk, opened the bottom drawer, and took out the stack of file folders he'd been working on when he'd left work Friday. Hobbes worked in the Psychological Branch. He was in the personnel section. He was a personnel analyst, and his supervisor was Winifred Simpson, a small, sparrowlike woman in her forties. Hobbes had been assigned to his job because he had a degree in sociology, and they had to put him somewhere after he had failed to qualify as an agent of the Operations Branch. Hobbes had a private office not because of the importance of his position, but because of the sensitive nature of the papers he handled.

Hobbes stacked the file folders on his desk and took a coding sheet from the middle drawer. His job was simple. The CIA was automating certain personnel records. Hobbes' job was to go through the files and code them on data sheets. The data sheets were then punched into cards. The cards were read into the computer, and the computer stored the information on its random-access magnetic discs. That was the extent of Hobbes' knowledge of his job. He'd been doing it for more than a year, ever since he had got out of the training program. Hobbes had grown to like the job. At first he had thought he would be bored. But that was before he began to read the files. In the beginning, he simply went through the files, picking out the data for coding, without letting his mind register what he was reading. Then one day he read a file. Each file contained photographs of the employee, as well as vital statistics. But what fascinated Hobbes was the history in each file, a kind of narrative written in bureaucratese of everything the CIA knew about an employee. And it knew a lot. It went to a great deal of trouble to know a lot. It knew about schools and grades. It knew about arrests. It knew rumors of indiscretions. It knew political leanings and activities. It knew about divorces and what had caused them.

It also kept a record of each employee's work history. A lot of this was dull stuff: secretaries and clerks; security guards and cafeteria employees. But once in a while Hobbes would get a file for someone whose classification was Field Operative. Some of these read like novels. Bribes, acquisition of state secrets from foreign countries, political manipulations—all these had come across Hobbes' desk in innocent-looking personnel folders.

When Hobbes started reading the folders, the number of files he processed dropped dramatically. That worried him. He worked through his lunch hour to make it up. Then he stopped working through his lunch hour, and no one said anything. He came to realize that no one was actually checking on the number of folders he processed. Winifred Simpson, his supervisor, stopped by occasionally and asked him if he had any problems. He always said no. Her nervous eyes would scan his office, and then she would leave.

Hobbes rose and prepared his tea. He took the cup to his desk and began to read the first file of the day. It was a disappointment: a cipher clerk in the Western European section of the Strategic Analysis Branch. The man had a pallid background and an even duller work history.

29

Hobbes coded the file quickly and picked up the next file. It was more interesting. A secretary in the office of the Deputy Director. Her picture showed a thin-faced woman with short-cropped pale hair in her late twenties. She had gone through a messy divorce when she was twenty-five. She was living with a lawyer with radical political connections. Hobbes was deep into the account of some rather eccentric political meetings the woman had attended since she started living with the lawyer when he became aware that he was no longer alone. He looked up to find Winifred Simpson standing before him, puffing nervously on a cigarette, her eyes darting at his face.

He leaped to his feet.

"Please—" Winifred Simpson waved him back in his chair. "May I sit?"

"Of course."

She sat on the only other chair in the room opposite Hobbes' desk. This was the first time in his memory that his supervisor had ever sat down in his office. She seemed more nervous than usual, her head making birdlike movements as she looked around the small cubicle.

"How are things going?" she asked.

"Fine."

"You've been coding files for what? A year now?"

"Over a year."

"Yes." She tapped ashes from her cigarette into the glass ashtray on Hobbes' desk. "Pretty boring work."

"I don't mind."

"Well, I appreciate your attitude. The other analysts hate coding and are always scheming ways out of it."

"It's not so bad, really."

"Nevertheless, Mr. Thomas, I want you to know I appreciate it."

"Hobbes. Thomas Hobbes."

She flushed. "Of course. I meant Mr. Hobbes." She brushed a hand over her temple. "This has been a busy morning for me."

30

"It's all right."

"Do you know Vernon Dooley, Mr. Hobbes?"

"No. I mean, I know who he is, of course." Vernon Dooley was the chief of the Operations Branch.

"Yes." She tapped the ash off her cigarette again, although there was little there. "Mr. Dooley needs some work done. I thought perhaps you would like to take it on as—" she waved a hand at the files on Hobbes' desk—"as a relief from this."

"Ah—what kind of work?"

"Oh, nothing you couldn't handle. A file search. Since you are probably more familiar with the personnel files than anyone in the section, I immediately thought of you. And then of course, I wanted to give you a little relief from all this coding."

"Really, Mrs. Simpson, I rather enjoy it."

"How could—" She stopped herself and puffed on the cigarette. "Mr. Dooley is very—ah—demanding. Don't misunderstand me—he has every right to be, with his responsibilities. I'm very grateful we have men like Mr. Dooley."

Hobbes took a cigarette from the pack that lay on his desk and lit it.

Mrs. Simpson looked at the cigarette pack. "I don't believe I've seen that brand."

Hobbes held the pack out to her. "Would you like to try one?"

"No, I'm fine. Now, Mr. Hobbes, what I'm getting at is that I believe you would work very well on this project. Mr. Dooley likes his people to obey orders."

"And not ask questions?"

"Exactly. And on an assignment like this, to be—ah— well, unobtrusive."

"I can see why you selected me."

Mrs. Simpson started to smile and then thought better of it. "May I tell Mr. Dooley I've found his man?"

"Can you tell me a little more about the assignment?"

31

"I've told you all I know. It will be classified work, of course. Need to Know. I don't need to know," she added matter-of-factly.

"How long?"

"Not long. A few weeks." She rose. "All settled then?" Hobbes nodded.

She paused at the door. "I'll be around after lunch to take you to Mr. Dooley." And then she was gone.

Hobbes picked up his cup. The tea was cold, and his hand trembled. When he had failed to qualify for the Operations Branch, he had resigned himself to the prospect of being a clerk, perhaps eventually working his way into a supervisory position such as the one Winifred Simpson held. But now he was going to work in the Operations Branch, even if it was only more clerical work, even if it was temporary. Somehow it corrected in some small but significant way the lie he had lived at the Lincoln Hotel, the wrong inferences he had allowed Peevey and the others to make, the fantasy life of his surveillances. Not only that, but he was to work for Vernon Dooley himself, a mysterious, half-mythical figure to Hobbes—a man he had only heard spoken of in whispered awe. *Superspook,* Darrin Semple called Dooley. Hobbes reviewed all this in his mind and then asked himself why the prospect didn't please him more. And the answer came immediately. He was *scared.*

Hobbes lit another cigarette with the gold Dunhill, unusual for him since he normally smoked at most five cigarettes a day. But then, he reflected, unusual things seemed to be happening to him in the past few days. First his decision to give up surveillances. Then the discovery that they had taken Commander Peevey away. His blurting out about the surveillances on Sunday at the domino table. Even the fact that he had stayed in the hotel playing dominoes until late in the evening. The Compatibles Singles Club had given a dance Sunday afternoon, and he hadn't gone—the first one he'd missed since joining the club two years ago. Now this assignment that not even his supervisor knew much about.

Hobbes pushed the files aside, leaned back in his chair, and smoked his cigarette. Impulsively he put his feet up on his desk, something he'd never done before. He thought of Winifred Simpson. She was a nervous little woman, and it made him nervous to be around her. But she had a ripe body, and he was mildly surprised that he'd noticed that. He wondered if she were married. He wondered about her sex life. He wondered what it would be like to hold her naked in his arms. He let his feet crash to the floor, rose, and began to pace his office. It was obvious why Winifred Simpson had chosen him for Vernon Dooley's assignment. Dooley wanted a robot. An intelligent drone. He fitted the description. Mr. Thomas! He laughed bitterly and lit another cigarette from the butt of the old one. He paced. He felt the sudden need for a strong drink, although he drank little. If the person you worked for for nearly two years couldn't even remember your name, what did that mean? Something. Something that made him want to smoke and drink and make love to Winifred Simpson.

FOUR

At eleven thirty Darrin Semple thrust his head into Hobbes' office. "Lunch?"

Hobbes couldn't look at Semple's tanned face. He shuffled the files on his desk. "I have to run an errand."

Semple came into the office and perched a slender hip on Hobbes' desk. "You seem distracted, Tommy. Did you flush something at the Compatibles Singles Club?"

Hobbes reddened and dropped his head lower over the desk, pretending to search for something among the files.

"C'mon," Semple said. "You can tell Darrin. Did you get your clock cleaned last night?"

Hobbes' eye fell on Semple's hip, elegantly sheathed in blue wool slacks. The image of that hip, starkly white against the tan of leg and back, flamed in Hobbes' mind. He staggered to his feet and went to the teapot.

Semple stood and stretched. He grinned, his white teeth flashing. "*I* had some weekend, I'll tell you. Little Vickie Prentice just can't get enough of this magnificent body."

34

Hobbes' hand knocked against the tin box he kept his tea bags in, sending them spilling across the floor.

"Hey!" Semple said. "What the hell's the matter with you? You act like you're about to crawl out of your skin."

"I'm awfully busy, Darrin," Hobbes said, on his knees gathering up tea bags.

Semple squatted and helped collect the remaining tea bags. "Has Winnie Simpson been riding your tail?"

"I've been assigned to Operations Branch," Hobbes blurted, and then immediately regretted it.

Semple whistled. He rose and stared at Hobbes. "Jesus! When?"

"I—I start this afternoon." Hobbes went back to his desk and sat down. "It's no big deal—"

"No big deal! Christ! It's just what you've wanted for two years, is all." Semple, grinning, thrust his hand across the desk. "Congratulations." Hobbes had no choice but to take the offered hand.

"Look," Hobbes said, "it's only temporary. And it's clerical."

Semple squinted speculatively at Hobbes. "Then why are you going around knocking into things?"

"I—I'll be working for Mr. Dooley."

"*Dooley!*" Semple breathed. His eyes widened. "Superspy himself?"

Hobbes shrugged.

"No wonder you're nervous. Listen, kid, this could be your chance. Impress Dooley, and you could be in."

Hobbes looked at his watch and stood. "I've got to be going, Darrin."

On the drive into Washington Hobbes couldn't get out of his mind the memory of Victoria Prentice's face as he had seen it over Darrin Semple's bare shoulder. He knew the vague anger he felt toward Semple was unfair; it wasn't his fault Hobbes had been following his girl.

It was Semple who had shown Victoria Prentice to

35

Hobbes. Semple was a lawyer on the CIA legal staff. He and Hobbes had met because of the proximity of their offices—the bull pen of young lawyers where Semple worked was just down the hall from Hobbes' office. Semple had introduced himself one day shortly after Hobbes had come to work for Winifred Simpson. He was a handsome, popular man a few years older than Hobbes, and for some reason he had cultivated Hobbes' friendship.

The relationship didn't extend beyond the office. Semple's social life, as he reported it from time to time, was beyond Hobbes' ken or experience. It centered primarily on women, and Semple had so many that Hobbes lost track of them. Semple talked of them the way another man might speak of a collection of art objects. He was a connoisseur of women, and his graphic, sometimes bawdy descriptions could evoke in Hobbes' mind vivid images of golden-limbed, laughing girls.

A month before, Semple had burst into Hobbes' office at lunchtime, his face flushed, his eyes dancing with excitement. "You've got to see this, Hobbsy." He refused to explain. He urged Hobbes down to the cafeteria and stopped him at the entrance. Semple swept an arm over the crowded cafeteria. "Pick her out, Hobbes. Pick out the most beautiful girl in here."

Hobbes hesitated, perplexed and slightly embarrassed. "Go ahead," Semple said. "Look 'em over, and tell me which one comes in first by five lengths."

But Hobbes had already seen her. She was sitting with two other women. Her dark, rich hair fell across her cheek as she leaned forward to say something. She was across the room, but even at that distance Hobbes could see the luster of health on her flesh and the light of intelligence in her eyes. Hobbes nodded toward her. "That one."

Semple slapped him on the shoulder and grinned. "Isn't she something? Miss Victoria Prentice, Attorney-at-Law, fresh out of law school and the legal depart-

36

ment's newest employee." He leaned down to Hobbes and whispered, "This is it, Hobbes. The right age, beautiful, a lawyer. I tell you, this one makes me think about hearths and two-car garages and joint checking accounts."

Semple led Hobbes back to his office and paced and drank Hobbes' tea. Hobbes had seen him enthusiastic about women before, had even heard him on other occasions claim that this was indeed it, but he had never seen him this agitated. "Can you believe it!" Semple exclaimed. "She even went to Columbia—had some of the same professors I did."

It seemed that Darrin hadn't wasted time. Victoria Prentice had been working in the legal department for only a week, and already Semple had taken her out twice and had discovered they liked the same things. Hobbes felt a mixture of envy and resentment—resentment because it hadn't occurred to Semple to introduce Hobbes to the girl or, apparently, to make any explanation for not doing so. When Hobbes had run across her at the Washington Athletic Club, his decision to follow her had sprung partly from the slight he felt at not being good enough to be introduced. The rest of his motivation had come from the feelings that were stirred in him when he looked at her.

The woman at the reception desk at the Veterans' Hospital didn't look up when Hobbes asked for Commander Peevey. She flipped through a file and pointed with a pencil. "Psychiatric ward. Third floor. Elevator's that way."

A reception area fronted the elevators on the third floor. Beyond was a wire-mesh wall with a locked door. A small man in a white smock stood behind a counter talking on a telephone. When he was through, Hobbes asked for Commander Peevey.

"You a relative?"

"Yes," Hobbes lied.

"You can see him for a few minutes."

"Are you the doctor?"

The man smiled. "Nurse." He took a ring of keys from his pocket and unlocked the door in the wire wall.

As they walked down a white hall unmercifully lit by fluorescent fixtures, Hobbes asked, "Why is he in the psychiatric ward?"

The little man shrugged. "That's where he was committed. He may be out of it. We've had him on sedation." He chuckled, "The old guy is strong as a bull. Didn't want any part of us." He stopped at a door and looked through a wire-reinforced window. "He's awake." He unlocked the door.

Commander Peevey lay on a narrow bed. His head was propped on two pillows. His eyes were inflamed and suspicious. One large hand lay on his stomach, knotted in a fist.

Hobbes tried to smile at the old man. "Commander Peevey—"

"Hobbes," Commander Peevey said. He spoke in a hoarse whisper. "Hobbes, are you behind this?"

Hobbes was momentarily stunned by the accusation. The nurse said in a low voice, "Don't let it get you. I told you he's out of it."

Hobbes swallowed. "No," he said to Commander Peevey. "I didn't know you were gone, even—"

"It's because of the war," Commander Peevey rasped, his eyes burning into Hobbes. "I didn't take that goddamn ship through their blockade. I didn't kill all my goddamn men and sink my ship. That's it, isn't it?"

"Now, now," the nurse said. He was busy arranging Commander Peevey's bed, tucking in the sheets at the bottom, plumping the pillows around his head. "You did just fine with that ship."

"I demand a board," Commander Peevey bellowed in a voice so abruptly full of strength that Hobbes jumped. "It's my right as an officer to present my side."

"Sure," the nurse replied. "You'll have it. But you know those things take time."

Commander Peevey seemed mollified. His great head rolled to one side, burying his cheek in the pillows, causing him to peer out at Hobbes with one eye.

"I'll leave you two to visit," the nurse said. He pointed to a cord at the head of the bed and said to Hobbes, "If you need me, flip the switch."

After the nurse had gone, Hobbes pulled a chair to the side of Commander Peevey's bed and sat down. Commander Peevey peered at him with one eye. Hobbes took out his cigarettes and held out the pack to the old man. Commander Peevey eyed the pack but didn't move. "Got a cigar?" he asked.

"No," Hobbes replied, putting the pack away. "I'll bring you some. I'll see if I can bring you some."

"I shook hands with Teddy Roosevelt," Commander Peevey said. He sat up abruptly and stared at his hand. "Did I tell you that?"

"Yes," Hobbes said, and quickly added, "but I'd like to hear it again."

Commander Peevey ignored him. He raised his hand to his face and stared at it. "Best damn President the country ever had, but they were too goddamn dumb to know it. I couldn't've been more than eight, maybe ten. My father pushed me out in front of that crowd. Right there on the courthouse steps in front of the whole goddamn town."

" 'Stick your hand out, Horace,' my father yelled at me. 'Stick your hand out.' And I did. And old Teddy grabbed my hand. Strong grip, hard, *hard*— And he took hold of my shoulder and said, 'Strapping lad!' he said. 'Do you like baseball?' he said. And I said, 'Yes, sir.' And he said, 'Bully for you, lad! Bully for you,' he said."

Commander Peevey stopped talking and stared at his hand. Slowly his eyes lifted. He looked around the room, as if trying to place it in his memory. Hobbes waited. Finally, the old man's eyes came to rest on Hobbes. He grinned. His teeth were worn stumps. His eyebrows were white wisps that swept at the ends up over his broad brow. "Hobbes," he said.

"Sir."

"Hobbes." The grin broadened. Commander Peevey fell back on the pillows and laughed. "I'm laid up here for a while, Hobbes."

"Yes, sir."

"Goddamn food is terrible. Whoever cooks it should be dragged out in the street and horsewhipped. Boiled eggs and Jell-O, for God's sake." He glowered at Hobbes. "That's their idea of a man's meal."

"The—ah—people from the hotel wanted me to give you their regards."

"What?"

"You know—Mrs. Crump, Dr. Marshall, Mr. Darling. . . ."

"Crap," Commander Peevey muttered. "Bunch of mice." Commander Peevey shot Hobbes a look of animated interest. "Did they send any food?"

"No, sir. I'll see what I can bring next time."

"Steak," Commander Peevey cried with sudden force. "I'd give my pension for one goddamn T-bone."

"Yes, sir. I'll see what I can do."

"And a newspaper." Commander Peevey's voice was fading. He turned his head away. "See that window?"

Hobbes looked up at the window over the bed. It was covered with a heavy wire mesh like that on the entrance door to the ward.

"Yes, sir," Hobbes whispered.

"Now, Hobbes," Commander Peevey said in a calm, steady voice, "you go rustle up my clothes and my suitcase. Don't forget my suitcase."

Commander Peevey was getting slowly out of bed. His legs projected from the hospital gown. His knees were enormous, the legs beneath as thin as pipes, gnarled and corded with varicose veins. Hobbes leaped to his feet.

40

Commander Peevey steadied himself on the edge of the bed. He was panting, and his forehead was sweating.

"Sir," Hobbes said, "don't you think—"

"Get moving," Commander Peevey panted. "Don't just stand there, man." He staggered to his feet. Hobbes put out his arms. Commander Peevey grasped Hobbes' forearms in his huge hands. His fingers were like clamps.

"It's about time I got out of here," Commander Peevey said. There was a strange light in his eyes. "I've put up with all the nonsense I'm going to."

"Yes, but—"

Commander Peevey leaned his weight on Hobbes' forearms, slowly forcing him toward the door. Hobbes tried to resist, and they pivoted slowly, as if performing a rehearsed movement. Hobbes felt his hip catch the white table beside the bed. Commander Peevey continued to bore in on him. The table tipped up. Commander Peevey's breath was rasping through his open mouth. His eyes were glazed. The table crashed on its side. Hobbes looked helplessly at the cord at the head of the bed. Commander Peevey was backing him slowly toward the wall.

The door was thrown open, and the small nurse and another, larger man, rushed into the room. They seized Commander Peevey by each arm. The old man's grip slowly broke from Hobbes' arms. The two men dragged the old man to the bed. The small man took a hypodermic needle from his smock and removed the protective plastic sheath with his teeth. They forced the old man back on the bed, his feet still on the floor. Commander Peevey was making a wounded-animal noise deep in his throat. The larger man forced Commander Peevey's arm out, exposing the vein behind the elbow. The small nurse knelt on the bed with both knees, bending over the arm. He plunged the needle into the exposed vein. Commander Peevey let loose a hoarse, angry sob. Through all this he never took his eyes from Hobbes' face.

"Hey! Hey!" the large man yelled.

Hobbes was amazed to find he had the large man's head

under his arm. He couldn't remember moving. The large man made a violent swinging motion with his shoulders and threw Hobbes against the wall. He pinned Hobbes there with his forearm, his face contorted with rage. The small nurse got off the bed and rushed over. "Okay, okay," he said. "No harm done."

The large man reluctantly let Hobbes off the wall. "That's assault, buddy," he said to Hobbes. "I could file charges."

"C'mon, now, Eddie," the small man said. "That's his grandfather there. He thought we were hurting him."

"Well—" Eddie said slowly, straightening his smock and feeling his head tenderly. He gave Hobbes a slow, angry look and left the room.

The little man grinned at Hobbes. "You pick on the big ones, don't you?"

Hobbes was looking at Commander Peevey. He still lay half on the bed, his feet on the floor. His eyes were dimming, the lids half-lowered. The nurse followed Hobbes' gaze. He went to the bed and said, "Give me a hand."

They got Commander Peevey into the bed, and the nurse arranged the covers over him. He patted Peevey's chest. "He'll sleep now." He looked up at Hobbes. "Is he really your grandfather?"

Hobbes didn't hesitate. "Yes," he said, "he is."

The nurse chuckled. "Pretty good guess, eh?"

Commander Peevey made a weak noise. The nurse bent his ear over his mouth. Commander Peevey's lips moved. The nurse nodded. "He wants to say something to you."

Hobbes bent his ear down to the old man's mouth. "Medium," Commander Peevey whispered weakly.

"What?"

"The steak," Commander Peevey whispered. "I like it medium."

Hobbes waited until they were in the reception area. Then he said, "I want to get him out of here."

"I'm sorry, buddy," the little nurse said. "That's not in my hands."

"But he's my grandfather. You can't keep him."

The nurse shrugged. "You're wrong there. We got a court order. We got 'em on a lotta the old guys around here." He paused and looked at Hobbes' face. "Maybe you should talk to somebody in Administration."

Hobbes nodded. The nurse picked up the phone. "I'll see who's in."

Dr. Dollarhide was a round, rosy man dressed in a vested tweed suit. He greeted Hobbes at the door of his office with a smile and a damp handshake. After he had Hobbes seated, he went behind his desk and picked up a file. He opened the file and studied it for a moment.

"You're his grandson?"

Hobbes nodded.

Dr. Dollarhide tapped the file with his stubby finger. "No mention of you here." He held up a hand and smiled. "Not unusual, though. Sometimes the old fellows simply forget." He looked down at the files again. "In fact, Commander Peevey put 'none' where it says living relatives." Dr. Dollarhide chuckled.

"I'm the only one," Hobbes said.

Dr. Dollarhide closed the file and rested his arms on it. "What can I do for you, Mr. Hobbes?" He shot his cuff and glanced at his wristwatch.

"I'd like to get Commander Peevey out of here. Today, if that's possible."

Dr. Dollarhide chuckled heartily. "Oh, my, no. Impossible, Mr. Hobbes. Quite impossible."

Hobbes felt the heat rise to his face. "He doesn't want to stay here. What right do you have—"

Dr. Dollarhide held up a hand, "Here, here, Mr. Hobbes. No need to raise our voices, is there? It's not me, you see. They've declared your grandfather incompetent. A danger to himself, don't you see?"

"Crap!"

43

"I beg your pardon?" Dr. Dollarhide was beginning to look alarmed. He eyed a row of buttons on his intercom.

"He's not incompetent. Who is this 'they' that decided he was?"

Dr. Dollarhide pawed through the file. Then his hand froze. He looked up at Hobbes. "Ah—it's all in order, Mr. Hobbes, I assure you. We have a court document."

"But who initiated it?"

Dollarhide flushed. He fingered a letter opener on the desk. "I'm not at liberty—you understand, that in matters of this kind, circumspection is—"

"The court order's public record, isn't it? Who initiated it? Was it someone at the hotel that had it in for Peevey?"

"The hotel?" Dollarhide looked perplexed.

"Never mind," Hobbes said wearily.

The intercom on Dollarhide's desk buzzed. He picked up a phone, listened for a moment and hung up. "If that's all, I have to get on with my work—"

"No. That's not all. What's the diagnosis?"

Dollarhide sighed heavily. "Very well. Wait here for a moment." He left the room at a fast waddle.

Peevey's file lay open on Dollarhide's desk. Hobbes stared at it, looked at the closed door, leaned across the desk, and riffled the papers in the file with his thumb. His hand stopped at a familiar blue and white letterhead. Voices came drifting through the closed door. Hobbes leaned back in the chair. Dollarhide came into the room and seated himself behind the desk. "Now, the diagnosis—"

Hobbes stood. "Never mind. I know you're busy."

"But I thought you wanted—" But Hobbes was already out the door.

Hobbes paused on the stone steps outside the building and lit a cigarette. He let the cigarette dangle from his lips as he shoved his hands deep in the pockets of his raincoat and read the brass plaque on the marble facade next to the entrance of the building.

VETERANS ADMINISTRATION
To Care for Him Who Shall Have Borne the Battle . . .

All he'd had a chance to see on the letter in Peevey's file before Dollarhide had come back into the room were the words "Re: Horace Arthur Peevey—Request to Commit to Veterans' Hospital" and the blue and white logo at the top. It was an emblem he saw every day—the seal of the Central Intelligence Agency.

FIVE

Vernon Dooley was a dark, densely built man with bulging brown eyes that gave him a perpetual look of disbelief. Now he looked up from his desk at Hobbes. Hobbes felt his spine tingle with a nameless apprehension.

"Thomas Hobbes," Vernon Dooley said.

"Yes, sir."

"I like my employees to be punctual, Thomas Hobbes."

"Yes, sir. I'm sorry. I had a personal errand at lunch, and Mrs. Simpson didn't say what time—"

"Also, I don't like excuses. Next time be on time." Dooley directed his gaze back at the papers on his desk.

"Yes, sir." Hobbes had the urge to wipe his forehead, but he didn't.

"This is a simple task, Thomas Hobbes. A file search. I take it you've done file searches."

"Ah—in a way—"

"Either you've done file searches, or you haven't, Hobbes."

"I'm familiar with the personnel files. But I've never done a search, no." Hobbes looked up to find Dooley studying him with a peculiar light in his eyes. Dooley's expression changed to one of indifference, and Hobbes couldn't help feeling he had caught him in some unguarded act.

Dooley leaned back in his chair. He took a toothpick from his shirt and rolled it between his fingers. "Pacifier," he said. He had a dry, flat voice. "Do you smoke, Hobbes?"

"Some, yes, sir."

Dooley smiled mirthlessly. "You smoke the way you do file searches?"

"Only five or six cigarettes a day."

"You're lucky." Dooley inserted the toothpick in the corner of his mouth. "I was three packs a day. I'm going cold turkey. Three days now. How the hell do you keep it down to five or six a day?"

"I don't really know."

Dooley sighed again and picked up a paper from his desk. "On this paper is a list of names. I want you to pull the files for the people listed. That's simple enough, isn't it?"

"Yes, sir."

"If you have questions, ask me. Don't speak a word about what you're doing to anyone."

"Yes, sir."

"Not a word. Don't even mention that you're on a different assignment. Got it?"

"Yes, sir."

Dooley pushed a button on the intercom on his desk. "I've had my assistant fix you up with a temporary office. We can't have the files out of this area."

A slender man with a sallow, sharp face entered the office.

"Get rid of that goddamn cigarette," Dooley bellowed.

The man stared for a moment in confusion at the cigarette in his hand. "Sorry, Vern. I forgot." He began to stub out the cigarette in an ashtray on Dooley's desk.

"Not there, goddamn it."

The man picked up the ashtray and hurried out. Dooley batted at the smoke in the air with his hand. The tall man reappeared empty-handed. "Sorry, Vern."

Dooley stared at him. Finally, he said, "Halladay. Hobbes."

Halladay extended a slender hand. Hobbes stood and took it.

"Have you got that office set up?"

Halladay nooded. "Two doors down."

"Did security put the files in?"

"All set."

Dooley handed Hobbes the paper on his desk. "You might as well get started."

The office was twice the size of Hobbes'. It was paneled. It had a thin green carpet on the floor. An upholstered chair stood against one wall beside a low table. The desk was walnut veneer. Behind it on the wall hung a Constable print. A large black steel safe squatted against another wall.

Halladay unbuttoned his suit coat and squatted in front of the safe. He began to twirl the dials. Hobbes was disconcerted to see a revolver in a holster clipped to the left side of Halladay's waistband.

Halladay swung the safe door open. The safe was packed with files tiered on steel shelves. Halladay removed an armful of files and stacked them on the desk. He counted them. "Forty," he said. "You count them."

Hobbes did. "Forty," he said.

Halladay closed and locked the safe. Then he turned to Hobbes. "Off with the coat."

Hobbes stared at him for a moment and then slowly removed his gray raincoat. Halladay took it and ran a hand down the lining. Then he threw it over the chair by the table. "Suit coat."

48

Hobbes took the coat off. Halladay searched it and deposited it on the raincoat. "Hope you're not ticklish," Halladay said with a grim smile. Hobbes stared at him. "Hold your arms out." Hobbes did. Halladay patted his torso and legs.

"Okay," Halladay said, buttoning his suit coat. "You don't leave until I search you again and escort you out. You don't leave until I've counted the files and put them back in the safe. Understand?"

"I—I guess so."

"I'll bring your lunch to you."

Halladay stepped to the rear wall of the office that was paneled in imitation walnut. He pressed a section of the wall and a latch-sprung door swung open. Inside was a sink and a toilet. "Okay?"

Hobbes nodded.

Halladay went to the outer door and stood with the knob in his hand. He held up a key. "You're going to be locked in. Any last requests?"

Hobbes swallowed. "No."

Halladay closed the door after him. Hobbes heard the tumblers in the lock turn.

The difference in these files was immediately apparent. The files Hobbes normally worked on were uniform in their construction: the information organized in sections, the sections composed of neatly typed government forms. The Operations Branch files were a hodgepodge. Some contained the forms he was accustomed to; most did not. Interspersed through all were handwritten memos, notes jotted on torn scraps of paper, lengthy situation assessments typewritten on coarse paper, single-spaced, by obviously inept typists. Even the photographs were a mixture. Some were the standard front and profile taken by the identification section. But others were little more than amateur snapshots, some taken from a distance through telephoto lenses with the subjects' features indistinct. One file he came across that afternoon

49

had no photos at all. After a cursory examination of the files he determined that there wasn't a dull one in the bunch.

He decided to improvise a routine that would allow him as much free reading time as possible. He examined the list Dooley had given him. There were eighty names, each followed by an identification number.

Hobbes went quickly through the forty file folders looking for matches with the list Dooley had given him. He found only one and put that file aside. He took a pencil from a drawer of the desk and placed a light check beside the name of the man on the list whose file he had found. Hardly half an hour had passed. He was apparently through for the morning, until Halladay brought his lunch.

He lit a Rothman, took the top file from the stack, put his feet up on the desk, and began reading.

Halladay stuck his head into Vernon Dooley's office. Dooley was sitting at his desk, his thick arms folded across his chest, chewing furiously on a toothpick.

"Dr. Beckman's here," Halladay said.

Dooley took the toothpick from his mouth and hurled it at his wastebasket. "Halladay," he said, "give me a goddamn cigarette."

"No dice, Vern," Halladay said, edging out of the door.

Dooley put his hand out and snapped his fingers. "Don't play games with me, Halladay. Give me a goddamn cigarette."

"No. Get your own. I'm not going to be the one—"

"Okay!" Dooley shouted. "I'll remember this! Get Beckman."

Halladay reappeared in a moment with a small bald man. Dooley glared at the man. "Beckman, do you smoke?"

"No," the man replied. "Never acquired the habit."

"Goddammit," Dooley said.

Beckman looked questioningly at Halladay. "He's trying to quit smoking," Halladay said.

"Ah," Dr. Beckman perched primly on a chair. "I suggest you make a list of all the disadvantages of smoking."

"Zero," Dooley said, glaring. "That list would have zero on it."

"Indeed," Dr. Beckman said, looking uncomfortable.

Dooley took another toothpick from his pocket and stuck it in his mouth.

"What did you think of Hobbes, Vern?" Halladay asked.

"The son of a bitch nearly gave me a coronary when he walked in here."

"I told you," Halladay said.

"What I can't figure is why haven't I noticed him before. Or you? Or any of us that knew Gordon?"

"He's been buried down in Winnie Simpson's section. The few people that see him around there never knew Gordon."

"Christ," Dooley said. "He's a ringer for Gordon, all right. At first glance, anyway. His mannerisms are all wrong, though. Gordon was an arrogant bastard."

"We can take care of that," Beckman said eagerly. "I've designed a training program—"

Dooley cut him off. "I don't mean to tell you your business, Doc, but can Hobbes pull this off? It's hard to believe that he's Vincent Hobbes' son. He seems like a pretty weak fish to me."

"Exactly!" Beckman exclaimed. "Dependent personality. Very malleable."

"But has he got the balls to go up against guys like Clawson and Fisher? Those bastards would kill their own mothers if the KGB gave them the word."

"We'll program his every move," Beckman responded, his eyes glittering with excitement. "Believe me, he is a much better subject than someone with—well, as you say, with balls."

51

Dooley sighed. "Okay. Tell me about him."

Beckman took a small notebook from his coat. His hands trembled slightly. "The mother died when he was three. The father didn't remarry, and there was no significant female figure during Hobbes' formative period. As you know, the father had eminent careers in the army and the CIA. He was a hero. He wanted Hobbes to follow in his footsteps. Hobbes applied for West Point but was turned down because the board felt he wasn't well rounded enough—good student, good IQ, but no extracurricular interests. His father got him his job with the CIA, but the personality tests indicated he was suited only for clerical work. Not enough aggressiveness for an agent. His father died shortly before he began work here. His life has been a pattern of trying to live up to his father and failing. As a compensation he has sought life situations that are nonthreatening and will allow him anonymity. His work history is a good example. He knows hardly anyone in his section. The work requires few decisions, no ego interactions. Even his living arrangement is typical—the youngest person there, other than Hobbes, is in his late sixties. He's surrounded himself with retired people, noncompetitive people."

"Jesus," Dooley said. "He sounds like a nut. The last thing I need is a nut."

"Ah, but I disagree, Mr. Dooley. He is precisely what you need. He is not psychotic. Neurotic, perhaps, but—"

"He can cope with his environment—is that the distinction, Doc?"

"Yes. But more important, he can be influenced—greatly influenced. He wanted desperately to be an agent in this branch. He wanted desperately to be like his father—heroic, manly. These thwarted desires can be used to motivate him."

Dooley chewed on his toothpick, staring at Beckman. Finally, he said, "I'm trying to place myself in his situation. I guess I would get goddamn frustrated. I guess I would store it up and just bust loose all at once."

Dr. Beckman nodded. "Very insightful, Mr. Dooley. That's probably exactly how you would handle his powerlessness. But Mr. Hobbes has been trained by the circumstances of his life in a different way."

"So how does he live with it?"

"Fantasy, Mr. Dooley. What you might call daydreams."

"Jesus, Doc—you shrinks astonish me with flat statements like that. You've never even met this guy."

"That's true. And of course, much that I conclude is educated speculation. But we've done a very thorough work-up on him. Mr. Halladay has provided us with the results of his excellent investigation."

Dooley sighed. "Okay. Tell me about these fantasies."

"Well—of course, I can't be sure of the precise form they take. But they probably entail scenarios where he has great power. He might identify with a strong-imaged movie star. Ah—he might identify with random figures—people he meets casually and that seem powerful. There are many ways to have these dreams, many ways to act them out—all harmless."

"Now, see, Doc, you're beginning to worry me. What if he suddenly decides he's John Wayne right in the middle of our project?"

Dr. Beckman permitted himself a small smile. "He probably decided long ago that he was John Wayne or someone like him. But you see, he decided it up here." Beckman tapped his forehead with a finger.

Dooley leaned forward in his chair, worrying the toothpick in his fingers. "And you'll guarantee he won't act it out?"

Beckman flushed. "Guarantee is perhaps a bit strong at this point. I would like the week we agreed upon to observe him."

53

Dooley turned to Halladay. "What's the setup on that office?"

"We've got a black-light screen in a painting on the wall in there. We can see Hobbes' every move through it from the office next door."

"How did he take the search?"

"Not a peep."

"You see," Beckman said eagerly. "Passive personality. I predict he will do what he is told and hardly question it, if at all."

"Jesus," Dooley said. "Maybe he's too dumb for this job."

"No," Beckman replied. "In fact, he is exceptionally intelligent, which is the perfect combination. Smart enough to understand what you want of him and passive enough to do it without question. If I am right, we will have no trouble training him."

Dooley eyed Beckman. "Assuming you're right and he passes the test this week, the question is this." Dooley leaned toward Beckman. "Can he impersonate George Gordon long enough to pull this thing off?"

"As long as you like," Beckman replied, his eyes glittering. "As long as you like."

After Beckman had gone, Dooley said, "Did you take care of the Peevey matter?"

Halladay nodded. Dooley studied him. "You look like you have something stuck in your craw. Want to spit it out?"

"It's Peevey," Halladay said. "I wonder if that was wise."

"Necessary." Dooley leaned forward, his eyes hard. "He's the only one that knew both Gordon and Hobbes. We can't take the chance that he'd spill something accidentally around the wrong ears."

"But, Christ, Vern! We could get in a hell of a lot of trouble—unlawful detention, kidnapping—"

"Bullshit! We've got a court order. The legal department did it up all nice and proper. Peevey gets a couple of weeks' rest and goes home a new man. It'll probably do the old bastard good."

Halladay sighed. "It just seems like a lot of trouble and risk for a small possibility."

Dooley smiled thinly. "Details. It's overlooking the details that can torpedo projects like this."

Halladay stood. Dooley eyed him. "You wouldn't've done it, would you?"

"I don't think so. I don't like the risk."

"Did you ever stop to think, Halladay," Dooley said with a slow smile, "that that's the reason I'm behind this desk and you aren't?"

SIX

The following Saturday an idea that had been germinating in Hobbes' mind sprouted full-blossomed into being.

The week had been strange. Each morning Halladay greeted him at the entrance to the office Hobbes had been assigned, searched him, and locked him in. Hobbes went through the files Halladay gave him from the safe, looking for the ones on Dooley's list. Then he read until Halladay arrived with his lunch and gave him another forty files. Although the files were the most fascinating Hobbes had ever read, he found it increasingly difficult to concentrate on them as the week pressed on. The locked door became a silent distraction. Once, on Wednesday, he got up from the desk, went to the door, and tested it to see if it was actually locked. It was.

He became obsessed with trying to remember the occasions during a workday he had come and gone through the door of his old office. He began to experience a stifling sensation.

Hobbes spent his evenings working on what Mr. Darling had begun to refer to as The Peevey Case. Commander Peevey had been moved from the psychiatric ward to a residential section of the hospital on Tuesday. Hobbes and Dr. Marshall formed a delegation of two from the Lincoln Hotel to visit Peevey each evening, but they were never sure the old man recognized them. Dr. Marshall was enormously upset at the vegetablelike condition of Commander Peevey, and he managed in turn to upset everyone at the Lincoln Hotel with his lurid descriptions of it. As the week progressed, the residents of the hotel increasingly looked to Hobbes for a solution to Commander Peevey's predicament.

At night, alone in his room, Hobbes became afflicted with ghostly images of the subjects of his past surveillances. Particularly strong was the memory of Victoria Prentice. He recalled her spirited walk, her slim, flashing legs, the intelligence that informed her glance. He told himself that these images were prompted by his decision to give up surveillances, that they were a kind of valedictory purging of his mind.

On Friday evening Dr. Marshall had said, as they left Commander Peevey's room, "What we need, Mr. Hobbes, is a good lawyer."

Now, as he awoke Saturday morning, the thought was there: Victoria Prentice was a lawyer—and, besides, a lawyer who worked in the right place to help Peevey. He'd told no one about the letter he had glimpsed in Dr. Dollarhide's files. But if anyone could get to the bottom of why the CIA had wanted Peevey committed, could, perhaps, even get the decision reversed, it would be a lawyer from Langley's legal department. He told himself that it would be best to go cautiously, to check out her apartment building one more time, to get a feel for how to approach her. He told himself that he wouldn't be breaking his vow to give up surveillances, that this was different; he would be doing it to help Peevey.

Then, as he was dressing, a thought struck him that

collapsed his carefully constructed rationalizations: Darrin Semple was a lawyer at Langley. One Hobbes already knew. He slumped down in a chair. If he really wanted to help Peevey, if that was his overriding motive, then he had to take the problem to Darrin. Sadly, he looked up Semple's number in his telephone book.

A kind of wary surprise showed in Semple's voice. Hobbes had never called him at home before. "What's up, kid?" Semple asked.

Hobbes told him about Peevey. Semple's voice took on a guarded edge. "Can't help you on that one, Tommy."

Hobbes felt anger heat his face. "*Why?* They have no right to put him there. Nothing's wrong with him."

"Listen, Hobbes. There's nothing I can do, and I can't discuss it with you. If you're smart, you'll let it drop."

"I won't!" Hobbes said stubbornly.

"That's up to you. I gotta run now, kid."

Hobbes finished dressing in a mood of elation. He had no choice! If he were to help Peevey, he would have to find a way to approach Victoria Prentice.

It was just nine o'clock when Hobbes arrived across the street from where she lived. The street was deserted except for two children who raced past Hobbes, pushing a bicycle. He was forced to step quickly out of their reckless path. They laughed and shouted to each other as they careened by. The sky was dark with the threat of rain. The children glanced over their shoulders at him. He imagined what they saw. A man in a gray raincoat, his brown shoes in need of a shine, his hands thrust in his raincoat pockets, his shoulders rounded as if the lowering sky was pressing down upon them.

He went across the street and found the alcove that contained the mail boxes. In the slot for her apartment was a card that had printed upon it, in a delicate Roman script, "Victoria Prentice."

"Can I help you?"

He spun around. She was there, not five feet from him.
"Ah—no—" he stammered. He stood rooted, staring back at her.

"Well," she said with a smile, "you're standing in front of my mailbox."

"What?"

"My mailbox—" She held up a ring of keys. "I'd like to get to it."

She opened the mailbox, removed her mail, and turned as Hobbes stood transfixed. He watched her walk away. Then the anger hit him. Anger at himself, What a fool! The perfect opportunity to approach her, to introduce himself, tell her he needed a lawyer, and he had been too scared to open his mouth.

He shuffled forlornly from the courtyard and crossed the street. He stood where he had stood before, with the vague idea of getting a cab. But none came, and he continued to stand numbly and stare across the street at the condominiums. He put his hand in his raincoat pocket, felt the package of cigarettes, and took one out and lit it. Some of the numbness left him. He looked up the street for a cab, and when he looked back, she was across the street, walking briskly, head down. She hadn't seen him or, if she had, hadn't known him. He laughed bitterly to himself. Probably had already forgotten what he looked like. The anger rose in him again. It was then that he decided to follow her.

Halladay didn't like to go to Dooley's home. It was a big old Georgian monstrosity, set on an acre of wild, overgrown Virginia land on the outskirts of McLean. Dooley's wife had money. Halladay didn't like to be at the home because it was so totally Dooley's domain. At least at the office, for all of Dooley's power and domination, Halladay felt he was on turf that he had his claim to. But at Dooley's house, Halladay had no claim, no constituency, no office to escape to and lick his wounds.

They were in Dooley's den, the three of them—Dooley, Halladay, and Dr. Beckman. Dooley stood in front of the huge fieldstone fireplace that was ablaze with burning logs. Dr. Beckman perched on the edge of a brocade-covered Regency chair. Halladay lounged on the sofa, trying to appear at ease. A coffee service stood on the low table in front of the couch. Behind Halladay a book-covered wall rose to the exposed oak beams of the ceiling.

Dooley took a sip from the coffee cup he held in his hand. In his other hand was a cigarette. In the fifteen minutes Halladay and Beckman had been there, Dooley had smoked three cigarettes, but nobody mentioned the fact.

Halladay was consulting a notebook. "He's been to the VA Hospital every night this week to see Peevey."

"What the hell for?" Dooley asked. "They're keeping the old bastard doped up, aren't they?"

Halladay nodded. "He goes with another old man from the hotel."

"I think it only natural," Beckman said, "that he's concerned about Commander Peevey. Peevey was a friend of his father's. He found him the accommodations at the hotel when he came to Washington."

Dooley shrugged. "It can't do any harm." He sucked greedily on his cigarette. "What's he doing at the office?"

"Nothing," Halladay replied. "Smokes. Reads files."

"Jesus," Dooley said. "We give him a job he can do in thirty minutes a day. We shake him down morning and night. We lock him in an office. And he doesn't even ask what the hell is going on?"

"It's authority," Beckman said. "He's learned not to question authority, and you represent that for him. It's a father figure transference—"

Dooley held up a hand. "Spare me the goddamn psychology, Doc. What I want are recommendations."

"I think we start training him next week," Halladay said.

"I agree," Beckman said. "We are prepared to begin Monday, if you say so."

"Okay," Dooley said. "But if Hobbes fucks up and gets himself killed, it's not only my ass that's hanging out. Both of you will go down with me."

"That's nice of you to tell us that, Vern," Halladay said.

"This is not a goddamn etiquette class, Halladay."

Halladay locked eyes with Dooley. He smiled lazily. "I see you've started smoking again, Vern."

"You son of a bitch," Dooley said quietly.

SEVEN

Hobbes stayed well back, on the opposite side of the street. She walked fast, her head down, her coat collar turned up. Hobbes couldn't afford to have her see him now. Before he had a plan. He needed a plan. His mind careened wildly.

She turned onto M Street, where a row of shops stretched awnings over the sidewalk. The clouds touched the horizon now. The air smelled of rain. She went into one of the shops. Hobbes waited under an awning a half block away, smoking. When she came out thirty minutes later, she had a small package under her arm. She went into another shop. For the next two hours, Hobbes followed her, inching along M Street, as she went into shop after shop. When she emerged from the final one, she had put all her packages into a candy-striped plastic shopping bag. It was raining now, a cold, stinging rain. Although nearly noon, the day was gray and dark.

She went into a restaurant. Hobbes delayed outside, giving her time to get seated; then he went in. It was dim in the restaurant. Candles in red glass bubbles hollowed out rosy circles on the tables. At the rear of the restaurant Hobbes saw the orange glow of a fireplace. He veered away from the hostess and into a small bar. He sat at the end of the bar, where it joined the wall. He unbuttoned his raincoat and shook out the wet folds. He leaned against the wall and ordered a martini. He lit a cigarette when the drink came and took a cautious sip that immediately warmed him. He took a larger sip, swiveling his eyes around over the rim of the glass, looking for her.

She wasn't in the section of the restaurant that he could see through an archway that connected the bar to the dining room. He relaxed. He felt safe. The drink was sending out pleasant waves of warmth from his stomach. Now, he thought. Now a plan.

He could have her paged. Have her come to the bar. And—and what? He passed a hand through his damp hair. He would level with her. Tell her about Commander Peevey. Elicit her sympathy. That was it. Sympathy for Commander Peevey. He ordered another martini.

When he thought about leveling with her, that didn't mean he would tell her he had followed her. Not that. He would say he had gone to her apartment to talk to her, and her sudden appearance had startled him. That was true. Before he'd had a chance to speak to her, she had gone. That was true, too. He ordered another martini.

He wouldn't have her paged, he thought. He would find her in the restaurant, go to her. More polite that way. Happened to be having a drink here and just happened to see you eating—and so on. By the time he had drunk half the third martini he had almost convinced himself he could do it. He fumbled for the pack of Rothman's on the bar in front of him, and they fell to the floor. He got off the stool and quickly gripped the edge of the bar. His head seemed to be floating off his neck. He willed it back with great effort. Then he stooped very carefully to get the cigarettes. He got a grip on the cigarettes and steadied

63

himself to rise. Take it easy, he said under his breath. He brought his eyes up first, to get used to the idea, and he saw her legs. He knew instantly they were her legs. He let his eyes travel up. Her back was to him. She was standing in the entry alcove shared by the bar and the dining room, putting on her coat. He rose very slowly, hardly breathing.

He was halfway up, in a kind of animal crouch, the cigarettes clutched in his hand, when she turned and looked directly into his eyes. They both froze, he in that awkward stoop, she with her hands lifting the shoulders of her coat around her. She stared at him, blank-faced, for a moment, and then she frowned, unpleasantly, and started to turn away. Cautiously he rose and felt behind him for the barstool. Then she was coming toward him with long, determined strides. He fell back heavily on the barstool.

She came very close to him. "You're following me," she said in a low, intense voice.

"Happened to be having a drink here and noticed . . ." His voice trailed off. He could feel the bar digging into his back. He smelled the faint odor of soap from her.

"Why?"

"What?"

"Why are you following me?"

He slumped over his hands. He couldn't look at her. "Needed a lawyer."

"What?"

"I—ah—" He looked up at her. Her face was stone, unforgiving. "Needed a lawyer."

The bartender moved toward them and asked if he could help her. She shook her head and sat on the stool next to Hobbes. "You'd better explain damn quick. I don't like men following me."

Hobbes tried to collect his thoughts. "It's true," he said. "I need to talk to a lawyer."

"How do you know I'm a lawyer?"

"I work down the hall from you—in personnel."

She turned and gave him a searching look. "I've never seen you."

"No. I've seen you, though. I—I work just down the hall—"

"Are you drunk?"

"I'm not used to drinking."

"You work at Langley?"

"In Personnel. Winnie Simpson's section."

She signaled the bartender and ordered a brandy. When she had it in her hand, she held it up. "You've got until I finish this to convince me not to call a cop."

"Don't do that!"

"Then you'd better start talking."

The martinis he'd had and her presence made it hard for him to organize his thoughts. The story came out brokenly. He carefully avoided any mention of Darrin.

Finally, she said, "What's your name?"

He told her.

"Well, Thomas Hobbes, that is a crazy story. Why would the agency want an old man committed?"

"I don't know."

"They couldn't have him in the hospital without a court order. Are you sure it isn't a simple case of senility?"

"No!"

"Okay," she said placatingly. "Don't get upset." She lit a cigarette and studied him. "Why didn't you see me at the office?"

"I don't know. Too many people around."

"Then at the mailbox, why didn't you tell me then, instead of following me around like—like—" She shuddered.

"You startled me."

"Let me get this straight." She leaned tensely toward him and said in a low, flat voice, "You live at an old people's home. This Peevey was committed to the VA Hospital. You follow me, instead of talking to me when you had the chance—"

"I see what you mean," he said dully. "It must seem like I'm the one that should be committed."

"Why do you live at an old people's home?"

"It's a hotel."

"But it's all old people—besides yourself?" He nodded. "Why?"

"I don't know. At first, it was temporary until I found a place. And then I got so I liked it."

She sighed. She drank the last of her brandy. She noticed him eyeing her empty glass. "I'm not going to call a cop," she said. "But that doesn't mean I buy your dumb story."

"Will you just check on it at the office? Find out if I'm telling the truth?"

"It's Saturday. I'm a very junior lawyer in the department. Assuming I could even find out anything, I couldn't help you."

"You could advise me on what to do."

"I'm not allowed to do private practice. And if what you say is true, if the agency did have him committed, it isn't going to do my career any good to go sticking my nose into it."

"But surely you could give me advice—"

"Commitments are not my field."

He sighed and stared into his empty glass. She looked at him for a moment and said, "This Peevey. What is he to you?"

"He was a friend of my father's. He—you'd have to know him. He is the least senile man you've ever met."

She was silent for a long moment. Finally, she said in a reluctant voice, "I guess I could read up on commitments." He turned eagerly to her. "Don't get the idea I'm going to do more than that. I could advise you what legal avenues to pursue—nothing more."

"That would be great."

66

She took a notebook and pen from her purse. "I'll look it up this afternoon. Where do I call you?"

Hobbes took a breath and said, "Since you can't take a fee, the least I can do is buy you dinner."

She shook her head. "Oh, no—even doing this much is against my better judgment."

"I just thought we could discuss it. . . ." His voice trailed off. He told her his phone number at the hotel.

She wrote the number in her book and put the book away with efficient movements of her slender hands. She stood and then hesitated, looking at him. "Do you know where the Embassy Restaurant is?" He nodded. "No," she said firmly. She turned and walked away. She hesitated at the entrance to the bar, turned again, and strode back to Hobbes. "Look," she said, "I'll be having dinner at the Embassy at seven. If you have dinner there, too, I can't prevent it. But I pay for my own. Is that clear?"

He nodded. He didn't trust his voice.

When Hobbes got back to the hotel, he went directly to his room without speaking to anyone. As he crossed the lobby Dr. Marshall, who was sitting at the domino table with Sophie Crump, called to him, but Hobbes pretended not to hear.

In his room Hobbes stripped off his clothes and took a shower. When he emerged from the bathroom with a towel around his waist, the spinning in his head had been replaced by a dull ache. He lay on his bed and stared at the ceiling, thinking about Victoria Prentice. He imagined what it would be like to have dinner with her. His closet door was open, and he saw his two gray suits hanging there.

He got up, went to the closet, took one of the suits, and hung it on the hook on the closet door. He ran his hand through his hair and began to pace in front of the suit. Then he went in the bathroom and stared for a long time at his face in the mirror.

67

Finally, he dressed in one of the suits and went down the stairs, through the lobby, and out into the street. Outside, the rain had settled into misting gray sheets that blew erratically across the pavement. Hobbes turned up the collar of his raincoat and ran for the garage where he kept his car. He drove back to M Street, parked in a municipal lot, and ran along the street and into a men's shop.

The man who waited on Hobbes showed him a suit made of light blue wool with a gold fleck in the weave. The suit seemed to scream at Hobbes. The salesman insisted that the suit was becoming. He said it brought out the color in Hobbes' eyes. Hobbes blinked his eyes at the mirror, took a deep breath, and said he'd take it.

The salesman said it was not possible to have the alterations done that day. But when Hobbes told him he also needed shoes, a shirt, and a topcoat, the salesman suddenly discovered that it could be done.

After the tailor took the measurements for the alterations, Hobbes selected a navy blue topcoat that was rain-resistant, a pale blue shirt, a pair of black loafers with shining gold links across the arch, and a tie in a shade of deep red. He wore the topcoat.

When he got back to the hotel, he went to his room. He took off his wet clothes, dried himself, and put on the blue shirt he had bought. It lay silken against his skin. He stared at himself in his bathroom mirror and tried to imagine what it was the salesman thought the suit would do for his eyes, but he couldn't and decided it had been sales talk.

He took off the shirt and hung it carefully in his closet. Then he lay on the bed in his shorts until it was time to go pick up the suit.

When Hobbes entered the Embassy Restaurant, he reluctantly gave up his topcoat to the cloakroom attendant. He was sure that every head in the restaurant was turning to discover the source of the penetrating blue light emanating from his suit.

Victoria Prentice was seated in a banquette along the far side of the main dining room, and as he followed the maître d' toward her, he saw her eyes attach themselves on him. By the time he reached the table he could feel the heat of his embarrassment in his face.

"I hardly recognized you," she said, after he had allowed the maître d' to seat him.

He laughed weakly and fingered the lapel of his suit. "A bit loud."

She touched the sleeve of the suit. "This is new?"

He nodded.

She withdrew her hand and studied him. "How new?"

He shrugged again and cleared his throat. "Uh—this afternoon—" He couldn't meet her gaze.

Victoria removed several sheets of legal-size paper from her purse. "I did the research on your problem this afternoon."

She took a pair of silver-rimmed reading glasses from her purse and put them on. They were oddly old-fashioned, almost austere in contrast with her thick hair and the fine line of her nose and jaw, and instead of detracting from her beauty, they somehow emphasized it.

She allowed him to light her cigarette and then, consulting her notes, said, "Your best chance is to ask the court to make you Commander Peevey's conservator."

"Conservator?"

She looked at him over the glasses. "Yes. You would be responsible for him. It is a relationship developed to protect people not legally competent to look after themselves: minors, mentally disturbed, old people like Commander Peevey."

"There's nothing wrong with Commander Peevey," he said with more heat than he had intended.

"Yes," she said gently. "I believe you. But that's beside the point. The court has acted. Of course, you could file a petition to have him reexamined and hope that he would be declared competent."

"What's wrong with that?"

"Time. It would take a great deal of time. And then there's the expense—for professional examination of Commander Peevey, the filing of reports with the court. That sort of thing."

"I see. And if I take the other way?"

"Not nearly so complicated. You simply file a motion to get the conservatorship transferred from the Veterans' Hospital to you. The question of Commander Peevey's competence to handle his own affairs is not in issue then."

"But if the CIA had him committed, couldn't they just reverse it? I'm sure it's some kind of administrative foul-up."

She removed her glasses and looked at him. "I made a phone call this afternoon—to my supervisor. It isn't any mistake."

Hobbes stared at her. "But how could they? Why?"

"I don't know. I was told to stay out of it."

"I appreciate your doing that. I hope it doesn't cause you any trouble."

"I thought I would prove that your imagination had run away with you."

"Your supervisor admitted Langley had Commander Peevey committed?"

"Not in so many words. But he was certainly familiar with Peevey's name. And he didn't leave any doubt that it was none of my business. I told him I was inquiring for a friend." She paused and looked embarrassed. "When he pressed me for a name, I invented one."

As they ate, Hobbes ransacked his mind for a way to see her again. "Look," he said. "Could you be my consultant on this—you know, help me with the paper-work?"

She shook her head. "I was told to butt out. And I in-

70

tend to do just that. I will say this, though—to get your old friend out of that hospital will take a lot of time and money, and assuming the petition were granted, you'd have to make arrangements approved by the court to care for him. I know you don't like to think about this, but maybe he *is* better off—"

"I won't let him stay there!"

"Would he do the same for you?"

"I don't know. All I know is I'm going to get him out."

Then she said a strange thing. "You know," she said, "that suit isn't loud at all. In fact, it's very becoming."

EIGHT

Hobbes spent a tortured night. Visions of his father and his childhood haunted his dreams. Before he fell asleep, the memory of his evening with Victoria Prentice sent him into agonies of self-recrimination as he replayed the scene in his mind time after time, each time his self-disgust at his performance growing.

He rose Sunday morning in a mood that touched the bottom of despair. He felt so little esteem for himself that, paradoxically, he seemed to have acquired a kind of reckless purpose, although he had as yet no target for it. He scrubbed his face mercilessly at his sink and felt a desire for action course through him that was as strong as lust.

He dressed and went down in the elevator. By the time he reached the lobby he knew what he would do. Sophie Crump was sitting wrapped in a shawl. Mr. Darling was on the lumpy old couch, reading a newspaper. Dr. Marshall was across the lobby, standing at the window with his hands behind his back. Hobbes paused in the entrance to the lobby. He looked at them, each in turn, with a strange, wild light in his eyes. He remembered again, with a stab of agony, his leave-taking of Victoria Prentice the previous evening. They had parted with an impersonal handshake. He had let her go without finding a way to arrange to see her again. He would never see her again, he thought, as he stood and looked at the old people in the lobby, because he had been a coward.

He launched himself into the lobby. Sophie Crump saw him first and called out to him. Dr. Marshall turned from the window with an expectant smile on his face that died when he looked at Hobbes. Mr. Darling looked up from his paper.

Hobbes motioned them together near the chair Sophie sat in. Mr. Darling folded his paper with maddening patience before he creaked to his feet and joined them.

"Are you all right?" Dr. Marshall asked Hobbes. Sophie Crump craned her neck to stare up at Hobbes' face.

"I saw a lawyer," Hobbes said. He told them what Victoria had said.

"It will take months," Dr. Marshall said morosely.

"I've got a plan," Hobbes said. "We'll take him."

"Take him?" Dr. Marshall asked. "How do you mean?"

"Take him out of there."

"Can we do that?" Sophie asked.

"You mean—" Dr. Marshall swallowed. "You mean without permission?"

"He's seventy-six years old, and he doesn't want to be there, does he? That's old enough to decide for yourself where you'll be."

"By God!" Mr. Darling cried, staggering with excitement. "Now you're talkin'!"

"But—but wouldn't that be illegal?" Dr. Marshall asked.

Hobbes shrugged. "Technically."

Dr. Marshall was pale. "I—I don't know."

"This is war!" Mr. Darling said to him. "Gird yer loins, Marshall. Join the front ranks!"

"I see," Dr. Marshall said to no one in particular. "I see."

"I'm with you," Sophie said, setting her false teeth in a determined grimace.

Hobbes looked at Dr. Marshall. The old man smiled palely and said, "I, too."

Mr. Darling slapped his leg. "Now we're cookin'," he said.

"How do we go about it?" Dr. Marshall asked.

"I was Signal Corps during the war," Mr. Darling offered. "Had combat trainin'."

"First," Hobbes said, "we need to know everything we can about the hospital. The layout, possible exits, the security routines—"

"Right!" Mr. Darling said. "Reconnaissance."

"I know something about hospital routine," Dr. Marshall said.

Hobbes studied each of the old people. "Here's what we'll do. Dr. Marshall and I will make a visit to Commander Peevey this afternoon. We'll look at the layout. Tonight, when we get back, we'll meet and draw up a plan."

Mr. Darling, in a paroxysm of excitement, reeled against Hobbes and clutched his shoulder. "By God! Now we're cookin'."

Commander Peevey's room in the residential section of the hospital had pale green walls. There was a bed, on which Commander Peevey lay, staring at the ceiling, a metal chest of drawers, two scuffed armchairs, and a table with a lamp on it.

Dr. Marshall perched nervously on the edge of the chair. His eyes darted furtively at the door that stood open into the hallway. Patients and their visitors ambled by. The echoing murmur of voices washed down the hall

74

and into the room. Hobbes studied Dr. Marshall for a moment and then said, "You stay here. I'll scout around."

"Scut food!" Commander Peevey rumbled suddenly from the bed, causing Dr. Marshall to jump.

Hobbes went to the bed and looked down into the old man's face. Commander Peevey peered up at him. He raised a palsied hand to his eyes and methodically rubbed each one with a big finger. "Hobbes?" he said.

Hobbes patted his arm. "Yes."

"My mind is just not working," Commander Peevey said. "Did I tell you that?"

"Yes," Hobbes replied. "Dr. Marshall is here, too." He motioned Marshall over to the bed.

Commander Peevey stared in confusion at Dr. Marshall. "Doctor?" he said. "I've had a stroke, haven't I?"

"No," Dr. Marshall said. "It's the drugs."

"Drugs!" Commander Peevey cried hoarsely. "Don't shit me, Doctor. I've had a stroke. Always knew I would."

"This is Dr. Marshall—from the hotel," Hobbes said.

Commander Peevey stared at him. "Hotel?"

"The Lincoln Hotel."

Commander Peevey's head swiveled back to Marshall. "The quack?"

Dr. Marshall smiled crookedly. "The quack."

"You haven't had a stroke," Hobbes said.

Commander Peevey cut his eyes at Hobbes with a hurt look. "You were the only one I could trust," he whispered.

Hobbes took a breath and said, "Now listen. You have not had a stroke. It's like Dr. Marshall said. It's the effect of drugs. We're going to get you out of here."

Dr. Marshall gasped. "Is that wise?"

Commander Peevey was staring up at Hobbes, his eyes suddenly lucid. "Thank God," he breathed. "Now?"

Hobbes shook his head. "In a few days. We're going to need your help."

75

"Really," Dr. Marshall whispered. "Is this wise?"

Hobbes held up a hand to silence Dr. Marshall. "Do you read me, Peevey?"

Peevey grinned. "Just tell me who I gotta kill."

"That's the spirit. Now listen carefully. Don't take any more pills. But you've got to make them think you have. Can you do it?"

Commander Peevey winked ponderously. Then his eyes clouded over again. "Scut food!" he shouted.

Dr. Marshall followed Hobbes to the door and said in an intense whisper, "What if he tells? In his condition, no telling what he'll say."

Hobbes shrugged. "In his condition, who'd believe him? If he doesn't get off those pills, we're going to have to carry him out of here."

Dr. Marshall groaned softly. "We'll never do it."

Hobbes patted him gently on the shoulder. "Yes, by God, we will!"

At the end of the hall were a reception area and elevators. Two nurses worked behind a counter. White-jacketed orderlies passed by, carrying trays, rolling gurneys. Bathrobed old men shuffled along the corridor with their visitors.

Hobbes leaned against the wall next to a cigarette urn and smoked. He observed that some of the patients were leaving with their visitors. When they did, they handed a pink card to one of the nurses. He came to understand that these passes allowed the patients and their visitors to walk outside on the grounds. He watched carefully as the nurses slipped the passes into metal holders that corresponded to room numbers.

A large nurse looked up at him. "Can I help you?"

Hobbes held up his cigarette. "It bothers my grandfather." He noted a door next to the elevators that led to a stairwell and filed that fact away.

Back in Peevey's room, Hobbes said, "I think we can do it."

Dr. Marshall turned pale.

When Hobbes and Dr. Marshall returned from the hospital, Mr. Darling and Sophie Crump were waiting in the lobby. A group of residents were gathered around the television set. Sophie Crump led the three men to her room behind the lobby desk.

"We can do it," Hobbes said.

"Hot damn!" Mr. Darling cried.

"It won't be easy," Hobbes added.

"Listen," Mr. Darling said, his eyes burning at Hobbes, "when we do it, take me along. I can't stand this waitin' around."

Hobbes said, "We'll all have to go."

"Good!" Sophie Crump replied. "I'm scared to death, but I wouldn't miss it."

"Okay," Hobbes said. "Be in my room in an hour. I want to make a sketch of the hospital ward while it's fresh in my memory."

"Oh," Sophie Crump said. "I near forgot. You had a call."

Hobbes turned back.

"Wait." Sophie went through the door ahead of Hobbes and took a slip of paper from the desk.

Hobbes stared down at the slip. In Mrs. Crump's spidery writing was Victoria Prentice's name and a phone number.

Mrs. Crump smiled slyly at him. " 'Bout time you got a girlfriend," she said. "Young fella like you."

Back in his room, Hobbes' hands were trembling so badly that he had to dial the number twice.

She answered on the second ring. The sound of her voice took the breath from Hobbes.

"I've been doing a little more research on your problem," she said, and described how Hobbes might file with the court an order to show cause why Commander

77

Peevey shouldn't be put into his care. Hobbes hardly heard her.

Hobbes cleared his throat. "Listen. Something's come up. I"—he took a deep breath—"I need to see you about it."

Silence. Hobbes prayed.

"I told you I can't get involved."

"I can't very well get a lawyer on Sunday." Hobbes tried to laugh. It came out a hoarse croak.

"It's that urgent?"

"Yes. Yes, it is."

Silence again. Hobbes' hands were sweating.

"All right. How about six o'clock?"

"I'll be there."

"No!" She paused. "Is there someplace at the hotel where we could meet?"

"Yes," he said eagerly. "I'll meet you in the lobby." He gave her the address of the hotel.

After Hobbes hung up, he sat on the edge of his bed and tried to think what he would tell Victoria Prentice. He ran his hands over his face and looked at his watch. He had three hours to think of some way to go on seeing her. He told himself he would think of something. He told himself he had to.

NINE

The three old people were gathered around Hobbes, who sat at the table in his room. He had carefully prepared a sketch of the hospital ward as he remembered it. Beside the sketch lay a sheet of paper with a list of numbered notes. As he described his plan for taking Commander Peevey from the hospital, he felt a strange sense of strength. The old people bent into the cone of light that came from the lamp on the table, and their intense attention to what he told them and the utter seriousness with which they bent their old faces down to see the sketch made Hobbes want to laugh and cry all at once.

"We'll need another room," Hobbes said, indicating the final item on his list. "The first place they'll look is his old room."

Sophie Crump nodded. "The one on the floor above his old one," she said. "It's the same, and he does so hate anything that's different."

"When?" Dr. Marshall asked.

Hobbes thought for a moment. "Tuesday," he said. "If

79

he can avoid those pills, maybe by then their effect will have worn off."

"And if not?" Dr. Marshall asked.

"Then we get him between us and drag him out."

"We can do it," Mr. Darling said stoutly.

"I'll see to getting his things moved up to the next floor," Sophie Crump said.

"We'd better do it ourselves," Hobbes replied. "Tonight, after everyone's in bed."

"We can do it," Mr. Darling repeated. His eyes glittered in the lamplight.

"Dr. Marshall and I will go tomorrow night for one last look," Hobbes said.

"I'll go," Mr. Darling said. "You might need help."

"No," Hobbes replied. "It's important that they not connect you and Mrs. Crump with Commander Peevey."

Mr. Darling gave a reluctant nod.

As the old people were leaving, Hobbes detained Mrs. Crump for a private word. "Ah—I'm having a visitor in about an hour, Mrs. Crump."

"A lady, Mr. Hobbes?"

"Yes, Mrs. Crump. I—I just thought I'd mention that we'll be talking in the lobby."

Mrs. Crump went to the door, closed it, and came back to stand close to Hobbes. "I'm not one of them sticklers on the rules, Mr. Hobbes."

Hobbes stared at her.

"I mean," she whispered, "if you want to have her up here—"

"No, no," Hobbes said. His face was crimson. "It's nothing like that."

Mrs. Crump was obviously disappointed. "Well"— she sighed—"keep it in mind, if the occasion should arise."

Hobbes showered and gave himself a close shave. He dressed in his new suit. Then he went down to the lobby

80

and sat stiffly on the lumpy old couch, suffering in silence the sly glances of the old people gathered around the television. Mrs. Crump obviously had told them about his visitor.

Victoria Prentice's arrival caused a shock of excitement to run through the old people. Hobbes, with constricted throat, went to meet her. She wore a pale blue trench coat, a red scarf around her slender neck. She nodded briskly at Hobbes.

"I've arranged for a place to talk," Hobbes said, indicating the french doors leading to the garden room.

"I'd like to meet your neighbors," Victoria said.

Mrs. Crump, Mr. Darling, and Dr. Marshall sat at the card table, playing dominoes. Hobbes led Victoria over and introduced her.

"Thomas has been telling me about Commander Peevey," Victoria said. "I hope you're successful in getting him out of there."

The three at the table turned startled faces up to Hobbes.

Hobbes said quickly, "Miss Prentice is the lawyer I saw."

The relief at the table was palpable. Dr. Marshall rose to his feet and smiled. "A pleasure, Miss Prentice. We appreciate your help."

The garden room was a glassed-over courtyard. Once it had abounded with plants, but now the flower beds were barren, and the soil was crusted over. Hobbes and Victoria sat on an iron bench.

"They're so thin," Victoria said.

"They're poor," Hobbes said.

"What is the big secret about Commander Peevey?"

Hobbes was startled. "What?"

"When I mentioned that you'd talked to me, they acted as if you'd been selling secrets to the enemy."

Hobbes took out his cigarettes and offered Victoria

81

one. He lit hers and then his. "Can I ask you a hypothetical question?"

"As a lawyer?"

He nodded. "What if someone were to—ah—help Commander Peevey leave the hospital?"

"That's abduction," she said without hesitation.

"Technically, I suppose—"

"There's no adverb in front of it," she said flatly. "And you'd be a fool to try. That's what those people were upset about—they're your fellow conspirators, aren't they?"

"Jesus!" Hobbes threw his cigarette down. "You make us sound like criminals. It's the agency that's committed the criminal act."

"That's not for you to judge." Victoria rose and walked to the french doors. She looked into the lobby at the old people. "You know," she said, "that if you go through with this crazy scheme, I'm bound by the ethics of my profession to report what you've told me."

"You'd *do* that?"

"I wouldn't have a choice."

Hobbes rose and walked to her. "Look. Just go see Peevey. Do that before you decide anything."

"It's not a matter of my deciding anything. It's the law."

He reached around her and opened the doors. "I thought you would be on our side."

She stared at his drawn face for a moment and then put a hand on his arm. "Let the law handle it. I'll help."

He looked into her face. "I don't have a choice either," he said.

She turned, walked quickly through the lobby, and out onto the street.

She saw Darrin pacing in front of her apartment building when the cab was still a block away. She nearly told the cabdriver to go on past, but she didn't.

As she was paying the driver, Darrin stood waiting impatiently. When she turned, he said, "Where have you been?"

"Hello, Darrin," she said quietly.

"Aren't you going to ask me in?"

"No."

"That's a hell of a way to treat the man you love." He gave her that melting smile of his. She felt the desire leap like a flame in her body.

"The agreement was that we wouldn't see each other this weekend, Darrin. The weekend isn't over."

"Agreement! Unilateral edict, you mean."

"What do you want, Darrin?"

"To see you."

"I told you I need some time to breathe."

"Now, that's just the thing, Victoria. That's why I want to see you. I don't understand this business of your feeling smothered."

"I don't either. But that's the way you make me feel."

He held his hands up in a helpless gesture. "Do we have to discuss it on the street?"

"You're not coming up, Darrin," she said flatly.

He nodded solemnly, then put his hands on his hips, his feet apart, and stared at the ground as he said, "Okay. We'll do it on the street corner. I've done a lot of thinking, Vickie. You were right. I see now that I smothered you." He looked at her out of the tops of his eyes. A lock of his thick, curling hair had fallen onto his forehead. She thought he had never looked more desirable. "But I love you, Vickie. So I surrender. Whatever you say goes."

"That's not the point, Darrin. I don't want to be the dictator. Don't you see—" She noticed she had her arm up in a declamatory gesture. She felt the tension in her body, as if her flesh had been strung too tightly on her skeleton. She let her hand fall. "Oh, for God's sake," she said. She brushed the hair back from her temples in a gesture of futility. "Come on up."

Darrin mixed drinks while she hung up her coat. When

she came back to the living room, he rose with a smile and handed her a drink. She took it and sat across from him on the couch.

"Darrin," she said in a trembling voice, "I'm not going to start with you again. Not now. Maybe never."

He nodded, giving her his best direct, sincere look. "Sure, kid. Like I said, you're the boss."

"My name is Victoria, Darrin."

"What?" He looked startled.

"Not Vickie. Not kid."

"Those are terms of endearment, ki—Victoria. I didn't mean anything—"

"I am twenty-six years old, Darrin. That makes me an adult. I'm not a little girl. I'm not a toy." She felt the anger flaming in her again. She took a cigarette from her purse and lit it.

"You never objected before," he said in a hurt tone.

"I mean, I never called you Darrie, or little guy, or anything, did I?" She felt petty for going on, but she couldn't stop herself.

"For Christ's sake, Victoria, I got the message." His face was dark with anger.

Victoria laughed. It was not a pleasant laugh. "There he is," she said.

"Who?"

"The real Darrin Semple. Sitting right there."

He put his hands over his face, his head bowed. "Christ, Victoria," he said through his hands, "have a heart." It was a gesture of supplication, of hurt and defeat, and it tore the anger from Victoria.

"Okay," she said quietly. "I apologize."

He took his hands from his face, like a magician presenting an illusion, to reveal his old melting smile. "See how you can cheer me up, just like that?"

She couldn't resist laughing.

He said, "I'd like to ask you something, but I don't want to make you mad again."

"What?"

"Where were you just now?"

"Why, Darrin?" she asked in a dangerous voice.

"Well, it's just that you look like a queen. You always look great, but that dress and the scarf—I mean, if there's another guy, I wish you'd just tell me. Okay? It would be kinder to just tell me."

"I've been helping someone with a legal problem."

"Is that smart? You know you aren't supposed to have private clients."

"It's not a client. It's a—friend."

"A guy?"

"If it matters, yes."

"Knotty problem?"

"I won't be cross-examined, Darrin. This is the very thing I've been talking about."

"Okay. Okay. No more questions about your private case."

"It's *not* a case—" She broke off and stood. "You'd better go now."

He got up quickly. "You're the boss." He walked to her and put his hands on her shoulders. "I appreciate your hearing me out."

She averted her face. She hoped he wouldn't notice how her legs were trembling.

He put his lips against her neck. She moaned softly. Her arms encircled his neck.

He led her to the bedroom and gently undressed her. Then he undressed. He approached her almost shyly. But she was reckless with passion. She wrapped him in her arms and legs. She forced his mouth hard against her breasts. In her final moment, it was as though she were alone at a destination he had brought her to. She flung her arms and made animal noises through her clenched teeth.

Later, as he smoked a cigarette, she lay with her hands behind her head, staring at the ceiling.

"God, baby," he said huskily, "I can't believe how I've missed you. It's only a week—it seems like a year." He gave her a quick look. "I mean, Victoria."

She smiled dreamily. "Under the circumstances, "baby" is okay. Light me a cigarette, will you?"

He fumbled beside the bed for his cigarettes, lit one, and passed it to her. She blew a stream of smoke at the ceiling. "Tell me something, Darrin—have you ever had a cause?"

He turned on his side and stared at her profile. "What kind of game is this?"

"I'm serious. Have you ever believed in something so strongly that you were willing to risk—well, if not everything, at least things important to you?"

"It's a test, right?"

"I know I haven't."

"What?"

"I've never believed in anything that strongly." She inhaled the smoke and let it trickle out of her nostrils. "I wish I had."

He grinned suddenly. "I signed a petition in law school to have the state bar exams brought up to date. Does that count?" He turned her head and kissed her.

Her passions were spent. She passively allowed Darrin to kiss her and stroke her body. Abruptly the memory of Thomas Hobbes' face when she had told him she would have to turn him in if he kidnapped the old man came flooding into her mind. She felt a sharp, sick pain at the memory. And it made her unaccountably angry. She turned to Darrin and let him make love to her again as a kind of retaliation against Hobbes and his lost, crazy cause.

TEN

On Monday morning Hobbes sat and stared at Vernon Dooley, for the moment too startled to do anything else. Dooley was leaning back in his chair, his feet up on his desk, a thick cigar in his mouth. Halladay leaned against the wall beside Dooley's desk, his arms folded, watching Hobbes.

"I'm sorry—" Hobbes stuttered. "What—what did you say?"

Dooley grinned, took the cigar from his mouth, and pointed it at Hobbes. "I said, we're going to make you an agent, Hobbes."

"But I haven't had the training—"

Dooley waved a hand. "Leave it to us." Dooley dropped his feet to the floor and leaned across the desk toward Hobbes. "Maybe you don't realize what it means to be an Ops agent. There are guys around here who would give their balls for a crack at it."

"I know what it means."

"Is that a new suit, Hobbes?"

"Yes, sir."

"Now there's a coincidence." Dooley winked at Hobbes. "The day you get promoted, you show up in a new suit. Have you got sources in the branch I don't know about?" Halladay laughed.

Hobbes managed a weak smile. "Ah—could I ask a question?"

"Shoot."

"Well—" Hobbes ran his hand through his hair. "What I don't understand is why I'm getting this—ah—chance. There must be others more qualified."

"Good question, Tom. The reason you were picked is that you fit a certain profile we were looking for. We had the boys in computing do a work-up on this assignment we've got, and your name bounced to the top."

"Assignment?"

"Right." Dooley opened a folder on his desk, shuffled through some papers, and took a photograph from them. He held the photograph out to Hobbes. "Take a look at this."

It was a picture of a man standing in the doorway of a building, caught in the act of putting on a topcoat. Either the photographer was inept or in a great hurry because the man's head was blurred on one side in a way that made it appear his cheek was being blown off by a high wind. His nose was a gray smear across his face.

"Remarkable, isn't it?" Dooley asked.

"Sir?" Hobbes looked up from the picture.

"The resemblance." Dooley got up and came around the desk to look over Hobbes' shoulder at the photograph. "You probably can't see it the way I can. I've seen the guy in person."

"Resemblance?"

"To you, Tom. You're a dead ringer for that guy." Dooley took the photograph from Hobbes and went back to his desk.

"You mean this man looks like me?"

Dooley nodded solemnly and puffed on his cigar. "There are some minor differences, of course," he said airly. "But we'll take care of them."

"Take care of them?"

Dooley chuckled. "When the special techniques boys finish with you, his own mother, if he ever had one, won't tell you apart."

"What will I be doing?"

Dooley's eyes narrowed. "Stand up, Hobbes." He came around the desk and put his hand on Hobbes' shoulder. "You read the security act and signed the oath when you joined the agency, didn't you?"

"Yes, sir." Hobbes could feel his forehead prickling with sweat under Dooley's unremitting gaze.

Dooley gave Hobbes' shoulder a rough shake. "You're our boy, Tom. The minute I showed you that photo, you were in. You'll be told what you need to know at the time you need to know it. You understand what I'm saying?"

"Yes, sir." Sweat was coursing into Hobbes' eyes.

Dooley dropped his hand. "Okay. Wipe your face, and let's have no more questions." Dooley went back to his desk. Hobbes took a handkerchief from his pocket and mopped his forehead. "Your training starts immediately," Dooley said. "You go with Halladay now, and I'll see you later."

As Halladay was leading Hobbes from the office, Dooley said, "Oh, Tom—"

"Sir?"

Dooley waved Halladay out of the office. When they were alone, Dooley said, "I just want to say this, Tom: Eventually, you'll understand the importance of this assignment. I don't mean important to me, although it is. I mean to our country. It's vital. I'm not a sentimental man—"

"No, sir."

"I'm not one to wrap myself in the flag. I've got a job, and I do it, and I do it well. My work speaks for itself."

"Yes, sir."

"But this assignment we've got for you requires a special kind of man. It requires a man who loves his country. To put it briefly, what the job wants is a patriot." Dooley leaned back in his chair and cocked his head, as though listening to the echo of that word ringing in the room. "Are you that man, Hobbes? Are you a patriot?"

"Well—I hadn't thought about it—"

"Think about it now, Hobbes."

"Well—yes, sir, I suppose so."

"Goddammit, man!" Dooley struck the top of his desk with the flat of his hand, making Hobbes jump. "Are you?"

"Yessir." Hobbes spoke so quickly his words slurred. "Yessir, I am."

Dooley sat back in his chair and smiled. "Good. Don't forget it." He bent over his desk and, without looking up, said, "That'll be all."

Halladay led Hobbes through a maze of hallways, down stairs, up stairs, through a tunnel joining two buildings, eventually arriving at a large, brightly lit room with a row of cubicles along one side. Hobbes followed in a daze. He was sure that he could never find his way out without a guide. The big room was empty. It echoed their footfalls eerily. Halladay left Hobbes alone in the room and then reappeared a few minutes later, carrying a black looseleaf notebook. He sat Hobbes in one of the cubicles and placed the notebook on the shelf that served as a kind of desk. Halladay opened the notebook. He explained that the notebook contained a description of everything that was known about the man who looked like Hobbes. Halladay explained that Hobbes was to memorize the facts in the notebook.

"This assignment—" Hobbes said.

"It's strictly Need to Know," Halladay said coldly. "Do you know what that means?"

90

"Ah—yes. I guess so."

"In this case, you will be told what you need to know at the time you need it. Got that?"

Hobbes sighed. "Yes, sir."

"I'll be back in two hours," Halladay said with a grim smile. "And we'll see how much you've learned."

Halladay left. Hobbes stared around the room for a moment, blinking in the harsh light. The place reminded him of a gymnasium. It increased his sense of disorientation to look out on its vast space. He turned to the notebook.

The first section in the book contained a terse summary of the man's history. (Hobbes was to discover that in this section, as well as the others, the man's name never appeared. He was referred to as "the subject.") The history was organized chronologically. The man had been born fourteen months before Hobbes, in Utah. He had gone through high school in Ogden. He had attended the University of Utah and graduated with a bachelor's degree in journalism. He had worked for a year for the Salt Lake City *Tribune* as a reporter and then had joined a news wire service. He had been sent to Vietnam by the wire service in 1972. He had been recruited by the CIA in Saigon and had continued to work for the wire service while secretly working for the CIA. When he returned to the United States, he went to work for the CIA full time. The last entry in the section was dated only two months before, and it made Hobbes' pulse race as he read it. It said:

Subject, by order Director, declared Extreme Danger to Agency. See Order DIR 77427.

Hobbes stared at the entry and then got up and walked across to the door. He pushed on it lightly. It was unlocked. He opened it just enough to put his head into the hall. The hall was empty. He stepped out. Just as he did,

Halladay appeared at the end of the hall. When Halladay saw Hobbes, his face clouded with anger.

"What's up, Hobbes?"

"Could I see you for a minute?"

Halladay followed Hobbes into the room. Hobbes turned and faced Halladay. "This guy," Hobbes said. "Is he a traitor?"

"Yes." Halladay stared at him coldly.

"Well, Jesus—I don't know. Nobody told me that."

"Do you want to talk to Dooley?" Halladay asked.

Hobbes shook his head. He felt trapped. He felt there was no way out of this assignment. If he complained, he would be taken back to Dooley. And Dooley would fix him with that steely glare and make him sweat.

"Why don't you get back to it then?" Halladay asked, and left.

The next section in the notebook contained a list of the man's personal characteristics: his likes and dislikes, his idiosyncrasies, his beliefs and prejudices.

The third section was in the form of questions and answers about the man. Hobbes understood that he was to memorize the answers. He was going through them for the second time when Halladay returned with another man. Halladay introduced the man as Dr. Beckman.

Halladay got three chairs from one of the cubicles and arranged them in the center of the big room. He sat Hobbes opposite himself and Dr. Beckman. The chairs were arranged in such a way that Hobbes' knees were nearly touching those of the other two men.

Dr. Beckman stared at Hobbes with a curiosity so clinical that it made Hobbes' flesh crawl.

Halladay opened the notebook on his lap and asked Hobbes the questions from the last section of the book. When they were finished, Halladay looked at Hobbes with grudging admiration.

"You're a quick study."

Dr. Beckman cleared his throat. "Perhaps I could ask some questions that aren't in the book?"

Halladay nodded.

"When were you divorced?" Dr. Beckman asked.

Hobbes stared in confusion at Beckman. "He—"

"*I*," Halladay thundered.

Hobbes swallowed, and began again. "I was never married."

"I see," Dr. Beckman replied. He removed his glasses, took a soiled handkerchief from his pocket, and cleaned them. "Perhaps you prefer the—ah—" Beckman held the glasses up to the light and studied them. "Boys, eh?" He looked at Hobbes with his naked, watery eyes and smiled.

"No." Hobbes looked at Halladay in confusion. "At least I don't think so. He—I lived with a woman in—wait—in Salt Lake City, wasn't it?"

Halladay leaned very close to Hobbes and said in a dry whisper, "You don't *know* if you prefer boys?"

Hobbes felt himself flush. "I don't. I lived with a woman."

Halladay leaned back. "That's better." He nodded to Beckman to continue.

Beckman put his glasses on. "Now, Mr. Hobbes, I will ask you a question that you do not have the answer to. But please make your best judgment as to how you might answer it if—well—as if your life depended on it." Dr. Beckman chuckled. "You had to kill in Vietnam, did you not?"

Hobbes felt a chill in the pit of his stomach. Dr. Beckman sat smiling, a serene-looking little man who appeared to have only the mildest of interests in the answer to the question he had posed, yet Hobbes couldn't dispel the feeling that Beckman had worded the question with infinite care.

Halladay sat with his arms folded over his chest, staring impassively at Hobbes.

"I guess—" Hobbes faltered.

"*What!*" thundered Halladay.

"Yes. Yes, I did," Hobbes said angrily. If that was what they wanted to hear, he would give it to them.

"And how did you feel about that?" Beckman asked quickly.

"What?" Hobbes stared at him, his mind numb.

"The killing. How did you feel about it?"

"Didn't like it—"

"Speak up!" Halladay shouted.

"I didn't like it!"

"*Why?*" Beckman was yelling now, too, leaning in toward Hobbes, his eyes glittering.

Hobbes took a deep breath, and said, "I—I'm not a killer. I did it out of necessity."

"*What!*" Beckman shouted. His face was shiny with sweat. "What did you do out of necessity?"

"I killed them!"

"Them? Them?"

"HIM, goddammit—HIM, then," Hobbes screamed.

Beckman leaned back in his chair, panting slightly. He took the handkerchief from his pocket and dabbed delicately at his forehead with it. "Excellent," he said quietly. He turned to Halladay. "Excellent."

Halladay nodded impassively. He stood abruptly. "I think we can go right to the tapes."

Beckman nodded and then said to Hobbes, "Really excellent, Mr. Hobbes. Keep up the good work."

Hobbes had no idea what he was being complimented on.

Halladay and Beckman left the room. Halladay returned alone, carrying a portable tape recorder, earphones, and a plastic container of tapes. He set up the recorder in the cubicle Hobbes had been using and showed him how it worked. The erase and record keys had been removed from the recorder.

94

"This is his voice," Halladay said. "Study that voice. Try it out. Tomorrow we'll have an expert in to help you get it down."

Hobbes spent the rest of the day listening to the tapes. Halladay brought him his lunch on a tray.

The voice on the tapes had a midwestern accent, not too different from Hobbes. But the voice was higher, and the man had the habit of lowering it at the ends of sentences. The tapes were taken from recordings of telephone conversations, with the responses of the other party deleted. The conversations were innocuous to the point of being dull. In some sections, words and even whole phrases had been edited.

At a little after five, Halladay came, gathered up the materials, and led Hobbes back through the maze to Dooley's office.

Dooley looked up from his desk. "I hear good things about you, Tom."

"Yes, sir."

Dooley leaned back in his chair and put his hands behind his head. He was in shirt sleeves, and there were dark circles of fatigue around his eyes.

"For the time being, you just go about your regular routine when you're not at the office. I don't have to remind you not to talk about this project, do I?"

"No, sir."

"As it turns out, your living arrangements are as good as any we could come up with—at least for the time being. That hotel—what is it? The Lincoln?—is low profile."

Hobbes was too weary and confused by the events of the day to be much surprised that Dooley knew the details of his living arrangements.

"Yes, sir," he said dully.

As Hobbes was turning to go, Dooley said, "Oh, and, Tom—"

Hobbes turned back. "Yes, sir."

"This—" Dooley picked up a sheet of paper from his desk and consulted it. "Victoria Prentice—"

Hobbes stared at him.

"What is she to you, Tom?" Dooley asked mildly.

"I—how?"

Dooley smiled. "Girlfriend?"

"No. Just an acquaintance." Hobbes felt his face flaming.

Dooley nodded. "Her office is near yours? That's how you met?"

Hobbes swallowed and nodded.

"Don't look so worried," Dooley said. "There's no rule against employees fraternizing. But it might be wise to cut down on social activity. You're going to be too busy for it anyway."

"Yes, sir. Is that part of the assignment?"

"What?"

"Digging into my private life."

"We have to know about our agents, Tom. It's the price you pay."

"Yes, sir."

"That'll be all, Hobbes."

ELEVEN

Darrin insisted he was going to spend Sunday night with Victoria. She had to marshal all her determination to get him to leave, and that had succeeded only when his stubbornness had finally caused her to explode in a rage. Darrin had left quickly, frightened by her reaction, promising to call before she had an opportunity to tell him not to.

The encounter with Darrin left her drained of emotion and energy. Despite that, she couldn't sleep. She finally got up at two o'clock and took a sleeping pill. When her alarm went off at seven, she awoke in a state of drugged lethargy. She put on a robe, shuffled to the kitchen, and tried to revive herself with strong coffee. But it seemed only to deepen her weariness. She considered reporting out sick at the agency. She told herself she had been there only a month, and it wasn't prudent to take the day off. Then she told herself she didn't give a damn about prudence, and she called her office and reported out sick. She was a very junior member on the staff of lawyers, and she rationalized that as such she really wouldn't be missed

97

much. She went back to bed and immediately fell into a deep, dreamless sleep. When she awoke, it was noon.

After a shower and breakfast, she felt revived and considered going into the office for half a day. But by this time it had occurred to her what it was she wanted to do with her afternoon. So instead of going into the office, she called the Veterans' Hospital, found out Commander Peevey's room number and the visiting hours that afternoon. When the time came, she took a cab across town to the Veterans' Hospital and went up to Commander Peevey's floor.

Commander Peevey's room was dim. The blinds were drawn, and the light was off. When she saw the vague outline of the man on the bed, she thought he was asleep. But then a surprisingly deep voice from the bed said, "Who's there?"

"Victoria Prentice." She stepped closer to the bed.

"Nurse?"

"No." She could see the huge old head now, crowned by fine white hair, and the eyes burning up at her out of the pillows. "You don't know me, but I'm a friend of Thomas Hobbes."

He was silent for a moment, looking up at her. Then he said, "What do you want?"

She searched for an answer and realized she really didn't know what it was she wanted. "I—Mr. Hobbes has told me a lot about you, and I just thought I'd like to meet you," she said weakly.

He held out a huge hand and stared solemnly into her eyes. She took his hand. It was strong and warm.

"How do you do?" he said.

She smiled. "How do you do?"

He motioned vaguely toward a chair. "Have a seat."

Victoria pulled up the chair and sat. Her eyes had completed their adjustment to the dimness of the room, and she could see his face clearly now. He smiled.

"So," he said, "I'm famous."

She nodded. "To me, at least."

"What did Hobbes have to say about me?"

"Well—he admires you. He's quite concerned about you."

"Say," Commander Peevey said, "you don't happen to have a cigar on you?"

Victoria shook her head. "I've got cigarettes."

"Can't stand 'em," he replied contemptuously. "Cigar's a man's smoke." He glared at her, as if waiting for her to contradict him. When she didn't, he grinned suddenly and said, "Hobbes tell you I got a helluva temper?"

She smiled. "I believe he mentioned it."

He sighed. "It gets me in trouble."

"I know what Mr. Hobbes is planning," she whispered, leaning closer.

His eyebrows shot up. "You and Hobbes sweethearts?"

She felt herself blush, and she was thankful it was dim in the room. "No," she said.

"Too bad," Commander Peevey said. "Hobbes could use a fine-looking woman like yourself. That's about all that ails that boy, you know. Hasn't got himself a woman."

"I'm—I'm sure he can find one."

"Nope!" Commander Peevey pronounced. "Too damn shy. A woman'd say boo to him, and he'd run like a scalded dog." He shot her a sudden look. "What'd Hobbes say he was planning?"

"To get you out."

"You in on it?"

"In a way," she replied.

"They had me drugged up like a dope fiend," he said. He motioned her closer and whispered, "I've been palming the pills since yesterday. Feel a damn sight better. Hobbes tell you I thought I'd had a stroke?"

She shook her head. He stared broodingly at the ceiling. "My daddy went with strokes. After the first, he couldn't talk, couldn't do a thing for himself. It was a blessing when he finally went. I've always had the dread that I'd go that way."

99

"Are you all right?"

"Fit as a bull calf." He thumped his chest with his fist. "All it was was the damn pills. If a nurse comes in, don't you let on. I gotta act like I don't have good sense, or they'll know I've been palming the pills."

"All right."

"When is Hobbes getting me out of here?"

"I believe he's planning to try tomorrow night."

"Good! That's not a damn bit too soon."

"Commander Peevey." Victoria hitched her chair closer to the bed. "I wonder if you know what Thomas is risking?"

"Risking?"

"He's going to try to take you out without permission of the authorities."

"Yes, he is, and I say, 'Bully for him!' "

"But don't you see—he'll be making himself liable to a charge of abduction?"

"Abduction!" Commander Peevey snorted. "It's no such thing. I want out of here!"

"But it's no longer your choice. The hospital has papers—"

"Papers!" Commander Peevey dismissed the hospital and its papers with a wave of a huge hand. "Let me tell you something, little lady. Come next June I'll be seventy seven years old. I didn't live all that time to be hog-tied by a bunch of papers."

"But aren't you concerned about what they might do to Thomas?"

Commander Peevey struggled up on his elbows and looked at Victoria from under the ledge of his white brows. "Does Hobbes know what he's getting into?"

Victoria bit her lip and nodded. "I've tried to tell him."

"Then it's his own damn business. Hobbes may be a rabbit in some things, but he's a grown-up man."

"But we could file in court. I'm a lawyer, Commander Peevey. We could force the hospital to release you through the courts."

Commander Peevey stared thoughtfully at her. "Did you tell Hobbes that?"

Victoria nodded.

"What'd he say?"

"Well, of course I couldn't guarantee it would work."

"What'd he say, dammit?"

"He said it would take too long."

"How long?"

"It might take a couple of months, but—"

"And Hobbes didn't want to wait?"

She shook her head.

"Good for him." Commander Peevey fell back on the bed. They were silent for a long moment. Then he said, "I thought you said you were with us."

Victoria didn't reply.

"Let me tell you something. You know what the insurance company's say my life expectancy is? Zero! That's what. Not a day, not a minute, but zero! Far as they're concerned, I'm dead now." He turned his head and looked at her. "So I haven't got two months to give to any damn court. I plan to do a lot of living in those two months."

They were silent again. Commander Peevey's heavy breathing filled the room, and Victoria decided that he had fallen asleep and was gathering herself to leave quietly when he said, "Lord knows, though, I don't want that boy to get sent to jail on my account."

Victoria sighed. "I don't think you could stop him."

Commander Peevey chuckled. "Got his back up, has he?"

"Yes."

Victoria stood and placed her hand on top of his. "This is between you and Hobbes. I see that now."

He captured her hand in his. "You didn't come here because you heard how fascinating I am. You came here because of Hobbes, didn't you?"

"I—I suppose so. Yes."

"So why don't you get behind him?"

101

"I'm a lawyer, Commander Peevey."

He snorted. "You were a woman before you were a lawyer, weren't you?"

"Yes."

"Well, for God's sake, try to remember that."

She squeezed his hand.

She could see his teeth flash. "Damn!" he said. "I haven't lost the old Peevey charm, have I?"

Hobbes drove home slowly. He thought about his day with a sense of wonder. Dooley's words to him kept bouncing around in his head, mixed up with words of his father. He thought particularly about his father's hope expressed in his last letter that Hobbes would distinguish himself in the service of his country. Somehow this phrase was juxtaposed in his mind beside the appeal Dooley had made for his patriotism.

Patriot; now that he thought about it, it was a strange word. When Dooley had asked him to accept that label, it had embarrassed him. It was not a word Hobbes was accustomed to using. It had the archaic ring of muskets and minutemen and redcoats about it.

Hobbes felt the hot premonition of peril, and he shuddered. He had no better idea what his assignment would be than he had had that morning, but he could guess that it would be dangerous. He didn't doubt that it would involve his impersonating the man in the photograph. A dangerous man.

It was true that Hobbes had fantasized being an agent, but he had separated that fantasy carefully from the reality of who he was. He was not agent material, he had told himself. But now fantasy and reality had run together in one brief day.

There was, as he thought about it in this new light, a headiness to the whole idea. A surge of power, a sense of having arrived, lifted his spirits.

When he entered the lobby of the hotel, several of the old people were gathered near the desk. He gave them the briefest glance as he proceeded across the lobby, and then he looked again and stopped short. There, in the midst of the group, was Victoria Prentice. She saw him and came over.

"Can we talk?" she asked.

He nodded numbly.

"I went to see Commander Peevey today," she said when they were alone in the garden room.

"Why?"

"I don't know. I suppose to try to talk him out of what you're planning."

"You had no right . . ." he began angrily.

"No," she agreed. "But it had the opposite effect."

"What do you mean?"

"He talked me into it." She turned and sat on a bench. "Oh, I don't mean that I'm going to be an accomplice."

He sat on the bench beside her. She turned to him. "Here's what I mean. I don't want to know anything about it. I'll forget we ever talked."

He nodded.

"I wanted you to know."

"I'm still going to do it."

"Please," she said with a pained expression. "Don't tell me." She stood.

"Don't go."

"That's all I had to say."

"Have dinner with me."

"I'm sorry. I'm not available."

"Not even as a friend?"

She smiled wryly. "I could use one."

He returned her smile. "No more than I could. Do friends have dinner then?"

"Friends definitely have dinner."

"I'll pick you up at seven?"

"I'll meet you."

He shook his head stubbornly. "Not friendly."

"I'll be in front of my building at seven."

103

TWELVE

When Victoria unlocked her door, her phone was ringing. She sensed it was Darrin before she answered.

"Where have you been?" he asked anxiously. "They said at the office you were sick. I've been calling all afternoon."

"I was out."

"I imagined all kinds of dire things."

"I can take care of myself."

"You sound strange." He paused. "I'm coming over."

"Don't. Don't do that, Darrin—" But he had hung up.

She put the phone down wearily. She dreaded Darrin's arrival. She didn't feel she had the energy to resist his smothering concern. She took a shower and was brushing her hair when he rang the doorbell. She slipped on a robe and went to let him in.

"You gave me a scare," he said. He looked quickly around the living room.

"Do you want to check the closets?" she asked.

"I was worried crazy about you. When they said you were sick, and then you didn't answer the phone—"

"I tried to tell you not to come over, but you hung up on me."

He took off his coat and put it in the hall closet. "Here's what we'll do," he said. "I'll get some pizza and a bottle of wine, we'll turn on the fire, and we'll just spend a cozy evening at home." He began pulling liquor from the cabinet Victoria kept it in. "But first, one of old Dr. Semple's magic home cures."

"Darrin—"

He measured gin into a mixing glass, holding it up to the light like an apothecary. "This will cure whatever ails you." He went into the kitchen and returned with ice.

"Darrin!"

He turned with a gay smile. "Darling?"

"I want you to go."

He shook his head, still smiling. "Wouldn't think of leaving you in your hour of need."

"I'm not in need, Darrin. And I have a—an appointment this evening."

He raised an eyebrow. "The friend with the knotty problem?"

"If it matters, yes."

He went on mixing the martinis. "Must be a challenging case, the amount of time you're devoting to it."

"It's not your concern."

"Oh," he said innocently, "I agree. Indeed I do." He poured the drinks and handed her one.

She took it and said, "Okay. One drink, and off you go."

"Really, darling," he replied, settling comfortably on the couch, "don't fret about me. You go ahead and get ready. I'll be fine."

"Darrin. Dammit."

"I'm really looking forward to meeting this knotty problem of yours."

She stared at Darrin's smiling face for a moment and then, with a weary sigh, went into her bedroom to finish dressing.

Hobbes' new suit badly needed cleaning and pressing. He rolled it in a bundle and, dressed in one of his old gray suits, went to the lobby and left the suit at the desk. Sophia Crump smiled at him as she slipped the suit into a cleaner's bag. "Tomorrow night," she whispered loudly.

He nodded.

"I'll tell you something, Mr. Hobbes." She crooked a gnarled finger to motion him closer over the counter. "I'm lookin' forward to it," she whispered. Her breath smelled of peppermint. "I ain't felt so alive in ages."

He patted her hand. "We'll pull it off, Mrs. Crump." He wished he was as confident as he sounded.

Hobbes got his car from the garage and drove to Victoria's apartment. He arrived ten minutes early. He parked in a loading zone in front of her building. He pulled up the collar of his new topcoat against the cold that seeped through the ill-fitting convertible top on the car. At ten after seven he decided she wasn't coming. He had his foot poised over the accelerator when he shut off the engine with an angry motion and got out of the car.

When Victoria opened the door to her apartment, she stared out at him with a distracted look. "Come in."

"I'm illegally parked," Hobbes said. He started through the door, and then he saw Darrin. They stared at each other.

"Hobbes!"

Hobbes couldn't find his voice. He stood frozen in the doorway, staring at Semple.

"You two know each other?" Victoria asked.

Semple stood. "I'll be damned!" he said. "Is this your knotty problem?"

"A friend," Victoria replied.

"Hobbes," Semple said slowly, as though trying to fit the name into his mind. Then, suddenly, he smiled. "Come in, man! Don't just stand there." Semple went to the bar. "What are you drinking?"

"Mr. Hobbes is illegally parked," Victoria said.

Darrin grinned. "Hobbes, a man with a lawyer like Vickie here shouldn't worry about little things such as parking tickets." He poured gin into the mixing glass. "Tell me—how did you two get together?"

Hobbes and Victoria exchanged a look. "We all work at the same place, Darrin," Victoria said.

Semple turned, walked to Hobbes, and handed him a glass. "Take off your coat, man. Relax."

"We have to go, Darrin," Victoria said.

Semple held up his drink. "Surely friends have time for a drink. We are friends, aren't we, Tommy?"

Hobbes sipped his drink. He didn't reply. "We're going, Darrin," Victoria said firmly. She took Hobbes' glass and put it on the liquor cabinet. "We're *all* going."

Semple sat on the couch and smiled lazily. "Maybe I'll wait around for you, Victoria. I worry when you're out." He looked at Hobbes. "Washington is such a dangerous place."

"Darrin," Victoria said, "don't be childish—please."

Semple settled more comfortably on the couch and smiled up at her.

Anger rose in Hobbes. "If Victoria wants you to leave—" he said in a strangled voice.

Semple looked at Hobbes with interest. "If Victoria wants me to leave—?"

"That's enough!" Victoria said.

"But Tommy was saying something to me," Semple replied in an innocent voice. "What was it you wanted to say, kid?"

Hobbes stared into Semple's grinning face and felt hate. "You'd better go," he said.

Victoria stepped quickly between the two men. "All right, Darrin," she said. "You win. Come on, Thomas— let's go."

Semple was on his feet now. His smile was gone. "Did I detect a threat in your words, Tommy, or am I being overly sensitive?"

Victoria took Hobbes' arm. "Let's go," she said. "Ignore him."

But Hobbes stood where he was. He couldn't take his eyes from Semple's face. "I guess you'd better go," Hobbes said.

Semple grinned suddenly. "I'm grateful, Hobbes. For years I've been keeping in shape—playing hours of handball, tennis, working out—and now you're going to give me a chance to have that investment pay off." He moved toward Hobbes.

Hobbes didn't see the blow until it was too late. Semple's right fist landed high on his temple. Vaguely he heard Victoria cry out. His head was roaring, and he found himself on the floor on one knee without remembering falling. Semple was standing over him.

"Rather disappointing, Hobbes," Semple said, panting. "For you to fold on the first swing."

Hobbes threw his arms out blindly and encircled Semple's waist. For a moment Semple struggled to keep his balance, and then both men toppled onto the floor. Hobbes hung on. He struck out blindly with his fist and felt it connect. Semple grunted. Hobbes swung again. He felt hands gripping his wrist and heard Victoria's voice loud in his ear.

He allowed himself to be pulled off Semple. He got shakily to his feet. His head throbbed. The anger was gone.

Semple was sitting up, his eyes dazed, a handkerchief held over his nose. The handkerchief was soaked with blood. Victoria's face was pale.

"Ice," Hobbes panted. "Get some ice in a cloth."

Victoria went in the kitchen. While she was gone, Semple held his nose and avoided looking at Hobbes. Victoria returned with ice cubes in a dishcloth. Hobbes knelt beside Semple, pressed the ice to the bridge of his nose, and tilted his head back. "Hold this," Hobbes said. In a few moments the bleeding had ebbed enough for Semple to get to his feet.

"I consider those sneak punches, Hobbes," Semple said thickly, still holding his head back with the ice on his nose.

"Next time you hit me," Hobbes said, "give me a copy of the rules first."

Semple laughed brokenly. He found his coat and clumsily put it on. "I've really got to go," he said with a crooked smile. "Now don't try to entice me to stay."

He turned and walked from the apartment.

Victoria sighed and put a hand over her eyes. "My God," she said.

Hobbes bent and began picking up the pieces of a glass that had been broken in the scuffle. She knelt beside him and helped. "Look," she said, "I really don't think I can go out after this."

"I'm sorry," he said. He stood and prepared to leave.

She stood beside him, holding the broken pieces of glass, and looked up into his face. "You've got a terrible bruise."

He touched his temple gingerly.

"Let me put something on it."

"It will be all right," he said.

She took the pieces of glass from him and went into the kitchen. When she returned, she insisted on helping him off with his topcoat. He sat dizzily on the couch while she went into the bathroom and returned with a tube of ointment and applied some gently to his temple.

She stood, removed her own coat, and hung it in the closet. "Listen," she said, "if you're willing to take potluck, I'll see what I can put together for dinner."

"If you're sure it's not too much trouble."

"No trouble. While I'm doing that, why don't you pour us a couple of those drinks?" She went into the kitchen.

He poured two drinks and brought them into the kitchen. She was standing at a chopping board preparing a salad. On the stove, a pan was beginning to simmer.

She took the drink and said, "My stew is always better the second day."

He leaned against the counter. The dizziness was coming and going in a plangent rhythm.

"You look awfully pale," she said. "Why don't you go in the living room and sit down?"

"I'd rather stay." Watching her slim hands wield the chef's knife had a soothing effect on his nerves.

"Darrin—" she said. She chopped a mushroom and pushed the pieces aside. "He and I—"

"You don't owe me any explanations," Hobbes said.

She glanced up at him. "But I do!" She sounded angry. "Can't you stand up for your rights?"

"All right," he said quietly. "You owe me an explanation."

"Darrin and I have—had a relationship." She turned and looked at him. "Did you know that?"

"Yes."

"How much did he tell you?"

Hobbes shrugged. "That he was seeing you. You said 'had—'"

She turned her back to stir the stew. "I'm thinking it over."

"I see."

She turned and held her glass out. "Get us another drink, will you?"

As he returned with the drinks, she was leaning against the cabinet, watching him. She took her glass, and said, "You and Darrin were friends?"

"In a way."

"I'm sorry."

"I'm not. It occurred to me that he felt more condescension for me than friendship."

"How did that occur to you?"

"Tonight—he was relieved that your visitor was me."

She stared at him. "Well, damn him," she said vehemently. "He shouldn't have been." She paused. Her eyes were large, and she swayed slightly against the cabinet. Hobbes realized she was getting drunk. Then he realized that applied to him, too. His tongue felt thick.

110

"Tell me," she said. "Have you discussed Commander Peevey with Darrin?"

"Yes. He told me to forget it. Very secretive about the whole thing."

"That's the way my supervisor was. Do you realize you could lose your job, among other consequesces?"

"I don't think so," he said. "They need me."

"A clerk?" She blushed. "I'm sorry."

"You're right—as a clerk, they don't need me. I've got a new job." She looked at him, waiting. "With Operations Branch. An agent—" He couldn't stop his tongue.

Her mouth parted as she stared at him. "One of the spooks? You?"

He nodded.

Suddenly she laughed. "Thomas Hobbes! Spy!"

He gave her a pained smile. "I wasn't supposed to tell anyone."

She leaned toward him with her finger to her lips. "They can torture me—I won't tell." She lowered her head and looked at him with drunken gravity. "Do you know what I've never been?"

"Is something burning?"

"Oh, God!" She jerked the pan off the stove and peered into it. "It's only burned on the bottom." She giggled. "We'll eat the top." She spun around to him. "Where was I? Oh! Do you know I've never been kissed by a spy? Now here you are—Thomas Hobbes, spy—to rectify all that."

She stepped close to him. "Spies are supposed to have a woman in every—what? It's not port. Hideout?" She closed her eyes and held her face up. "You will, won't you? Rectify that?"

He bent and gently placed his lips on hers.

THIRTEEN

The following morning Hobbes was joined in the training room by a small man with a large head and a mouthful of the most perfect teeth he had ever seen. The man smiled constantly. He carried a tape machine under one arm, and he introduced himself as Cramer, the voice man from the special techniques section.

Cramer set up the tape machine in a cubicle and began teaching Hobbes to speak in the voice of the man on the tapes.

Cramer showed Hobbes how to hold his tongue to achieve the desired accent. He showed Hobbes how to take a breath at the beginning of a sentence and trail it out at the end, so his voice would drop off like the voice on the tape.

At eleven o'clock Halladay and Dr. Beckman came in. Cramer gave them his full set of teeth.

"Apt pupil," he said.

"Good," Halladay said.

"Thing is," Cramer said, "we can't achieve pitch. Mr. Hobbes' voice is lower."

112

"Can't he raise it?" Halladay asked.

Cramer beamed and shook his head. "He'd be hoarse in a day. Now, it would be different if he'd had vocal training. But his vocal cords aren't toughened up."

Cramer played part of the tapes and then played a tape he had recorded of Hobbes imitating the voice.

"Very good," Dr. Beckman pronounced.

Halladay frowned. "The accent's good. But not the pitch. Any suggestions?"

Cramer shrugged and flashed his grin. "A cold!"

"Of course," Dr. Beckman said enthusiastically. "That would account for the lowering of the voice."

"I don't know," Halladay replied. "We'll have to think about it." He turned to Hobbes. "You've got an appointment." He told Cramer to come back after lunch, and the little man left the room.

Dr. Beckman left them in the hallway. Halladay led Hobbes to an elevator, and they descended beneath ground level. On the way down Hobbes remembered again, as he had many times since, the evening with Victoria, especially the feel of her cool lips on his. He even imagined for a moment that he could smell the lingering essence of her hair.

They had never got around to eating the burned stew. After the kiss, they had had another drink, and by the time Hobbes was through with his he was floating in a rosy ambience composed entirely of Victoria's presence. She had excused herself at one point and disappeared for what seemed to Hobbes at the time as hours. Finally, he had gone looking for her and found her curled up like a child on her bed, fully clothed and sound asleep.

With the excessive care of the drunk, Hobbes had removed her shoes, found a blanket in the closet, and covered her with it. Then he had turned out the lights in the apartment and left.

"Hobbes!" Halladay said, and Hobbes realized with a start that it was the second time he had said it. Halladay stood holding the door of the elevator open. Hobbes

113

stepped out and followed him to an unmarked metal door with no handles. In the wall beside it was a slot. Halladay inserted a plastic card into the slot, and the door slid back into the wall.

Inside they passed through a corridor into a long, narrow room. Men in white smocks sat at the tables on which was distributed an array of laboratory equipment. A bald man rose from his chair and came over. The man wore an orange badge and a black name tag that said "R. Bishop."

"Is this our boy?" Bishop asked.

Halladay nodded. "Bishop, Hobbes," he said.

Bishop didn't offer to shake hands. Instead, he took Hobbes' jaw in his hand and turned his head first one way and then the other. "Not bad," he said.

"What do you think?" Halladay asked.

"Step into my parlor," Bishop said. He led them into a small room. It was crammed with photographic equipment: spotlights, reflectors, cameras on tripods. In the center of the room was a high stool with an upholstered seat. "Hop up here."

Hobbes sat on the stool while Bishop fiddled with lights and took several pictures from different angles of Hobbes' face.

"What do you think?" Halladay repeated.

"Well"—Bishop gathered photographic plates from the cameras—"unless the camera shows up some serious discrepancy, I think he'll do."

"What kind of discrepancy?" Halladay asked.

Bishop sighed the sigh of the professional besieged by the questions of amateurs. "Bone structure, for one. The jawline is damned important. People pick up first on three features of the face: jawline, and that includes the contour of the neck; the nose; and the mouth."

"Eyes?" Halladay asked.

"That comes later, when you're in close. I'm speaking of initial impression. Now the nose we can take care of.

The mouth is a little more difficult, but you'd be amazed how we can alter that with these new plastics—you can do everything but smash him in the face, and they won't give way. But the jaw is tough. He and Gordon are going to have to have similar structure here—" He extended a finger and traced a line from Hobbes' chin to his ear.

Hobbes looked quickly at Halladay. But Halladay was listening intently, apparently unaware that Bishop had spoken the name of the man Hobbes was to impersonate. Hobbes sounded the name in his mind. He wondered if it was the man's first or last name. Knowing the man's name was exceedingly important to him, yet he couldn't say why.

"The eyes can be handled," Bishop was saying. "We can get the color with contacts and reshape them with the plastic cosmetics. You can cry, swim, anything, and they won't run."

"When will you know?" Halladay asked.

Bishop weighed the photographic plates in his hands and looked at a clock on the wall of the room. "Come back after lunch."

"Okay," Halladay replied.

"I'll work through my lunch hour," Bishop said in a way that indicated Halladay had missed the point.

"Good for you," Halladay replied dryly.

The room Halladay took Hobbes to was square, with mauve walls, and just large enough for the teak table and four chairs around it. The floor was covered in a thin all-weather carpet. On one wall hung a cheap reproduction of a Van Gogh. There were two doors, the one they had entered through and, opposite that, an aluminum-clad swing door with a small window through it. As with every other room Hobbes had ever been in at Langley, this one had no windows.

A man dressed in white backed through the swing door and laid down identical plates of steaming roast

115

beef, mashed potatoes, and bright orange carrots at three places that had been set at the table. The man left without a word.

Halladay stabbed a carrot with his fork, raised it to his eyes, and dropped it back on his plate. "I swear that goddamn carrot has been dyed," he said. He settled back in his chair and lit a cigarette.

Hobbes tried the roast beef. It was tough and tasteless. The door they had come through opened, and Vernon Dooley walked in. He nodded to Hobbes and Halladay in turn and then sat at the vacant place at the table, opened his napkin with a snap of this wrist, and began voraciously to eat every scrap of food on his plate. While he did this, Halladay smoked and stared moodily at the Van Gogh print. Hobbes picked through his food, trying to find something palatable, and finally gave up and sipped his water.

When Dooley was finished with his meal, he wiped his mouth on the napkin, threw it on the table, and lit a cigar. He held the cigar up for inspection. "Don't let them tell you that you don't inhale these suckers." he said. As if to underscore his words, he coughed. Then he took a mighty draft of smoke from the cigar and blew it at the ceiling. "So now you know his last name," Dooley said.

Hobbes sat up. "Sir?"

"Gordon. Don't tell me you didn't catch it?"

"No, sir. I did. You mean that was intentional?"

"Jesus," Dooley said with disgust. "We may have our arcane ways, Hobbes—but we aren't cracked."

"No, sir."

Dooley inspected the end of his cigar. "Friend Bishop has a very raw ass right now, let me tell you. Not that it matters in this case. It's a question of discipline, is all. When I want somebody to tell you something, I'll let them know." He looked at Halladay with narrowed eyes. "Right?"

"Christ, Vern," Halladay said plaintively, "what did you want me to do? Slip a cork in Bishop's mouth?"

116

The waiter reappeared to clear the table and then brought coffee. After he had gone, Dooley turned to Hobbes. "We're at the commit point on this assignment, Hobbes," he said. He smiled cheerfully. "Point of no return."

Despite Dooley's smile, Hobbes felt a chill in his blood.

"And since that's the case," Dooley went on, "I thought it would be appropriate to let you know the rest of it."

"The man who took the pictures," Hobbes said, "Bishop. He said my face might not be right."

Dooley waved this away with the cigar. "He invents problems. All those technical types do. It justifies their rating. No. I think we've found our man." He looked at Halladay for confirmation. Halladay nooded, without interrupting his gloomy inspection of the Van Gogh.

Dooley leaned forward on the table. "Okay. Here's the picture, Tom. The man's name is George Gordon. No middle name. You've read his file, so I won't bore you with that stuff." Dooley's voice was warm and confidential, and this sudden change of style put Hobbes more on guard than ever.

"About a month ago, we discovered that certain representatives of a country not sympathetic to our interest had managed to tinker with Gordon's head. They managed to get him to do some things for them. To put it plainly, Tom, the bastard turned traitor."

Dooley sat back in his chair, put a hand behind his neck, and for a moment worked his head as if he had a stiff neck. "When you find a traitor, you don't always rush him right out to the firing squad. First, you see if he knows you've found him out. In this case, Gordon didn't. He thought he was still free to work his dirty business, and that no one was the wiser. Okay. That being the case, you ask yourself, can we use this to our advantage?"

"Now I have to give you a little more background. Gordon was slipping information to these guys. Oh, shit. I

117

might as well tell you—you'll know soon enough." Dooley paused dramatically and stared at Hobbes.

"These people work for the Russians." Dooley continued to stare at Hobbes.

Hobbes felt compelled by Dooley's look to say something. The tension transmitted from those dark eyes was like a steel prong against Hobbes' forehead. "Ah—" Hobbes said. He was beginning to sweat. "The Russians."

"They work for them," Dooley said. "Yes. What do you think of that, Hobbes?"

"Well—" Hobbes shrugged and swallowed hard. "Well—interesting—"

Dooley laughed mirthlessly. "Interesting. You have a talent for understatement, Hobbes. Anyone ever told you that?"

"No, sir."

Dooley studied the end of his cigar, then leaned forward and brushed the ash off against the rim of his ashtray as delicately as a surgeon performing brain surgery. "We are in the era of détente, Hobbes. You know that, of course."

"Yes, sir."

"The Russians are our good buddies now." Dooley put the cigar in his mouth and spoke around it. "We sell them grain at cut-rate prices. We let them buy our most advanced computers. We send trade delegations, concert pianists and jazz bands over there, not to mention tourists. The tourist business from America is big in Russia now, Hobbes." Dooley smiled. "It's all very reassuring, wouldn't you say?"

"I guess so." Hobbes took his handkerchief from his pocket and wiped his forehead. Dooley watched him do it with a tight smile.

"Well, don't you believe it, Tom," Dooley said. "Those bastards will cut our throats for a plugged nickel the first chance they get. And do you know why they haven't yet?

118

Because right here"— Dooley stabbed the table top with a rigid forefinger—"right here at Langley we are maintaining the last line of defense."

Dooley sighed, and sat back in his chair. Halladay was staring impassively at Hobbes.

Dooley leaned forward again with an intense smile. "So the State Department says we are in the era of détente. And while they're out giving the store away to the Reds, we are busy taking it back. Our friend Gordon is a case in point.

"Their boys got to Gordon. Convinced him they'd take him back to Russia and make him Commissar of Virgins or some goddamn thing. We don't know exactly what lever they used. But Gordon had them sticking out all over him. He was a womanchaser. He boozed too much. He was known to spout the weak-kneed liberal line when he had a few too many. It could have been a lot of things."

Hobbes cleared his throat. Dooley paused and tapped the top of the table with his finger, while he looked at Hobbes expectantly. Hobbes said, "If he was so—so erratic, why—"

"Why'd we have him working for us in the first place?" Dooley grunted and stubbed out his cigar in the ashtray. "Hindsight, Hobbes. All this stuff is hindsight. Sure, we knew he had a few weaknesses. We don't object to that— in fact, it makes me a little easier about a guy if he has some of the human frailties, know what I mean?"

Hobbes didn't, not exactly, but he nodded anyway.

"What we didn't know was the rotten streak he had down at the core. That stinking soft spot that makes a man turn on his country. No matter what the motive or what the bad guys have got on you, you've got to have that soft spot, or you won't turn." He studied Hobbes, as if trying to see inside him and determine if he had a similar soft core.

"Gordon had been giving them stuff for several months

119

before we caught on to his act. Junk stuff. NATO arms inventories. Polaris sub exercise schedules. Junk." Dooley made a moue of disgust. "And typical."

"Typical?" Hobbes asked. Once again he had to take the handkerchief from his pocket and wipe his forehead.

"Yeah," Dooley replied. "It's a way to build an agent up for the big score. Have him get junk for you—stuff you already know, so you can check him out. At the same time you're getting him in deeper, inch by inch, until he can't say no to the big one." Dooley paused to grin with a kind of bitter pride."Shit. We taught the Russians that game ourselves."

Dooley took another cigar from his coat and carefully lit it while he studied Hobbes' perspiring face. "Halladay," he said,"see if you can get more air-conditioning in this goddamn coffin." Halladay got up and went through the swinging door.

"So now we come down to it," Dooley said softly. "See—Gordon had been set up for the big one. They told him what they wanted." He waved a hand. "Never mind what, now. They put the final twist of the screw to our friend. He steals the goods. We find out. We knew what it was he stole. We stop him. But we still want to deliver to the Reds. Follow me?"

Hobbes shook his head.

"Information! It was information they wanted. So we give it to them. Except it'll be *our* version."

Hobbes nooded. "I see, " he said sickly.

Dooley puffed on the cigar. The heat and the cigar smoke, combined with the reaction of his stomach to the things Dooley was telling him, made Hobbes faintly nauseated. He picked up his water glass and took a large swallow.

"What do you think, Tom?" Dooley asked in a mild voice.

"Think?"

"About the assignment."

120

"Oh—well, I'm not sure."

"Not sure, Tom?"

"Exactly what it is."

"Take a guess, Tom." Dooley's voice was a velvet purr.

"Well—I suppose I'm to deliver this—this information?"

Dooley leaned over the table, smiling, and patted Hobbes on the shoulder. "Good, Tom. Good thinking."

"That's it then?"

"That's it, Tom."

Hobbes frowned. "Ask it," Dooley said. "Go ahead."

"Well, why not just make Gordon deliver it?"

At that moment Halladay came back in the room. "That goddamn thermostat is stuck again," he reported.

"Never mind," Dooley replied. "We're through. You'd better get back down to the lab. Those photos ought to be ready."

Hobbes rose to go. "Oh," Dooley said, "I didn't answer your question, did I, Tom?"

"No, sir."

"Gordon can't deliver because he's dead. So you'll just have to make the delivery for him, won't you?"

FOURTEEN

Bishop had the photographs of Hobbes clipped to a wire that was strung across the room. While Hobbes and Halladay watched, he measured Hobbes' face in the photos with a pair of wooden calipers and jotted down figures in a notebook.

"You see," Bishop said as he worked, "I've enlarged these photos to the exact scale of the one we have of Gordon. I take known references in the photo of Gordon: lettering on a street sign in the background and the tie he was wearing. Then we take a facial feature—we used Gordon's nose. We know the dimensions of the lettering and the tie, and we estimate the length of the nose and triangulate. That gives us the distance Gordon was from the film itself. We factor out lens distortion, and we've got the exact reference position. Then I blew up the photos of our friend here—" he nodded at Hobbes— "to those specs."

"Terrific," Halladay said.

Bishop turned to him. "I've learned not to expect you

122

guys to appreciate what we do," he said, "but you don't have to be sarcastic."

Halladay sighed wearily. "Just get on with it, Bishop. We've got a lot to do."

Bishop's face took on a petulant set. He went to a table and opened a folder lying there. He took a photo from it and pinned it beside the photos of Hobbes.

"That's your boy," Bishop said.

Hobbes stared at the photo. The face was long, with a square jaw and a full mouth. The nose was straight and a little too narrow for the other dimensions of the face. The eyes were wide-set, light, with a look of intelligence and something else—a kind of defeated cynicism. Hobbes' flesh crawled. It was like looking at a picture of himself that had been clumsily retouched.

Bishop opened the notebook. "Look at this," he said with a note of triumph.

Halladay peered at the notebook. "Yeah?"

Bishop stabbed at figures in the notebook with his finger "Length of the mandible. Angles. Look. Look at this. Length of the nose. Septum."

"So?"

Bishop snapped the book shut. "So you've got a winner."

"What will you have to do?" Halladay asked.

"Less than I had expected," Bishop replied. "Contacts, of course. A little darkening of the eye sockets. The hair. The major difference is the bulb of the nose. But we can alter it with plastic skin."

"From the time I give you the go-ahead, how long will it take?"

Bishop shrugged. "Four hours."

"Okay," Halladay replied. "Don't make any plans for Sunday."

Bishop groaned. "Sunday! Don't you guys ever do anything during normal working hours?"

Hobbes' pulse raced. Sunday was five days away.

Hobbes cautiously mentioned his misgivings to Halladay as they were going back up in the elevator. "You'll be ready," Halladay replied coldly and in a way that barred further discussion.

Hobbes spent the rest of the afternoon being tutored by Cramer. By the time he left that evening his head was ringing with the sound of George Gordon's voice

When Hobbes entered the lobby, the three old people converged on him, quivering with excitement.

They met in Sophie Crump's room to go over the plan one last time. Dr. Marshall reported on his visit to Commander Peevey the previous evening and assured them that the old man was clearheaded and capable of navigating on his own. They arranged to meet again in the lobby thirty minutes before visiting hours.

Once Hobbes was alone in his room, he let the weariness take him. He lay on his bed and stared out the window. The sky was clear and high, shot through with the yellow rays of the dying sun.

His mind relaxed. Then his body. He drifted toward sleep. Just before it took him, he thought of Victoria Prentice, smiled, and slept with the smile still on his lips.

The phone woke him.

Hobbes' leg was asleep, and he massaged it as he picked up the receiver. Then he heard Victoria's voice and forgot his leg.

"I'm sorry about last night," she said.

"Don't be."

"Is tonight still on?"

"Yes."

"I'd like to go."

"What?"

"I'd like to help. May I?"

"You don't have to do that."

"I want to."

"I appreciate your saying that. But I won't let you run the risk. "

"Now, listen to me, Thomas Hobbes," she said breathlessly. "I am asking this for myself. Do you understand?"

"No."

"You said once it was something you had to do—didn't you?"

"I suppose I did."

"Well—it's something *I* need to do."

"If that's what you want."

"Do you remember kissing me?"

"Yes."

"It was nice."

"For—for me, too."

"We were pretty drunk."

"Yes."

"Maybe we should try it sober, sometime."

Mr. Darling greeted the news of Victoria's participation with an angry outburst. "We already got our squad!"

"She can be a great help," Dr. Marshall said gallantly.

Sophie Crump grinned impishly up at Hobbes and patted him on the arm. "We need her, " she said, "don't we, Mr. Hobbes?"

Hobbes felt himself blush.

When Victoria arrived, Mr. Darling was polite to her, his petulance gone. They drove to the home in Hobbes' car.

Two nurses were on the duty desk at the end of the hall when Hobbes and Dr. Marshall got off the elevator at Commander Peevey's floor. One of them gave Hobbes a nod of recognition.

Commander Peevey was propped up in his bed, the covers pulled up to his chin, his eyes gleaming with anticipation. "Close the door," he said in a hoarse whisper. When the door was closed, he threw back the covers. He was dressed. He got spryly out of bed, went to his closet, got a topcoat and a hat, and put them on. Then he turned to Hobbes. "Ready when you are."

Hobbes looked at his watch and nodded. Commander Peevey stepped into the closet, and as Hobbes closed the door, the old man gave him a grin and a thumbs-up sign. Hobbes moved to the bed and turned on the nurses' call switch.

At the duty desk, Sophie Crump was in animated conversation with one of the nurses. The nurse was flipping through the pages of a patient register. Another nurse was writing in a patient chart.

"He's not on this floor, dear," the nurse said patiently.

Victoria was sitting in a chair in the lobby.

"Oh, dear," Sophie Crump said. "I was sure this was the floor. He's my brother."

"Yes," the nurse said. "Well, we don't have a Peabody. Let me call downstairs. He's probably on another floor."

Behind the nurse, the red call light for Commander Peevey's room went on. The other nurse looked up with open irritation. The nurse on the phone was saying, "Peabody, P-E-A-"

Victoria got up and walked casually to the nurses' station as the second nurse came from behind the counter and went down the hall toward Commander Peevey's room. Victoria leaned over the counter, took a pink pass from the box there, found Commander Peevey's room number in the rack, and slipped the card into it. Then she turned and strolled across the lobby and through the door to the stairs.

The nurse came bustling officiously into the room. Hobbes looked up. Dr. Marshall turned from the window.

"Can you tell me where my grandfather is?" Hobbes asked.

The nurse stared at the empty bed. "He's not here?"

Hobbes gestured at the empty room.

The nurse was flustered. She pushed back a strand of hair that had escaped from her cap. "Peevey," she said. "Right?"

Hobbes nodded.

126

"Well, he's around here somewhere," she said. "Maybe the TV room?"

"He was so drugged he didn't know his right name."

"Right!" she said. She kept pushing at the loose strand of hair and biting her lip. "Maybe the doctor took him out for tests. I just came on. If you'll come with me, I'll check at the desk."

Hobbes said to Dr. Marshall, "You go. I'll wait here in case they bring him back."

The nurse bustled off with Dr. Marshall in her wake.

Hobbes closed the door after them, went to the closet, opened it, and motioned Commander Peevey out. They stood by the door, waiting. Commander Peevey couldn't stop chuckling.

When Dr. Marshall and the nurse got to the duty desk, the elevator doors were just closing on Sophie Crump.

"Did you check Peevey off the floor?" the nurse with Dr. Marshall asked the other accusingly.

"No. Why?"

"He's not in his room," the nurse said irritably. She began flipping through a book, then slammed it shut. "He's not listed out in the doctor's log." Her eyes went to the sign-out rack and widened. She took the pink card from the slot for Commander Peevey's room. "What's this doing here?"

The other nurse craned her neck to see the card. "I'm sure I don't know," she said, catching the other's irritability.

"He's not allowed on the grounds," the first nurse snapped.

"Oh, dear," Dr. Marshall said. "Oh, dear." He wrung his hands and was secretly pleased with his performance.

"Someone will have to go down and find him, " the first nurse said pointedly.

"You answered the call," the second nurse said in a tone that absolved her from further responsibility.

127

The first nurse slammed the card down and strode to the elevator. Dr. Marshall wrung his hands.

"We'll find him," the nurse said as the doors closed on her.

Dr. Marshall turned slowly and looked at the other nurse. She was bent over a file, oblivious to his presence. He shuffled slowly up the hall and stationed himself at a point near the door to Commander Peevey's room where he had a view of the lobby and the duty station.

The door to the stairs opened, and Victoria Prentice appeared. She walked quickly to the nurse and said breathlessly, "There's an old man in the stairwell."

"What!" the nurse said.

"In the stairwell. He's—he's confused. I tried to help him, but he's too big."

"A lot of white hair?" the nurse asked urgently. She was already moving toward the stairs.

"Yes," Victoria said. "He was headed *up*," she called as the nurse ran through the door.

Dr. Marshall stepped to the door and rapped twice on it. It opened, and Hobbes and Commander Peevey came out. The three of them strode rapidly down the hall, where they were joined by Victoria. Hobbes opened the door to the stairwell and looked in. Mr. Darling was on the landing. The voice of the nurse echoed from above, calling Commander Peevey's name. Mr. Darling motioned them frantically into the stairwell. They went down the stairs rapidly, and at the first floor the others waited while Victoria went out. She was back in a moment. "All clear," she said, suppressing a giggle. Commander Peevey guffawed.

They walked rapidly along a corridor and out a side door into the night. Hobbes' car was parked in the lot on that side of the building. Sophie Crump came from the shadows of the parked cars and embraced Commander Peevey tightly in her thin arms.

"Here, here," Commander Peevey cried, prying her arms loose. "Control yourself, woman!"

FIFTEEN

Commander Peevey didn't like his new room. "Another whole flight up," he groused. Victoria sat in Peevey's easy chair. Hobbes leaned against the door, smoking a cigarette. Sophie Crump, Dr. Marshall, and Mr. Darling, exhausted by the night's events, had retired to their rooms.

"Well"—Peevey sighed—"it will have to do." He went to his wardrobe and removed a bottle of brandy and a cigar. "I'd say this calls for a drink."

After he had served the drinks, Peevey turned to Hobbes. "Now. What was it you said in the car?"

"The letter was in your file at the hospital. It had the agency emblem."

"Damn!" Peevey said. "You're sure?" He lit his cigar.

"Positive. 'Request for Commitment' and your name."

Peevey rolled the end of the cigar in his brandy and put the cigar in his mouth. "Even if I had been too senile to take care of myself, it's not Langley's business." He stared at Victoria. "You say you work in Legal?"

"I've tried to find out why they had you committed.

My supervisor told me to mind my business and keep my mouth shut."

Peevey nodded. "It was no mistake then. They had a reason."

"What?" Hobbes asked.

Peevey shook his head. "I don't know. But with those screwballs that are running Langley these days, nothing would surprise me." Peevey paused and looked embarrassed. "I appreciate what you two did. I hope it doesn't cause you any trouble."

"The important thing," Hobbes replied "is to keep you out of that place. You've got to stick close to your room."

"I can't do that!" Peevey replied. "I'm going to get to the bottom of this. Someone is going to pay for turning me into a cabbage."

"Listen," Hobbes said, "if you stick your nose out of the hotel, they'll pick you up. Let me see what I can find out."

"You?" Peevey looked incredulous.

"I've got a new assignment. I'm working for Dooley."

"Dooley! When did this happen?"

"Just this week. So will you stay in your room?"

Peevey nodded slowly. "I'll give it a few days. But if you don't come up with something, Hobbes, I'm going to."

Victoria smothered a yawn. "You'd better take this young lady home," Peevey said.

The Dooleys were having a dinner party when Halladay arrived at their house. Large, new cars clogged the drive. Halladay had to park at the gate. A maid showed him into the den. As they passed the closed door to the dining room, Halladay heard laughter.

Dooley was dressed in a dark suit, his cheeks flushed with drink. He strode impatiently into the den and closed the door.

"Peevey's out," Halladay said.

130

"What!"

"Apparently he wandered away from the hospital."

"Jesus Christ! What kind of security do they have?"

"He couldn't have gone far. He was heavily sedated."

"What are you doing about it?"

"Staying in touch with the D.C. police."

Dooley paced in front of the cold fireplace. "Are they sure no one else was involved?"

"It just happened tonight. The police are investigating. But who would want to get him out?"

"I don't know. Maybe we should put some men on it."

"We can't do that, Vern. We aren't allowed to operate here."

"I know, I know." Dooley looked at his watch. "You keep on top of this. I want him back in that hospital. I know that old bastard. He can be trouble."

Halladay sighed. "Okay."

Dooley was at the door. He paused. "You don't seem to agree."

"I think it was a mistake in the first place. We wouldn't have this problem if Peevey hadn't been put in the hospital."

"I've got guests waiting," Dooley said. "So I'll say this once. That old man knows Hobbes—knew his father. I don't want him mucking around in this Gordon thing. I want him out of the way until it's over." Dooley paused, his eyes bulging at Halladay. "You got that?"

Halladay met Dooley's gaze for a moment and then averted his eyes. "I got it," he said.

Hobbes stopped his car in the loading zone in front of Victoria's apartment building. She had been silent during the drive. Now she sat up and stretched. "I don't know what's wrong with me. I feel like I could sleep for days."

"Reaction," Hobbes said. "Was it worth it?"

"Yes. He's quite a man. I can see why you couldn't stand the idea of his being in that place." She slid down

131

in the seat and put her hands on top of her head. She looked at him out of the corner of her eye. "You know, you are a strange man. Freshman spy. Abductor of old men. Living in a retirement hotel. How did you get into all that?"

He lit a cigarette and cracked the window on his side. The night air was sharp with a premonition of winter. "I don't know," he said. "The way I got into most things in my life—by accident, not choice."

"Peevey and your father were friends?"

"In a way. They admired each other. My father didn't really have friends. Just associates, some of whom he admired more than others."

"Was it because of Peevey that you decided to live at the hotel?"

"I suppose—and it seemed easier at the time than looking for another place." Hobbes sat up abruptly. "Say! When I first came to Washington, Peevey met me at the airport. He said I looked like—" Hobbes broke off his sentence.

"Looked like what?"

"Ah—nothing important." He passed a hand across his face. "He thought I looked like someone he'd worked with."

Victoria stretched out a hand and took the cigarette from Hobbes. "You acted like you'd been struck with lightning. That's nothing important?"

"I can't talk about it."

"Secret stuff?"

"Something like that."

She smoked the cigarette and studied his profile. "If you hadn't fallen into all these situations, what would you have chosen to do?"

"I don't know. I always thought I wanted to be an agent with Operations Branch."

"And now?" She passed the cigarette back to him.

He flexed his jaw. "That's what I want. I want to be the best agent I can be."

"Better than your father?"

Hobbes gave a short laugh. "My father was the *best.* No—I'd just like to, well, to *acquit* myself decently."

"My father was a lawyer," she said. "I was the youngest. Both my brother and sister became lawyers, so my fate was sealed."

"You don't like being a lawyer?"

"No. . . . It's all right." She gave an embarrassed laugh. "The thing is, I had this secret yearning to live in a warm climate and write poetry."

"You'd make a lovely poet."

She looked at him. "Now how would you know that?"

"The name. Victoria Prentice, Poet. It has the ring."

She laughed, then looked at him with a small smile. "Is it fair to say that we're both sober?"

"Eminently."

"Well, then—" She put her hand behind his head and brought his mouth down to hers. She broke the kiss much too soon for him. He reached for her, but she slid over the seat and out of the car.

She held the door and peered in at him. "Good night, Spy."

"Good night, Poet."

He watched her until she was lost in the shadows of the courtyard. He waited until he saw the lights go on in her apartment, then started the car, and drove slowly home.

"Good news, Hobbes," Dooley said the next morning. He held the door of his office open for Hobbes with a smile.

He motioned Hobbes to a chair, went behind his desk, and pushed a button on an intercom. In a few moments the door opened, and Halladay and Dr. Beckman entered.

Dooley said to Beckman, "Tell him the good news."

"You'll go to the meeting only lightly disguised."

"That's the good news?" Hobbes asked incredulously.

"Sure," Dooley said. "You can ask anyone in this business—the fewer gimmicks you have to rely on, the better chance you have."

"Of course," Dr. Beckman said. "We'll have to do the hair, and you'll wear contacts, but—" Beckman paused dramatically and held the edge of his palm over his leg. "That's it!" He brought the hand down.

"It was Doc's idea," Dooley said expansively, taking a new pipe from his pocket. He began to fill the pipe from an enormous can of tobacco that stood on his desk.

"I simply put two needs together with one solution," Beckman said modestly. "We had the problem of the pitch of the voice and then the facial differences—the nose primarily. It will be quite simple, really, Mr. Hobbes. I'm having the lab prepare the virus culture now."

"Virus culture?"

Dooley chuckled. He was lighting his pipe, throwing up a smothering cloud of blue smoke. "It's sort of a reverse inoculation, right, Doc?"

"Right," Beckman said smugly.

"Wait a minute," Hobbes said. "What does that mean?"

"We're going to give you a cold," Beckman replied.

"A cold!"

"Perfect disguise," Dooley said. "Red eyes, swollen nose, husky voice—"

"And you won't have to pretend," Beckman added. "I guarantee it."

"Swell," Hobbes muttered.

"What's that?" Dooley asked.

"I said, that's swell."

"Don't worry," Dooley said, puffing mightily on his pipe. "Doc will load you up with penicillin afterward."

"When—when do I have to have this virus?"

"Oh, it works very quickly. The culture we're working up is potent. I should think Friday night would be time enough," Beckman said.

Dooley felt the tip of his tongue with his fingers and eyed the pipe. "How do people smoke these goddamn things?" he asked. "It feels like my tongue is coming out."

"You're supposed to break the pipe in, Vern," Halladay said.

Dooley sighed, put the pipe in an ashtray, and took a cigar from his coat pocket.

Hobbes spent the morning with Cramer on voice training. Now that the artifice of the cold had been decided upon, Cramer ignored pitch and concentrated entirely on accent.

A little before noon, Bishop appeared with a black satchel and examined Hobbes' hair under a magnifying lens, pausing occasionally to refer to a photo of George Gordon and to make notes. Then he handed Hobbes a small capsule.

"Contact lenses," Bishop said.

He instructed Hobbes on the proper way to insert and remove the lenses.

"Wear these at the office, so you'll get used to them," Bishop said. Then he left.

Hobbes ate a lonely lunch that was brought to him in the training room. After lunch, Cramer reappeared with a movie projector and portable screen. He set up the projector and for the rest of the day showed Hobbes film clips of George Gordon and coached him on how to move as Gordon did. The films were home movies, and in them Gordon was waving at the camera, or mugging, or, in one, doing a clumsy dance in front of a Christmas tree with a drink in his hand. Cramer didn't explain how he had come by the films, and Hobbes didn't ask.

At the end of the day, as Cramer was packing up his equipment, Dooley appeared and motioned Cramer out of the room. Dooley sat on a chair, crossed his legs, and threw an arm over the chair back.

"Well, Tom," Dooley said, "today is Wednesday."

There was an uncharacteristic hesitation in Dooley's manner.

Hobbes dragged a chair over and sat in front of Dooley. He took his Rothmans from his pocket and lit one.

"Loan me one of those," Dooley said.

Dooley blew a stream of smoke at the ceiling and said, "You know you get a raise, don't you?"

"No. I hadn't thought of it."

"Sure," Dooley said. He flicked ashes off the cigarette on the floor with his little finger. "You're moving up, Tom."

"That's good. Thanks." Dooley's strange uncertainty was beginning to make Hobbes nervous.

"Did you ever use a gun, Tom?" Dooley asked suddenly.

"No—no, sir."

Dooley waved a hand. "Doesn't matter."

"Why do you ask?" Hobbes felt his spine tingle with apprehension.

Dooley laughed with false heartiness. "It was just a thought. You know—if you could handle a piece, that you might feel better—" Dooley left the sentence unfinished. He took his shoe in his hand and examined a scuff mark.

"You mean there's a chance—ah—that I might need one?"

Dooley shrugged casually. "No, no. Remote. Very remote."

Hobbes cleared his throat. "I—I don't have a very good idea of what the risks are, I guess."

Dooley raised his eyes to Hobbes'. "You just do what you're told," he said. "And there won't be any. Believe me, if you've never used a gun, you're better off without one. After this assignment, we'll send you out to the farm."

"The farm?"

"The training school. You'll like it. Fresh air, good food, regular hours."

136

"I was wondering," Hobbes said tentatively. "I understand I'm going Sunday—"

Dooley's eyes narrowed. "Yes?"

"And—well, I was wondering how long I'd be gone."

"That's a reasonable question."

"And where I'm going."

"That's pushing," Dooley said mildly. He ran a thumb over the scuff mark on his shoe. Then he raised his arms and rested them on top of his head and looked at Hobbes speculatively. "You'll be gone a few days. I can't tell you exactly, but in any case, it shouldn't take over a week."

"A week!"

"What's the matter?"

"I guess I thought I would just go deliver the papers, and that would be it."

"These fellows don't work that way, Tom. You have to go through the rigamarole."

"Rigamarole?"

But Dooley didn't explain. "Don't worry. You can handle it," he said. "You'll know everything you need to know at the time. Have you ever been in Canada, Tom?"

"No. Is that where—?"

"Any relatives or friends that live up there?"

"No."

"You're sure? Think about it."

"No. I'm sure. Is that where I'm going?"

Dooley nodded solemnly. "The initial meeting is in Vancouver. From there they'll take you someplace— someplace nearby. They may do the whole business in Vancouver. My guess is they will."

"Will I be going alone?"

"Let's just say that help won't be far away. In a case like this, Tom, it's better you don't know what the back-up is. You look over your shoulder once too often and the boys you're meeting might get nervous."

"So I'm going to Vancouver Sunday?" Hobbes tried to get used to the idea. He couldn't.

"Did I say that, Tom?"

"But I thought—"

"The assignment, Tom. The assignment starts Sunday."

Dooley watched him in silence and then leaned forward. "You'll be in Washington for a couple of days. You'll arrive at Dulles on the London flight Sunday night."

Hobbes stared. "I'm—I'm already in Washington."

Dooley smiled. "Thomas Hobbes is in Washington. George Gordon is in London—or I should say our Communist friends think he is."

"Oh."

"You'll go to Gordon's apartment from the airport. You'll live there for a couple of days. You'll come out to work here each day. Then—off to Vancouver."

"Oh."

Dooley rose and patted Hobbes on the shoulder. "You'll like it, Tom. Your friend Gordon lived well."

"Something I've been wondering—"

"Yes?"

"George Gordon—how did he die?"

Dooley smiled. "Like he lived. Spectacularly." He made a diving motion with his hand. "Flaming plane crash."

"And the papers he stole?"

"Microdot. It burned with him."

"So I'll be delivering another film?"

"Right."

"And they'll have to look at it first, before they—before they what?"

"Ah, that's a question, Tom. I'll tell you my personal opinion. I think they had something on our boy. I think the big payoff is maybe the negatives of films that could've brought him down or tapes of the same kind of thing."

"How will I know? I mean, won't they expect me to know?"

"Don't make a big thing of it, and don't, for God's sake, act surprised."

"I'll do my best." Hobbes felt faintly dizzy. Some unnamed dread seemed to be closing in on him.

"Sure you will. You know what's riding on this—or—" Dooley paused and abruptly sat down again. "I guess you don't. Not in detail."

Hobbes swallowed. "No." He was torn between the anxiety of not knowing and his dread of what Dooley might tell him.

Dooley moved his chair closer to Hobbes. "It's a list of names." Dooley's face was close enough for Hobbes to smell the tobacco on his breath.

" A list of names," Hobbes repeated.

"Yeah." Dooley leaned even closer. "People behind the Iron Curtain."

"Oh," Hobbes said leadenly.

"Officials in Communist governments. A couple in Russia itself."

"Russia."

"Who"— Dooley put his mouth beside Hobbes' ear— "who work for us." Hobbes could feel Dooley's breath hot in his ear.

Dooley sat back, dropped the cigarette on the floor, and ground it under his heel. "Of course, the names won't be the right ones." Dooley's eyes glittered. "Don't you see the double-barreled opportunity we've got here, Hobbes?"

Hobbes shrugged.

"Double-barreled!" Dooley cried. "We not only protect our guys, but get rid of a few who have been a pain in the ass to us." Dooley laughed. It was not a pleasant laugh.

Hobbes didn't reply. Dooley gave him a peculiar look. "You don't look too well, Tom."

With effort, Hobbes said, "You mean these people—on the list I'll be delivering—will be—will be—?"

Dooley made a chopping motion with his hand.

139

"Heads will roll, as they say, Hobbes." He grinned. "Now do you see the importance of what you'll be doing?"

Hobbes passed a hand across his eyes. "How many?"

"What?"

"How many people will I be condemning?"

"Whoa! Let's just slow down a little there, boy. You just remember that it's not us that goes around in jackboots kicking people's doors in in the middle of the night. You keep this in mind. Those people—those that work for us—you'll be packing the mail for them, do you understand? Their lives are in jeopardy, and by God, Thomas Hobbes is going to save them—and their families. Do you get that, Hobbes?" Dooley was leaning toward Hobbes, his forehead perspiring lightly, his eyes bulging.

"I see," Hobbes said.

"Good! You just keep that in mind." Dooley leaned back, took a cigar from his pocket, and rolled it between his fingers. "You pull this off, Tom and you could get a department commendation out of it."

"Oh."

"You don't know what that could mean to your career. I'll put you in for it personally."

Hobbes didn't know how to reply.

Dooley lit his cigar. "We've got a code name for you on the assignment." Dooley smiled. "I think you'll like it, Hobbes."

"Yes?"

Dooley looked solemnly at Hobbes. "Patriot, Tom. Your code name is Patriot."

SIXTEEN

On the drive from Langley to the hotel that evening Hobbes searched his mind for something to tell Commander Peevey. He had promised to investigate Peevey's commitment and report that evening. Several times during the day he had attempted to muster his courage and ask Dooley about it. But those bulging brown eyes of Dooley's had dissolved his determination. Tomorrow, he told himself—I'll get to the bottom of this thing tomorrow. He would tell Peevey that he hadn't had the opportunity to confront Dooley. Which, in a way, was true.

As he wearily made his way across the lobby, Sophie Crump's face appeared at the door to her room. She put out an arm and motioned frantically to Hobbes. Hobbes entered her room. Dr. Marshall sat in a chair with a cup of tea balanced on his knee.

"It's the police," Sophie said in a quavering whisper. "They were *here!*"

Hobbes stared at her. "About Peevey?"

"Yes," Dr. Marshall said. He stood and placed an arm around Sophie's shoulders.

"Did they find him?"

"No," Dr. Marshall replied. "They wanted to see you."

"Me!"

"They asked all kinds of questions," Sophie cried.

"I'm afraid we did a dreadful amount of lying," Dr. Marshall said with embarrassment.

"They left a card," Sophie held a card out to Hobbes. "Said for you to call."

Hobbes looked at the card. "I might as well get it over with," he said.

Hobbes went directly to Commander Peevey's room. Peevey was sitting in his easy chair, dressed in tweed trousers and vest and reading *The New Yorker* magazine.

"Hobbes!" Peevey exclaimed, getting to his feet. "What did you find out?"

"Nothing yet. The police were here."

"So Darling informed me." Peevey went to the highboy and got down his bottle of brandy. After he had served himself and Hobbes, he said, "Do you think they're on to us?"

Hobbes sipped the brandy. "I don't know. They may just be checking people that knew you. In the meantime, you've got to stay here."

"But goddamn it, I'm a prisoner in my own place. This isn't a hell of a lot better than that hospital."

"Victoria is looking into filing papers that would reverse the commitment."

Peevey gave him a sour look. "That could take months."

"A couple of weeks, she said."

Peevey grinned suddenly. "There's a woman, Hobbes! You got her nailed down yet?"

Heat rose to Hobbes' face. "No."

"Well, by God, if you don't get her nailed down pretty soon, I might go after her myself."

Hobbes grinned. "Why do you think I want you to stay in your room?"

Peevey threw his head back and boomed a laugh at the ceiling.

Hobbes went to his room and called the number on the card. The man who answered was polite. Hobbes was asked to stay in his room; two detectives would be there within the hour.

Hobbes went into his bathroom and washed his face and the back of his neck with cold water. He stood for several moments staring at his face in the mirror until, gradually, it became not his face he saw but George Gordon's. He shuddered, broke away from the mirror, and went into his room to wait for the detectives.

The two detectives wouldn't sit. Hobbes felt compelled to stand, too. The younger of the detectives seemed to be in charge; he did the talking. The older detective stood with his hands in his pockets and looked around the room.

"Now, Mr. Hobbes," the younger detective said, "we know you took a Horace Peevey from the Veterans' Hospital last night."

"I see."

"We know others were involved, but it appears to us that you led the abduction."

"Is that what it was?"

"Yes, sir. According to the law, that's what it was."

"Are you arresting me?"

"Look," the detective said in a confidential tone, "we don't want to haul a lot of elderly people in. It wasn't a violent crime. If you'll just tell us where we can find Horace Peevey, we'll forget it."

"No."

The detective sighed, turned to his colleague and said, "Read him his rights."

After that had been done, the younger detective said, "Any second thoughts, Mr. Hobbes?"

Hobbes shook his head.

The detectives took Hobbes to the municipal jail. They performed the booking process in a high-ceilinged room that echoed their voices. They fingerprinted him. They took the contents of his pockets and gave him a receipt. He was stripped, searched, and put through a chemical shower. They gave him denim pants and a shirt that were starched to the consistency of cardboard. They asked him if he wanted to call anyone. He shook his head mutely. They told him he would be taken to court in the morning and arraigned. Then the younger detective asked him once more if he would tell them where Commander Peevey was. Hobbes wouldn't. A jailer led him into the bowels of the jail. He unlocked a cell door. Inside the cell, a gaunt black face stared out at Hobbes. Hobbes went into the cell, and the jailer locked the door and left. Hobbes could hear the jailer's leather soles striking echoes down the corridor for a long time after he disappeared.

"Hey, man, you got smokes?" The black face materialized beside Hobbes. It was attached to an emaciated body that made the prison shirt seem suspended from a clothes hanger.

Hobbes felt in his shirt pocket and found the pack of Rothmans they had allowed him to keep. The black man took one and looked at it.

"This is a bad cigarette," the black man said. He lit it and exhaled with great satisfaction. He went to a bunk and sat on it with his feet folded under him. The cell smelled of disinfectant and cold concrete.

"I'm Lawrence," the black man said.

"Hobbes." Hobbes, for the first time, took a clear look at his cell mate. He seemed terribly young.

"You been in this here jail before?"

Hobbes shook his head.

"It's the pits, man." Lawrence blew on the lighted end of the cigarette, making the coal glow. "I'm goin' up to Danbury next week."

Hobbes walked to a bunk and sat on the edge of it. He took a cigarette from his pocket and lit it.

"Now, Danbury," Lawrence said, "is tough. But the food's good. And they got the rules, and if you go with them, you sur-vive. Dig? But this here jail—" Lawrence made a face. "It's a zoo." Lawrence laughed. "We're the animals, see? Any day now the screws are goin' to bring their kids in to throw peanuts to us." Lawrence doubled over his knees and laughed. "Hope you like peanuts, man."

Hobbes smiled weakly.

Lawrence leaned toward Hobbes and stared at him. "You don't talk much, man."

"I—it's my first time."

"What—in D.C. slammer or just in jail?"

"In jail."

"Oh, yeah?" Lawrence scraped the coal off his cigarette against the edge of the bunk and carefully put the butt in his pocket. He stood, hitched up his pants, and began to pace the cell with his shoulders thrown back and his legs stiff. "You can ask me anything," he said. "I'll take care of you. Don't worry your head. Any dude makes noises at you, you tell Lawrence, dig?"

"I—I appreciate that."

" 'Round here, when Lawrence say do it, they do it, man." He made a cutting motion in the air with his hand. "So you just tuck in with me. When we're out in the yard or down at the cafeteria, you just tuck in with me."

"All right."

Lawrence stopped beside Hobbes. He bent from the waist until his face was inches from Hobbes' face. He grinned hugely. "You're my man."

"Ah—fine—"

"I *like* you, man!"

From the corridor, a voice yelled, "Hey, A-rab! Stuff your face!" Laughter echoed eerily in the corridor.

Lawrence ran to the cell door, his face twisted with fury. "I know who you was!" He shouted. "I'll feed you your balls, turkey!" The laughter died out to murmurs that sounded like water gurgling through a pipe.

Lawrence turned from the door with a satisfied grin. "They call me A-rab, because of *Lawrence of Arabia*, see? That movie? You see it?"

Hobbes shook his head.

Lawrence laughed. "Bad movie! All these dudes runnin' around on horses, dig? Out on the sand dunes? Doin' women, shootin'." Lawrence sighted an imaginary rifle. "Whippin' ass with sabers." He whirled and cut the air with an imaginary saber.

As he watched Lawrence spin around the cell, acting out the movie, Hobbes had a vivid vision of the world unseen beyond the cell walls dematerializing, being eaten away by some corrosive force that reduced it to wisps of fog so that soon all that would be left would be this square of concrete supporting him and Lawrence, adrift in the void, like shipwrecked sailors.

Lawrence was staring at Hobbes, his face covered with a light sheen of sweat from his exertions. "Dig?" he asked.

SEVENTEEN

The uniformed officer at the desk made a call on his phone. In a few moments a young man in a civilian suit appeared and introduced himself to Victoria as a detective.

"You say you're his lawyer."

"Yes."

The detective scratched his nose. "He didn't call anyone."

"I found out from the people where he lives."

"Uh-huh. Well, you can see him, sure. If he agrees."

"I can't imagine that he wouldn't."

The detective took Victoria to a room with steel mesh walls and a drain in the center of its concrete floor. He motioned her to take a seat at one side of a long table. Victoria placed her briefcase on the table. The detective went through a door. A few minutes later Hobbes appeared followed by a guard. The guard went out the door and locked it.

Victoria couldn't stop staring at Hobbes. The prison

clothes he wore gave him a defeated air. He smelled strongly of disinfectant. He smiled and sat across from her. "They said my lawyer was here."

She opened her briefcase. "I had to promise Commander Peevey I would have you out tonight to keep him from charging down here." She took a paper from the briefcase and studied. "I'll file a writ. I'm going to try to get you released on your own recognizance."

He was examining her face. "I'm sorry I got you involved in this."

"I'm a lawyer," she said briskly. "It's my profession."

"Sure."

She put down the paper and sighed. "I don't know why I'm doing this. But I guess it's the least I can do since I'm your accomplice."

"They don't know that." He stood suddenly and came around the table and looked down at her. "Can a prisoner kiss his lawyer?"

"It's one of the rights guaranteed under the Constitution." She stood. "Anyway, it should be."

When Dooley entered the visiting room ten minutes later, his presence seemed to squeeze all the air out of it. Dooley's face was a stone mask with protruding brown eyes. The young detective was with him. Dooley's eyes fastened to Hobbes'.

"What the hell do you think you're doing?"

"Talking to my lawyer." Hobbes returned Dooley's stare.

After a silent moment of tension, Dooley pointed a thumb toward the detective. "Take her and wait outside."

"I have the right to be present," Victoria said heatedly.

Dooley turned on her. "This is a matter of national security. You're in trouble just being here. So move!"

"I'm his lawyer . . ." Victoria began.

Dooley spun back to Hobbes. "Tell her!" he barked.

"It's okay," Hobbes said. "Wait outside." She got up and reluctantly followed the detective out of the room.

Dooley leaned on his hands on the table and put his face inches away from Hobbes' eyes. "Have you gone nuts?" When Hobbes started to speak, Dooley shut him up with a look. "I can understand the deal with Peevey. Okay, so the old man means something to you. But for Christ's sake, why didn't you ask me about it? And why did you bring that dame in here? Do you want to torpedo the fucking assignment?"

Hobbes remained silent. Dooley stared at him. Then he passed a hand across his face and wearily sat in a chair across from Hobbes. "Give me a cigarette." Hobbes passed him the pack and his lighter.

"I tried to tell you," Dooley said, "how important this assignment was. Didn't I get through, Hobbes?"

"You got through. But—"

"Shut up!" Dooley leaned across the table and glared at Hobbes. For the first time Hobbes noticed that he was tieless, his eyes were red-rimmed, and he wore the pants and coat from two different suits under his topcoat. "Fortunately we can fix it this time, Hobbes. Fortunately for you. You just tell me where we can lay hands on Peevey and you take a walk."

"Can I say something?"

"Say it!" Dooley stuck the cigarette in the corner of his mouth, hooked his elbow over his chair, and squinted at Hobbes.

"Commander Peevey is not senile. He was out at that hospital, drugged, a prisoner—"

Dooley held up a palm. "Spare me the goddamn agonizing details. Just get to the point."

"I won't let him be taken back there."

Dooley's jaw clenched. "Listen to me, Hobbes," he said in a deadly tone. "You don't know what you're talking about. Peevey's being there is a matter of grave importance—"

149

"Because he knew Gordon?"

Dooley stared at him. "How did you know that?"

"It wasn't hard to figure. And that's not a good enough reason to have him there. Commander Peevey was a loyal employee of the CIA for over twenty-five years, and before that he was a naval hero—"

"No one is questioning that, Hobbes. But he's outside our control now. And he's an old man—vulnerable—a weak link."

Hobbes took a deep breath and said, "If he goes back, I'm not doing the assignment."

"Now wait a minute, Tom." Dooley suddenly switched to a reasonable tone. "You know how important it is that you work this assignment, don't you?"

"I mean it," Hobbes said. "I won't do it."

Dooley struck the conference table with a fist. "Goddammit! You will!"

Hobbes felt strangely calm, as if he were the eye and Dooley the hurricane raging around him. He closed his eyes and shook his head. He heard Dooley sigh heavily, and he opened his eyes to see him slumped in his chair, his topcoat gaping, the cigarette dangling from limp fingers. "Okay," he said. "Peevey stays out. You win this one, Hobbes."

Hobbes nodded, afraid to say anything.

"You'll have to let the D.C. cops have a look at him. For all they know, you sank him in the Potomac."

Hobbes gave Dooley a suspicious look.

"C'mon, Hobbes. What have I got to gain by double-crossing you?"

"He's at the hotel."

"Didn't the cops check there?"

Hobbes told him how they had switched Commander Peevey's room. "You've got a warped mind," Dooley said.

Dooley went out of the room and returned in a few minutes. "Your clothes are outside. Go get dressed."

"Where's Victoria?"

"I sent her home."

"She won't be in any trouble? She was just trying to help a friend."

Dooley waved a hand. "The whole troop of Brownies gets off scot-free, Hobbes." Hobbes turned and started to walk away. "Where do you think you're going?"

"Home." Hobbes turned.

"You're going with me," Dooley said. "I'm not letting you out of my sight."

"But—"

"No buts," Dooley said. "You've reached the limit of my flexibility."

Hobbes saw that he meant it. He walked slowly back to where Dooley stood waiting.

Dooley's car was a dark brown Ford. Dooley and Hobbes sat in the back seat, while an impassive man in a blue suit drove. Occasionally a radio transmitter under the dash would squawk faintly.

"You're going to be my guest for a while," Dooley said. Somewhere he had found a cigar, and he was filling the interior of the car with its blue smoke.

"I thought you said the hotel was perfect—"

"That was before I knew your hobby was kidnapping."

The car turned onto the Washington Memorial Parkway and began to leave Washington behind.

Dooley puffed complacently on his cigar. "I'm not taking any chances on this assignment, Hobbes, so forget your girlfriend for the duration. There'll be plenty of time afterward." Dooley puffed on the cigar and looked out at the freeway lights flashing by. "You'll like my house," he said with a touch of pride. "Old country house. Very comfortable."

Hobbes didn't reply. Dooley turned to him. "Tell me something," he said, "just to satisfy my curiosity. What made you pull that stunt at the Veterans' Hospital?"

151

"I don't know," Hobbes replied. "I haven't thought about it."

Dooley was silent for a long time. In the distance the city of Arlington lit the sky with a cold light. Finally, Dooley stirred, and said, "You know what you are?"

"No."

"You are a fucking enigma."

Hobbes didn't know exactly how he expected Dooley to live, but it certainly wasn't in the big stone English mansion they arrived at. Dooley took Hobbes through the darkened house, up a carved oak staircase, to a spacious bedroom, and left with the announcement that they would have dinner in thirty minutes. On the bed was Hobbes' scuffed two-suiter suitcase. He opened it and found his clothes and toilet kit.

Hobbes undressed and got into the shower and scrubbed the smell of the jail out of his pores. Then, dressed in cotton pants and an old Oxford shirt, he went downstairs. Dooley was waiting for him at the foot of the stairs. He led him to a paneled study, where their dinners were waiting on TV tables in front of a crackling fireplace.

After they had finished their meals, Dooley poured snifters of brandy from a cut crystal decanter on a sideboard.

Dooley waved his cigar at the room. "Some place, eh?"

Hobbes nodded. "Very nice."

"My wife's. Been in her family for ages." Dooley laughed uncomfortably. "I sure couldn't afford it on a government salary."

"No."

"You'll meet her in a bit," Dooley said.

"All right."

"I was just a poor Nebraska farm boy," Dooley said. "You were from where?"

"A lot of places. My father was career army; then CIA."

"Oh, yeah. Listen, Tom—you make yourself at home around here. There are servants. What ever you need. . . ." Dooley's voice trailed off.

Hobbes understood that Dooley was uncomfortable in the role of host. He seemed oddly naked here in this luxury. He seemed stripped of the power he wore like a toga at the office.

There was a timid knock at the door. Dooley got up and opened it, and a small blond woman came hesitantly into the room.

"This is Mr. Hobbes," Dooley said. "Louise, my wife."

Hobbes stood. "Mrs. Dooley."

"How do you do, Mr. Hobbes? I hope your room is comfortable." Her speech was halting. She was like a timid doe. She was older than Dooley, her face crosshatched with a network of sere wrinkles. But she had a singular grace that shone through her timidity, a kind of physical self-assurance that only very beautiful women have. And despite her age, she was beautiful in the way very old china is beautiful: fragilely, delicately.

Louise Dooley left the room with a shy smile for Hobbes. Dooley threw his cigar into the fire place. "Lou doesn't like me to smoke," he said, although she had given no indication she noticed he was smoking. "Do you still get by on five or six a day?"

"Lately, I'm afraid not."

Dooley grinned. "We've put a bit of a strain on you?"

"Something like that."

"You'll commute to and from Langley with me," Dooley said abruptly.

"I see."

"That okay?"

Hobbes smiled. "What are my choices?"

Dooley laughed. "You're right. You don't have any."

153

"Can I make phone calls?"

"Hell, yes, Tom. You're not a prisoner." Dooley paused. "All the calls go through the board at Langley. They'll be taped."

"Oh."

"You've got to get used to our ways."

"Sure."

"Let me tell you something, Tom." Dooley got up and stood with his back to the fireplace. "You could have a great future with us. I like the way you operate. We can overlook the Peevey thing. You look like that doesn't please you."

"I just wonder how much of it is for effect—to keep me in line until I do the assignment."

Dooley grinned. "See, that's what I like about you. You consider the angles. And in this business you have to. Look, I'll level with you. Sure, I want you to pull off this job. It's important for all the reasons I've told you. But more than that, it will prove something to some people at Langley. There are factions there, Tom. It's no secret. There are those that want to turn us into bean counters—statisticians who count missiles and troops and send reports up to the National Security Council, where they die a death of attrition. The big rallying cry is détente for those birds. They like to imagine that the Iron Curtain is made of Jell-O now. That the Communists are ready to be God-fearing Christians if we'll just not do anything to upset them." Dooley turned and spit into the fireplace. "Just once," he said, "I'd like to put some of those yo-yos into a field operation in Eastern Europe and let them see how goddamned soft the Communists are.

"Think about this, Tom. Here we've got the doves saying the Commies have seen the light. They're letting the Jews emigrate. They're sitting down at the negotiating table at Helsinki. They're opening up diplomatic channels.

"But the Jews go out on quotas. Eastern Europe is still closed to free emigration. They're robbing us blind at

154

Helsinki. The diplomatic channels may be open, but to what? What have we gotten out of it? Nothing. So—if we can get that microdot into the right hands, it's going to cause a hell of a purge. One so big that they can't hide it. And who do you think they'll blame? Who do you think the Communists will put the finger on? Us. They'll scream we subverted their people. They'll close off some of those phony diplomatic channels goddamn fast. And believe me, we'll be better off for it."

"And your faction?"

Dooley grinned. "Our star will rise. And. Tom—you can go up with us."

"My delivering the microdot will do all that?"

"Not that alone, of course. But it's a step—a big one. And combined with some other things I've got cooking, it will add up, believe me."

Hobbes fell silent. He thought about what Dooley had said, and it didn't seem real to him. Dooley's plotting and manipulations seemed like the rules and strategies for some elaborate game. Hobbes wondered what plotting and strategies were going on in the other factions. It occurred to him that perhaps all the opposing efforts would cancel each other out, and the world after all would remain the same.

EIGHTEEN

In the two days since Dooley had got him out of jail, Hobbes had learned to walk and sit and move like George Gordon.

The evenings at Dooley's house had been quiet and boring. The meals were excellent. Hobbes saw Mrs. Dooley infrequently. She seemed to spend her time in a separate wing of the house. Hobbes read books from Dooley's large library. Many times he started to call Victoria, but he couldn't bear the thought that the recording of the conversation would be listened to by faceless bureaucrats at Langley—perhaps, worst of all, listened to by Dooley himself.

On Friday, as they were riding to Langley in the back of the Ford, Dooley said, "What's bothering you, Tom?"

"Nothing."

"Something is. And whatever it is I want to get it out of your system before Sunday."

Hobbes saw a chance and took it. "I'd like to see Commander Peevey."

Dooley gave him a pained look. "Still don't trust me, do you?"

"Maybe I do. I'd just feel better if I could see him. And Victoria Prentice."

"Jesus," Dooley said irritably. "You got a list?"

"No. That's all."

Dooley was silent for a moment. Then he said, "Tell you what. Tonight we'll drop by your hotel on the way home. If that woman lawyer happens to be there, well—I'll leave that for you to arrange. Okay?"

Hobbes phoned Victoria at her office as soon as he arrived at Langley that morning. The relief in her voice made his spirits lift. She agreed to be at the hotel that evening.

When he had hung up, he went back to the training room. He felt better than he had in days. At the end of the day Hobbes reported to Dooley's office and found Dr. Beckman and Halladay there. Beckman was carrying a medical bag from which he took a syringe.

"This is the day," Beckman said cheerfully.

The shot hurt. Hobbes massaged his arm.

"Tomorrow morning," Beckman said, "you should have a dandy cold."

"Thanks," Hobbes replied.

"Any chance it will wear off before he's through?" Dooley asked.

"If it goes untreated, the symptoms should last ten days," Beckman replied. "I'll check him Sunday and give him a booster if he needs it."

On the ride to the hotel Dooley chuckled and said, "Not many people get to call the time and place for a cold."

"I'd rather be surprised."

"You worry me, Hobbes," Dooley said. "You're beginning to develop a sense of humor."

When they reached the hotel, Victoria hadn't arrived

157

yet. Hobbes and Dooley went up to Peevey's room. Peevey let them in and then glowered down at Dooley. "Vernon," he said, "I want a straight answer. Were you behind having me put in that hellhole?"

"Hobbes," Dooley said, "why don't you go downstairs and wait for your friend?"

"He stays," Peevey said.

Dooley shrugged and sat in Peevey's easy chair. "Horace," he said, "you got caught in the middle of a sensitive situation."

"Don't give me any of your Langley funny talk," Peevey said. "Did you have me put in the hospital?"

"The company did, yes," Dooley replied.

Peevey barked out a laugh. "The company! No one's responsible—"

"I'm responsible," Dooley said, his face darkening.

"I want an explanation!"

"It's classified," Dooley said. "Need to know, and you don't have the need, Horace. Just let me say that it's extremely important—vital—"

"Vital! That I be turned into a cabbage?"

"Perhaps that was a mistake. But you're out now. I want you to lie low for another week, ten days. Stay in your room. Don't talk to anyone."

"On whose orders?" Peevey glared at Dooley.

"Let me put it this way," Dooley said. "If you don't do as I say, you'll be putting Hobbes in a very serious spot."

Peevey turned to Hobbes. "That true?"

Hobbes nodded. "I guess so. I guess it could do that."

Peevey was silent for a moment, his broad brow wrinkled in thought. "I won't do anything to put Hobbes in danger."

"That's the spirit," Dooley said. He stood. It occurred to Hobbes that Peevey had promised very little.

When they came down, Victoria was waiting in the lobby. Dooley looked at Hobbes' face. "Five minutes," he

158

said. He went across the lobby and out the front door to where his car waited.

In the garden room Victoria said, "Are you in trouble?"

"No. Everything's okay now. The charges have been dropped, and Commander Peevey is free."

"But where have you been? Why haven't you been home?"

"It's a job I have to do. Another week and it will be over."

"Spy business?"

"Yes." An idea took shape in his mind. It frightened him. But the risk seemed small compared to the possible rewards. "Starting Sunday, I'll have a place here in Washington."

"A place? Where?"

"I don't know yet. But when I do, will you come?"

"I thought spies always watched each other."

"Langley won't be watching because they don't want some other men who might be watching to know they're interested in the place."

She gave him an incredulous look. "These are grown men?"

Hobbes laughed. He put his hands on her shoulders. She came reluctantly into his arms. "Will you come?" he said against her hair.

"I don't know."

"Will you think about it?"

"I'll think about it."

He took her chin in his hand, tilted her face up, and kissed her. "I'll call you."

In the car Dooley said, "That is a beautiful woman, Hobbes."

"Yes." Hobbes' eyes had been hurting for some time. Now the stench from Dooley's cigar was making him faintly nauseated.

"Don't do anything foolish, Hobbes. Just keep your eye on the ball until this job is over. Okay?"

"Okay," Hobbes lied.

"Say"— Dooley leaned over to peer into Hobbes' face— "you don't look too good."

Saturday morning Hobbes woke with a raging fever. Then the chills began. One moment he couldn't pile the covers high enough, and the next he was kicking them off and soaking in sweat.

At nine o'clock Dooley came into the bedroom to see what had happened to him. He took one look at Hobbes' ashen face and hurried from the room. Hobbes didn't know if it was moments or hours later that he felt one of his eyes pried open and found Dr. Beckman's face floating like a balloon over his head.

Beckman examined Hobbes' eyes and looked down his throat. Then he went into the bathroom and washed his hands. When he returned, he said, "Well—we may have overdone it a bit."

"Jesus, Doc," Hobbes heard Dooley say, "that's the understatement of the year. How the hell is he going to go on the job in this condition?" The voices seemed to Hobbes to be coming from the distant end of a tunnel. Through the distortion he could tell that Dooley was furious, and he wondered idly why that was so.

Hobbes felt his arm grasped, smelled alcohol, and felt the sting of a needle in his flesh.

"That will back it off," Beckman said. "Keep him in bed, feed him aspirin, and by tonight it should be a good healthy cold."

"Doc"— Hobbes heard Dooley's steel-edged voice— "you goddamn better be right." For a moment Hobbes felt grateful for Dooley's concern; but then he remembered why Dooley was concerned, and he let himself slip down into a delirious sleep.

When Hobbes awoke again, dusk was darkening the room. He sat up, sneezed, and switched on his bedside lamp. His throat was scratchy, and his sinuses seemed packed in cotton; but compared with the way he had been that morning, he felt marvelous.

He washed his face and combed his hair. He dressed in slacks and shirt and went downstairs. Dooley was at the desk in his study, bent over a folder of papers. When Hobbes entered, he closed the folder and rose.

"How are you?" Dooley said.

"Starved."

"Great! We'll fix that." Dooley went out the door. When he reappeared a moment later, he said, "I've ordered you up a feast."

Dooley put his hand on Hobbes' forehead. "Fever's gone. Looks like Doc came through."

"Would you really have had him shot if he hadn't?"

Dooley laughed. "I was a little pissed off, wasn't I? But it looks like everything's okay now. Your voice is great."

"I'll bet." Hobbes felt as if his voice were emerging from a point somewhere near his left ear.

Hobbes ate in the study while Dooley worked at his desk. As he was finishing his meal, Dr. Beckman arrived. He examined Hobbes with obvious relief and left shortly thereafter, leaving behind a sleeping pill.

But Hobbes didn't have to use it. He went to bed at nine with a book, and by ten o'clock he was asleep.

Sunday morning Hobbes' cold had settled in. His head felt a size too large, and his eyes and nose were red and swollen.

Downstairs he found Dooley, Halladay, and Dr. Beckman waiting for him in Dooley's den. Dooley was smoking a cigarette and pacing in front of the dead fire. A coffee service was laid out on the desk, and Hobbes helped himself. As he poured coffee, he was aware of the three men looking at him.

"What do you think?" Dooley asked.

161

"It'll do," Halladay said.

"With the contacts and the hair," Dr. Beckman said, "it will be perfect."

"Good morning," Hobbes said.

"Voice is good," Dooley said nervously, "don't you think?"

"It'll do," Halladay repeated dryly.

"It's nice to see you fellows, too," Hobbes said.

Dooley lit another cigarette from the stub of the first and looked at his watch. "We'd better roll."

"Nice of you to offer breakfast," Hobbes said, "but I don't think I've the time."

But the others were already out the door. Dooley came back to motion impatiently to Hobbes. Hobbes sighed, put his half-drunk coffee down, and followed him out.

Hobbes didn't think he was going to be able to tolerate the contacts in his inflamed eyes. But Beckman administered eye drops, and the pain subsided.

Working from photographs, the technician Bishop trimmed Hobbes' hair. He carefully shaved away patches at each temple that he instructed Hobbes to shave when he shaved his face. He washed Hobbes' hair and tinted it with a rinse. Then he had Hobbes change into a brown English wool vested suit, brown slip-on shoes of soft leather, and a beige topcoat of cashmere.

When Dooley came to get Hobbes, he pulled up short and whistled. "Jesus," he said. "George Gordon."

"With a cold," Bishop added.

Bishop put an expensive leather suitcase on a lab table and opened it. It was stuffed with a gaudy array of clothes. On the bag was a TWA tag and a British customs' sticker.

"These clothes are your size," Bishop said to Hobbes. "Don't get them mixed up with the clothes in the apartment because they don't fit you."

Dooley carried the suitcase, and they left the building.

Dooley's car was waiting at the door. Halladay was in the back seat. They made the trip to Dulles Airport in under fifteen minutes. The sky was leaden, and there was a smell of snow in the air. Hobbes spent the trip bundled in a corner dabbing at his tender nose with tissues.

At the airport a man in coveralls stood beside a gate in a fence to a service road beside a runway. He opened the gate as they approached and waved them through. Tiny flakes of snow were beginning to float in the cold air as the driver accelerated down a lane beside the runway.

The car pulled to a halt beside a corrugated steel door in a large building.

As the car idled, Dooley turned to Hobbes. "This is it, kid," he said. "If you need to talk to me, call and say Patriot. They'll patch you through. Got that?"

Hobbes nodded. His mouth was dry.

"Give me your wallet," Dooley said. Hobbes handed it over.

Dooley took a wallet from his coat pocket. "The address of the apartment is on the driver's license. Take it out now and memorize it."

Hobbes found the driver's license and looked at it. George Gordon's picture stared back at him. He said the address to himself three times, put the license back in the wallet, and put the wallet in his pocket.

Dooley slapped him on the shoulder. "Good luck, Hobbes. See you at the office tomorrow."

Hobbes took the suitcase and got out of the car with Halladay. Halladay rapped on the steel door, and it began to rise. Hobbes glanced over his shoulder at the car before he stepped through the door. Dooley was slumped in his seat, a cigar in the corner of his mouth, staring broodingly out at the snow that was now beginning to fall in large, wet flakes. Inside the building huge crates were stacked on pallets. A man in overalls greeted them, punched the button to close the door, and led them through an aisle between the crates to a small glassed-in office at the rear

163

of the building. Halladay and Hobbes went in the office while the other man waited outside.

Halladay handed Hobbes a passport. "Diplomatic visa," he said, "made out to George Gordon. When you get in the customs' building, go directly to a door on your left marked 'Special Handling.' And do it like you've been there many times before, because you have. They'll put you right through."

Hobbes put the passport in his coat pocket.

"Take a cab to the apartment," Halladay went on. "Gordon's car keys are in the middle desk drawer. The desk is in the living room." Halladay held up a key ring. "Key to the apartment and to the desk. When you want the car in the morning, call on the intercom down to the doorman, and it will be brought around front for you by the parking attendant. Got that?"

Hobbes nodded.

Halladay led Hobbes out of the office and to a small door. Halladay looked at his watch. For five minutes they stood silently at the door. Finally, the door opened, and a man stuck his head through. "Unloading," he said.

"You're on," Halladay said, and pushed Hobbes through the door.

Hobbes had been briefed on what to expect, but he was nevertheless disoriented by the crush of people making their way down a fluorescent-lighted hallway. Hobbes let himself be swept along. Over his shoulder he saw at the end of the tunnel an unloading tube terminating at the door of an aircraft. He knew the plane was a Boeing 747 because he had been told it was.

Ahead he saw the door marked "Special Handling," and he angled through the crowd for it. He went through the door and found himself confronted by a baggage counter behind which stood a man in a blue customs officer's uniform.

The man smiled and said, "Mr. Gordon!"

Hobbes froze.

164

"London again, eh?" the man said, and Hobbes imagined he saw him wink.

"Uh—that's right. London again."

The man was staring at him in a peculiar way.

"Should we get at it?" the man said, looking down at Hobbes' hand.

Hobbes followed the man's gaze and then said, with relief, "Oh." He put the suitcase on the luggage counter.

The customs officer picked up a clipboard with a passenger manifesto attached to it and ran his finger down the list. Hobbes had recovered enough of his composure to remember to take the passport from his coat pocket and drop it on top of the suitcase.

The customs officer made a check on the manifesto with his pen and smiled again at Hobbes.

"Anything to declare?"

"No."

"Got yourself a bit of a cold over there, did you?"

"Yes," Hobbes said. This time he definitely saw the customs officer wink.

"Get it from the birds?" The man laughed.

Hobbes croaked out a laugh. "That's where I must've gotten it." He had no idea what the man was talking about. He shoved his hands in the pockets of his topcoat and averted his eyes, pretending to be considering some grave thought. Then, suddenly, the numbing realization came to him that he had reverted to his normal habits of speech and posture, that, since entering the room, he had been Thomas Hobbes and had forgotten completely all his training. He stole a look at the man. He was busy stamping the passport as if he had noticed nothing. Hobbes swore to himself that from now on he would be George Gordon whatever the circumstances.

The customs man finished his business quickly. Hobbes put the passport in his pocket and picked up his suitcase.

"If I ever get to London when you're there," the customs officer said with a sly smile, "maybe you'll introduce me to some of those birds."

Now that his panic had left him, Hobbes realized what the man was talking about. Hobbes gave the man his best George Gordon smile. "If you do," he said, "you'd better bring your vitamins." He left the customs officer laughing.

The apartment had the closed-up smell of disuse about it. Hobbes switched on the hall light and peered into the living room. Outside the windows the snow was throwing a white curtain across the afternoon. As he stood in the hallway studying the shadowed forms of the furniture in the living room, Hobbes felt the hair on the back of his neck rise with the advent of some emotion that was at once familiar and nameless.

He put the suitcase down and went through the living room, switching on lights. The furniture was leather and chrome, featuring a suede couch under heavily draped windows. Hobbes pulled the drapes. The air outside the window was thick with snow, obscuring whatever view existed there. He drew the drapes again and looked around the room. A walnut bookcase was built into one wall. On its shelves were an expensive stereo system and some small abstract iron sculptures, but there were no books. In the wall opposite the couch was a gas fireplace. Hobbes went to it and got the gas log going. The flickering flames comforted him. Above the fireplace was a framed batik painting. Hobbes stared at it. It was done in arresting shades of orange and brown. It depicted the face of a woman. Her mouth was an orange slash. Her eyes were huge and somehow seemed to Hobbes to be filled with pain.

Hobbes got the suitcase and took it into the bedroom. The bed was very large. In the closet Hobbes found suits and shirts, all of the same flamboyant style as the clothes in the bag.

166

After he had unpacked, Hobbes explored the rest of the apartment. The kitchen was functional and cold—all tile counters and chrome appliances. The refrigerator contained a carton of tonic bottles, half a shriveled lime, and an unopened bottle of chianti. Over the tiled breakfast bar was a cupboard crammed with bottles of liquor of various description. Hobbes took down a scotch bottle, found a glass, pried an ice-cube tray from the refrigerator freezer, and poured himself a drink. He lit a cigarette and stood leaning against the counter, drinking scotch and thinking.

He finished his drink, rinsed out the glass, and went into the living room. A brown telephone rested on a table beside the suede couch. He considered calling Victoria, but the possibility that Dooley had the telephone bugged deterred him. He decided to go out and call her from a public phone.

Then, as he stood in the middle of the living room, he identified the strange emotion that he had felt upon entering the apartment. It was as though, at long last, he had finally come home.

NINETEEN

Outside, the streets were covered with a slick half inch of snow, and more was on its way. He found a pay phone stall a block from the apartment.

Victoria answered on the first ring. "Have you been thinking?"

"Yes. I don't know, Thomas—have you got a cold?"

"Yes, Listen, the apartment I've got isn't far. I just want to talk to you."

There was a long pause. "I could come tomorrow night."

"Fine." He gave her the address.

"To talk," she said.

"Right."

Hobbes trudged through the snow back to the apartment building. As he was putting the key in the door, the phone began to ring. He went to it, set his mental attitude in that of George Gordon, and answered it.

"Gordy!" The woman's voice was high-pitched with excitement. "When did you get back?"

"Tonight." He wondered who the woman was and if he was supposed to know her well enough to recognize her voice.

"What's the matter with your voice, baby?"

Hobbes forced a chuckle out. "Caught a cold in—where I was."

"I've been calling for days." Her voice contained a childish plaintiveness. "You could let a person know."

Hobbes decided to try a strategy. "I'm sorry, Gloria," he said.

"Gloria!" she shrieked. "Gloria! This is Jeanette!"

"I'm sorry. Sure, Jeanette."

"God, Gordy, you know how to cut a person, don't you?"

"I said I was sorry." Hobbes let irritation show in his voice.

Instantly she became apologetic. "Okay, honey," she said. "I know you're probably tired from the trip." She paused then giggled. "Not too tired, if I know you. It's snowing like crazy," she announced, as if he couldn't know.

"Look, Jeanette, I've got to get off the line. I'm expecting a call."

"Business or pleasure?"

"What?"

"Listen, baby, it's Sunday."

"Oh?"

"My night off, dummy. And I'm so cold."

"I've really got to get off this line—"

"Who are you expecting?" she asked suspiciously.

"I told you, I've got a call—"

"All right," she broke in. "All right. You told me once I don't need an invitation, didn't you?"

"I what?"

"Just come on over and snuggle up any old time you feel like it, you said."

"Now look—"

169

"I'll be there in twenty minutes."

"Now wait a minute—" But the line had gone dead.

Hobbes sat on the suede couch and tried to think what he would do if the woman appeared. He knew he had to get rid of her before she became suspicious. His mind fantasized a situation in which Jeanette would accuse him of being an impostor, would accuse him of murdering the real George Gordon and taking his place. He imagined her running hysterically into the night, screaming the news. He groaned, picked up the phone, dialed the number he had memorized, and said, "Patriot."

An impersonal voice said, "Hold on."

Ten seconds later Dooley's voice came booming over the line. "Hobbes!"

"Yes, sir."

"Can you talk?"

"Yes," Hobbes said, surprised by the question. "Sure."

"Okay. What's the problem?"

Hobbes told him about Jeanette. Dooley groaned. "You called me away from my dinner for this?"

"I thought it was important," Hobbes said stiffly.

Dooley sighed. "Listen, Tom, Gordon was a swinger. You knew that."

"I didn't expect, that—ah—"

"That you'd have to handle that problem so soon?"

"Yes."

"Well, you're going to have to handle it."

"But I don't know anything about her."

"You know what they were up to, don't you?"

"I—I guess so."

"What else do you need? Enjoy yourself."

"Wait! I—I can't do that."

Dooley sighed again. "Okay," he said wearily. "Don't be there when she gets there."

"What?"

"Stand her up. Go get a cup of coffee somewhere. That would be true to form. Gordon was a prizewinning bastard."

"Okay," Hobbes said, relieved by the simplicity of the solution. "I'll do that. Thanks."

"See you in the morning, kid," Dooley said.

Hobbes put on his topcoat. Then it occurred to him that he didn't actually have to go out. He could simply make Jeanette think he had.

He checked the lock on the door, put out the lights in the living room, and went into the bedroom. Wearily he stripped his clothes off, throwing them onto the bed carelessly. His throat was aching, and his eyes felt as if they were embedded in grains of sand. He went naked into the bathroom, removed the contacts from his eyes, and put them in their container. A red silk dressing gown hung on the back of the bathroom door. Hobbes examined it. Over the left breast were the initials G.G., monogrammed in heavy gold thread. He put the dressing gown back, turned the shower up as hot as he could stand it, and stepped in.

He was standing with his neck bowed, letting the hot spray pound off his spine, when he imagined he heard a laugh. He decided it was the noise of the drain playing tricks on his imagination. He let his mind drift back to the memory of his last encounter with Victoria.

The shower door opened.

Hobbes turned his head toward the door, his eyes wide. A slender girl stood there smiling at him. She was naked. Through the steam her body was a golden aura. She laughed and stepped into the shower. "Move over, baby," she said. She put her body against his, her arms around his neck, closed her eyes, and held her mouth up to be kissed. Beads of moisture from the shower glistened in her long blonde hair.

"How . . ." Hobbes began, but she covered his mouth

171

with her own. Her tongue probed his teeth. He pulled away. "How the hell did you get in here?"

She made a hurt moue. "You gave me a key, Gordy. Jesus, do you give so many out you can't remember?"

He tried to disengage from her. "You scared the hell out of me."

"I thought you were expecting me," she said in a little-girl voice. She giggled. "You sure got out of your clothes fast. They're all over the bed." He felt her hand probing between them, and instinctively he cringed away.

She looked at him peculiarly. "What's the matter, baby?"

He tried to laugh. "Nothing. I—I've got this cold."

She continued to peer at him through the steam. "You look funny. Your eyes—they're all puffy."

Suddenly Hobbes remembered the contacts. He pulled her roughly to him.

"That's better," she breathed against his chest. She moved her body sensuously against his, and despite himself, he felt his body begin to respond. "Jeanette will take care of her poor, sick baby," Jeanette said in a voice hot with passion.

He placed his hands on her round hips and pulled her closer. She moaned under her breath. "Listen, Jeanette," he said into her ear, "get out of here for a minute, will you?"

Her hand went between them again, and this time she found him. "What's wrong with here?" she murmured. "I don't think you can wait." Despite her slimness, her breasts were surprisingly full. Hobbes could feel her nipples hard against his chest.

He croaked out a laugh. "That's—that's just it, baby. I have to go, and it hurts like hell."

She laughed. She gave him a final squeeze and turned and stepped gracefully from the shower and his sight. When she reappeared, she was wrapped in a white towel.

172

"Don't be long," she said. He heard the bathroom door open and close.

He stepped hurriedly from the shower and, without bothering to dry off, went to the medicine cabinet, took out the contacts, and put them in his eyes. They stung furiously. He took the eyedrops from his shaving kit and applied a drop in each eye.

He put on the red dressing gown and cautiously opened the bathroom door. The bedroom was cloaked in darkness. The light from the bathroom made a narrow path across the floor and onto the bed. His clothes were no longer there. Jeanette's pale hair gleamed from under the covers. "C'mon, baby," she said urgently.

He remained in the doorway. "Ah—listen, Jeanette, this cold is worse than I thought. I'm really tired."

Instantly she was out of the bed and across the room, pressing her naked body against his, holding his head in her hands, and crooning her hot breath into his ear. "Poor baby." The smell of alcohol mingled with the scent of her breath. She took his hand and led him toward the bed.

"Really, Jeanette—"

She put her fingers on his mouth. "Save your strength, darling." She sat him on the bed. He heard the clink of ice against glass and liquid being poured. She handed him a glass and held her own up for a toast. He took a tentative sip and coughed. "What is that?" She was kneeling in front of him on the carpet, and he averted his eyes from the golden roundness of her naked body.

"Campari, darling—your favorite."

"With this cold, I can't taste a thing."

She cocked her head and stared up at him. "I've never seen you sick before, Gordy."

"No."

"I like it—taking care of you. You seem—well—you seem gentler. More needy, you know?"

173

He tried out one of Gordon's sardonic smiles. "It's just a cold, Jeanette—not a lobotomy."

She laughed. "There's the old Gordy!" She held her glass high over her head in a mock toast, her eyes gleaming. Her breast was pulled taut by the elevation of her arm, the nipple tilted upward. Hobbes felt himself flush with something more than just embarrassment.

He passed a hand across his eyes and tried to convey regret. "I don't think I'm going to be able to—you know—tonight, at least."

She placed a cool palm on his forehead. "Don't you worry, baby," she said. "You don't have to do a thing. Jeanette will take care of it."

From the living room came the sound of the doorbell. Hobbes heard it with a mixture of alarm and relief. Jeanette gave him a suspicious look. "I thought you weren't expecting anyone."

He rose, confused. "I'm not. You'd better get dressed."

She stood defiantly before him. "Just get rid of whoever it is."

"No, now look—" The doorbell rang again, insistently. He bolted out of the bedroom door, closing it behind him.

He opened the front door slightly and put his eye to the opening. Victoria's dark eyes smiled up at him.

"Victoria! What—what are you doing here?"

She held up a paper bag. "I brought you some medicine."

"Listen," he said desperately, "something's come up—I can't—"

"Do I have to stand in the hall?" She gave him a peculiar look. "What have you done to your hair—and your eyes?"

From the bedroom door came Jeanette's demanding voice. "Gordy! What's going on out there?" Hobbes could hear bare feet approaching behind his back. He closed his eyes. When he opened them, he saw Victoria staring up at him.

She backed into the hall, the paper bag clutched to her. "I thought you were different," she whispered. "I thought you were so different."

He fumbled at the door with fingers grown clumsy. He ripped it open finally. Victoria's back was receding down the hall. He ran after her. "Victoria!"

He got to the elevator too late to stop it. The door closed, and he caught one last glimpse of Victoria's face between the rubber lips of the elevator doors. Then she was gone. Hobbes looked wildly around. The door to the stairs caught his eye, and he rushed to it and had the door open before he remembered how he was dressed. He swore, spun, and ran back to the apartment.

Jeanette stood in the doorway wrapped in the towel, her wide eyes peering at him as he approached, the dressing gown flying out behind him, his bare feet slapping the hallway carpeting.

"What's going on?" Jeanette asked.

He brushed past her. "Goddamn," he said under his breath. "Oh, goddamn."

Jeanette spun to follow his flight. "What in hell is going on?" she said.

Hobbes tore into the bedroom and began feverishly to put on a pair of pants, dancing on one leg, the dressing gown tangling his arms. He ripped off the dressing gown and threw it across the room. He pulled the pants up and searched for his shirt. Jeanette stood beside the bed, regarding him with narrowed eyes.

"Who was that woman?"

"Dammit!" The zipper of the pants caught a wad of cloth from the shirt. He tore frantically at the tangled cloth.

"Why'd she call you Thomas?"

Hobbes froze. He looked up into Jeanette's blue eyes.

175

They stared at each other across the bedroom. Then Hobbes' shoulders slumped wearily. "What the hell," he said in a defeated voice. He limped to the bed, still working at the zipper, and sat heavily on it.

Jeanette's face took on a knowing look. "You told her your name was Thomas, didn't you?"

Hobbes nodded wearily. He gave up on the zipper and lay back on the bed and stared gloomily at the ceiling.

"You bastard," Jeanette said in a husky voice.

Hobbes didn't hear her. He was mentally calculating how long it would take Victoria to get home. He was planning what he would say when he called her.

Jeanette fell on the bed beside Hobbes and gripped the front of his shirt in her fist. She shook him roughly. "You bastard."

She squirmed her body across the bed until her chest was resting on his. She stared into his face. She put a pointed red fingernail on his chin and traced his jawline up to his ear. "Maybe that's your real name," she said huskily. "Maybe you gave me the phony name." She leaned down and gently bit his chin. "Huh?"

Hobbes roused himself from his misery. He pried himself out from under Jeanette and stood. "Look," he said in a strangled voice, "I've got some business to take care of."

Jeanette lay on her back, and looked up at him. The towel had fallen away from one side of her body. "Insurance business at eight o'clock on Sunday night?"

"What?" Hobbes stared down at her.

Jeanette laughed. "Don't tell me that was a lie, too? I'll bet your real job is seducing women, right? Right, Gordy, or Thomas, or Harry, or whatever the hell your name is?"

"No," Hobbes said.

"Sure." Jeanette stretched lazily, and the rest of the towel fell away from her body. She smiled at him. "You look weird, Gordy. Your shirt is all scrunched up, and

176

half a yard of it's sticking out of your fly, and your hair's going every which way. I've never seen you with a hair out of place. It's very sexy, Gordy."

"You're going to have to leave."

She flushed with anger. Hobbes couldn't help noticing with a sense of wonder that the flush spread down her neck to the cleavage of her breasts. She reared up on her elbows and struck the bed with her fist. "Goddamn, Gordy. What's the matter with you?"

"I'm—I'm in love."

Jeanette's eyes widened. "You're kidding!"

"No," Hobbes said.

"With the woman at the door?"

"Yes."

Jeanette laughed. She held her naked flanks and shrieked with laughter. She rolled on the bed, gasping for breath. She turned on her stomach and pounded the pillow. "The great Gordy!" she cried. "The use-'em-and-leave-'em kid! In love!" The golden orbs of her hips flared from her slim back in front of Hobbes' fevered eyes.

He spun and went into the living room. He put on his coat and went out the door. Out on the street, he ran clumsily through the snow to the pay phone.

Victoria answered as he was about to conclude that she wouldn't. Her voice was faint and flat.

"Listen," he said, "I can imagine how it seemed to you. But it's part of the job—the assignment—" He realized he wasn't making much sense. His words were tumbling over each other.

Victoria's laugh was void of humor. "You have a strange job."

"Dammit!" He ran his hand through his hair in a gesture of frustration. "I—I can't explain the whole thing. Please believe that what happened is a result of the job. It wasn't my idea. I was trying to avoid it. I mean nothing happened! It just seemed—"

"I have to go," she said wearily.

He took a deep breath. "Okay. I don't blame you. But give me a chance to explain."

"I don't intend to go through this, just when I've got my life straight again."

"But you won't. Please. Let me explain."

There was a long silence on the line. Hobbes held his breath.

"Is that woman still there?" Victoria asked finally.

"Yes." He groaned. "But she's leaving."

She sighed heavily. "I don't know why, but I'll give you your chance."

"Will you come over then?" he asked eagerly.

"No! I won't go near that place. I—I'll meet you at the hotel tomorrow night."

"I don't know if I can—"

"Forget it," she said harshly.

"No! Wait! I'll be there."

Hobbes went slowly back to the apartment. Jeanette came from the bedroom while he was sitting on the couch, brooding over a cigarette. She was dressed, and she had brushed her hair and put on fresh makeup. Through his gloom Hobbes couldn't help noticing what a beautiful woman she was.

"Well, baby," she said cheerfully, "I hope your lady treats you the way you've treated me. That's all I can wish for you."

He looked up at her from under the hand he had over his eyes. "I'm sorry, Jeanette."

She smiled crookedly. "You've got a bad case, honey. She must be some woman if she can soften up George Gordon this way."

At the door she paused and looked at him over her shoulder. "You know," she said, "you're a different person. Two weeks, and you're not the old Gordy anymore. So I'm not really losing anything, am I?" And she left.

Hobbes paced the living room. He went to the kitchen

and poured himself a substantial amount of scotch. He took the bottle with him and went into the bedroom. He fell onto the bed with his clothes on and drank. The lilac smell of Jeanette lingered on the sheets. His head hurt, and his eyes ached with a simmering fever. He fell asleep with the empty glass in his hand. He dreamed Victoria and Jeanette were in bed with him. Somehow he was paralyzed, and the two women were clawing at his flesh, tearing at his limbs, trying to divide his body between them.

TWENTY

Hobbes stamped his feet in the doorway of the apartment building, waiting for Gordon's car to be brought around. He sneezed mightily, and the doorman smiled at him. "It's the season for colds, Mr. Gordon."

The sky was steel blue. The snow plows had come and spun a low bank along the sidewalks. The doorman was punching a path in front of the apartment building with an aluminum snow shovel.

Hobbes recognized the car as it came in sight. It was a dark blue Jaguar. Hobbes had been briefed about the car at Langley.

The Jaguar negotiated the frozen streets effortlessly. Leather cradled Hobbes' body, and the heater warmed him. He had awakened that morning still clothed, lying across the bed, the empty glass at his side.

When Hobbes arrived at Dooley's office, he found Dooley in a sweat suit, down on the carpet doing push-ups. Dr. Beckman and Halladay sat watching.

Dooley got to his feet puffing. His fleshy face was shining with sweat. He wiped his forehead on his sleeve and grinned at Hobbes. "I'm licking it, Hobbes." He went huffing over to his desk and picked up a glass of murky-looking liquid. "Liquid protein," he said, and threw his head back and downed it.

Hobbes took out his cigarette pack and then put it back.

"Smoke!" Dooley commanded. "It's part of the program. I've got to get used to it."

Hobbes lit a cigarette, and Dooley winced. "I won't tell you I'm used to it yet." He sniffed at the cigarette smoke like a beagle picking up a rabbit scent.

Dooley sat at his desk, took a towel from a drawer, wiped his face with it, and draped it around his neck. "It was in the *Post* Sunday. This doctor in Florida came up with the perfect quit-smoking plan. Exercise and diet, see. You get to feeling so goddamn good, as you quit, that you—that you—" Dooley looked at Beckman.

"Positive reinforcement," Beckman said.

"Right. Positive reinforcement," Dooley echoed. "You get programmed to believe that quitting is why you feel good." He stared at Hobbes, as if he expected him to add something to help convince both of them of the truth of what he had just said.

"Good!" Hobbes said with forced enthusiasm.

Dooley sighed, picked up a file folder, and looked over the top of the folder at Halladay. "You know, that goddamn doctor overlooked tapering off. If you cut down as you feel better, then the psychological effect would be more telling, wouldn't it?"

"Vern," Halladay said wearily.

"Just kidding," Dooley said, and then chuckled unconvincingly. "Let's get down to business." He looked at Hobbes. "Tomorrow you're on your own."

"Yes," Hobbes said.

"I mean, we can't send anyone in there tight with you, you know? Those boys would smell it a mile off. They're pros, these lads are."

181

"We've been through that with him," Halladay said. He lit a cigarette.

Dooley waved at the smoke with both hands. "So I'll go through it again," he said irritably.

Halladay shrugged. But Dooley didn't go on. Abruptly he asked, "Who's your initial contact?"

"Anthony Clawson," Hobbes said.

"You don't know him, right?"

"I've known Tony off and on for two years. We spent some time together in London."

"Yeah," Dooley said angrily. "He's the bastard that got his hooks into you—into Gordon. Damned Limey. But he's smooth, Tom. Don't underestimate him."

"Yes, sir." Hobbes became aware that Dr. Beckman was leaning forward in his chair and examining his face. Hobbes shifted uncomfortably.

"Any fever?" Beckman asked.

"A little," Hobbes said. "At night."

Beckman nodded with satisfaction.

"Who will be with Clawson?" Halladay asked.

"A man called Leo Fisher. I met him once in New York."

"That son of a bitch is an officer in the KGB," Dooley said.

Hobbes had heard this before. His mind drifted to Victoria. Halladay brought him back to reality.

"He's a killer."

"What?"

"One of their top ones," Dooley added. "He has an A rating."

"A rating?" Hobbes felt a tingle in his spine.

"Assassin. The Russians are subtle, aren't they?"

"How—how do I handle him?"

"You don't," Dooley said. "He's not dumb, but he's not bright either. He'll take his direction from Clawson. You just play it the way we said."

"What if something goes wrong?" Hobbes asked.

182

"We won't leave you in there without backup," Dooley said. "You have a number to call."

"An office to go to in Vancouver," Halladay added.

Hobbes had heard this before, too. He wasn't reassured. "I see."

"Don't worry, Tom," Dooley said soothingly. "Our fellows will be around in Vancouver."

Dooley stood and extended his hand. The sweat suit made him look somehow older and less powerful. Another time it might have made Hobbes feel easier, but at that moment he wished Dooley were in his suit, his hair combed, looking invulnerable.

Hobbes took Dooley's hand. Dooley looked him in the eye. Hobbes braced himself for one of Dooley's speeches. Instead, Dooley simply nodded and said, "Good luck."

Toward the end of the afternoon Halladay took the car keys to the Jaguar from Hobbes and left him sitting in the training room with nothing remaining to do but wait for his return.

When Halladay came back, he dropped the car keys into Hobbes' hand. Hobbes looked at them. A miniature license plate had been added to the ring. It was dented and scratched, as if it had been on the ring for a long time. On the back the name and address of a veterans' organization were embossed.

"That's the license number of Gordon's Jag," Halladay said. "The microdot is exactly in the center of the zero."

Halladay took a pocket magnifier from his coat, unfolded it, and held it out to Hobbes. Hobbes centered it over the zero. He could just make out a dot, a half shade darker than the background.

Hobbes parked the Jaguar in the basement garage of Gordon's apartment building and made his way to the elevator. The parking attendant waved to him from a glass-walled booth.

During the day Hobbes had formulated a plan for getting from the apartment to the Lincoln Hotel. If, as he had been told, the Russians were watching the building, then Hobbes knew he couldn't have them follow him to the hotel; they might connect Thomas Hobbes and George Gordon.

He was alone in the elevator when it reached Gordon's floor. He let the doors open and close in case someone was watching the floor indicators below. He got off on the floor below. The foyer was deserted. He ran down the stairs to the garage level and peered through a wire-enforced window into the garage. The attendant was bent over a desk in his booth talking to a man in a topcoat.

Hobbes slipped out the door and, staying between the wall and the front bumpers of parked cars, made his way in a crouch to a place twenty feet from the ramp to the street. He peered around the last car. The attendant and the man were now out of the cubicle, walking toward the rear of the garage. Hobbes pushed away from the car and went up the ramp at a fast walk.

It was cold. Clouds blanketed the sky, and the streetlights shone frostily against the gray snow. The streets were clogged with commuting traffic, but the sidewalks were nearly deserted. Hobbes walked for two blocks and suddenly stopped and spun around, feeling in his pockets as if he had forgotten something. The block he was in was deserted. Dimly, in the next block, he could see a young boy skipping along the sidewalk and behind him a man in a short, heavy jacket hurrying as if to catch the boy. Hobbes turned and continued to the coffee shop he had selected.

He had been in the coffee shop before on one of his surveillances. He walked briskly through the coffee shop to a rear door that connected with the lobby of a small hotel on the next block.

He hurried through the lobby and out onto the street. A doorman was sitting in a booth next to the entrance, warming his hands over an electric heater. He saw Hobbes and came stiffly from his booth.

"Cab, sir?"

Hobbes nodded, and the doorman blew his whistle and waved his arm. A cab pulled up. Hobbes handed the doorman a dollar bill and climbed into the back seat of the warm cab. As he gave the driver the address of the Lincoln Hotel, he looked out at the sidewalk. The doorman had gone back to his booth, the sidewalk and the lobby were deserted. Hobbes settled back in the seat.

The opposite door of the cab opened, and a man leaned in. "Hey, Bill," he said.

Hobbes hardly heard him. His concentration was centered on the gun that the man held on the seat beneath the driver's line of vision, the muzzle tilted at Hobbes' stomach.

The man put his finger to his lips. Hobbes continued to stare at the gun. The driver turned his head and said through the wire-mesh partition, "You gettin' in, mister, do it fast."

The man with the gun got in and closed the door. "Christ, fancy running into you in this traffic, Bill."

Hobbes continued to stare at the gun. The man slid the butt of the gun across the seat and jabbed Hobbes in the thigh with the barrel.

"Uh—hi—" Hobbes said.

The cab pulled out and stopped for a red light at the corner. The driver put his arm along his seat and looked over his shoulder. "Say," he said, "you two are twins, right?"

TWENTY-ONE

Hobbes sneezed. The man beside him said, "That's quite a cold you've got, brother."

Hobbes tried to pierce the shadows shrouding the man's face. The nose was narrow. The eyes caught the light from an approaching car. They glittered with icy amusement. Hobbes recognized their color. The contact lenses he wore were the same color.

The man moved closer until his thigh pressed against Hobbes. The gun barrel gleamed dully on his lap. "Where are we going, pal?" he whispered.

Hobbes considered the question. He could see no purpose in lying. In another few minutes they would be there. "A hotel," Hobbes said.

"Okay," the man whispered. "When we get there, you act normal, see? I'm a friend. If anything goes wrong, I pull the trigger. I'm very nervous, get it?"

The man didn't sound nervous at all.

"Now this hotel," the man went on in the same hoarse whisper. "You got a room there?"

Hobbes nodded.

"Anyone else there?"

"No."

"Fine." The man settled back in the seat, but the gun barrel never wavered.

When the cab stopped in front of the hotel, the man took a blue stocking cap and a pair of dark glasses from his coat pocket. He pulled the cap low on his brow and put on the glasses while Hobbes paid the cabdriver.

Hobbes walked ahead, the man a pace behind with his hand holding the gun in his jacket pocket. Sophie Crump, Dr. Marshall, and Mr. Darling sat at the domino table in the lobby. Victoria wasn't in sight.

Sophie saw them first. "Mr. Hobbes?" She was looking at him peculiarly.

"Don't stop until we get to the room," the man said in a low voice.

"What have you done to your hair?" Sophie Crump called.

Hobbes shrugged. "Ah—new style."

As the elevator doors were creaking closed, Hobbes heard Mr. Darling say, "It's not manly, a person dying his hair—"

The man searched the room quickly. He locked the door. He motioned to Hobbes to take the chair by the telephone. After Hobbes was seated, he removed the stocking cap and glasses.

He stared at Hobbes. "Jesus," he said softly, "where'd they find you?" His gaze broke from Hobbes face and darted around the room.

"You have coffee?"

Hobbes nodded.

"Fix us some." The man sighed wearily and lit a cigarette. The gun was out of his pocket now, and the muzzle followed Hobbes around the room like an eye.

The man sat at the telephone table with his coffee. He had Hobbes sit on the bed across from him. "You know who I am." It was not a question.

"George Gordon," Hobbes said.

187

Gordon sipped his coffee. "I've been watching the apartment for a week." He smiled. "Imagine, if you can, my surprise to see myself get out of a cab Sunday afternoon with a suitcase and walk right into the goddamn place." His smile widened. "You were a disappointment to Jeanette. You trying to ruin my reputation, pal?"

"Can I have a cigarette?"

"One of mine," Gordon said. He removed a cigarette from his pack and tossed it and a lighter to Hobbes.

Gordon settled back in the chair and crossed his legs. "I called Jeanette Monday morning. She wasn't too glad to hear from me."

Hobbes paused in the act of lighting the cigarette. "She knows?"

"That there are two of us? No. I just called and said this is Gordy. That's all you have to do with Jeanette. She takes over from there. I got the whole sordid story played back."

Hobbes smoked his cigarette in silence, while Gordon studied him. Finally, Gordon said, "That goddamn Dooley. He never misses a beat. The cold is a stroke of genius. Let me guess—I'll bet Beckman came up with that one. Right?"

Hobbes didn't reply. He was measuring the distance between himself and the gun.

Gordon's eyes narrowed. "Now, pal—I know what I'd be thinking right now if I were in your place. This gun is a thirty-two special—nothing fancy. Just a good, competent killing weapon. And it's my favorite, see? I can hit the moving silhouette of a man at fifty yards nine times out of ten. I hope you get the message."

Hobbes nodded slowly.

"What did the old lady call you? Hobbes?"

Hobbes didn't reply.

"Okay, Hobbes. I'm going to tell you a story. You correct me where I'm wrong."

Hobbes continued to gaze silently at George Gordon.

188

"It took me awhile to figure it out," Gordon said. "I mean, I stake out my apartment for a week—right? And nobody from Langley is anywhere near the place. There are people watching around the clock; but they aren't from Langley, and I'll bet I don't have to tell you where they're from.

"But that's what I expect. Langley thinks I'm dead, so there's no point in watching a dead man's place, is there? The boys who are watching know I'm not dead—I made sure of that. So I figure the deal's still on. I'm about to show myself at the apartment, just to reassure the guys who are watching, when I see myself get out of that cab." Gordon laughed. "Jesus! So I sit up around the clock on the place. I froze my butt off Sunday night, let me tell you. Then Monday morning here comes my car, and you get in."

Gordon paused to drain his coffee cup. He put the empty cup on the floor and pushed it with the toe of his shoe toward Hobbes. "Fill 'er up, pal—and move very slowly."

While Hobbes was getting the coffee, Gordon turned in the chair to keep the gun on him. "While I'm standing around in the cold watching Jeanette twitch her beautiful ass into my apartment building and imagining what's going on up there between you two, I figure out that only half of my little plan has taken. Dooley has bought that I'm dead in the plane. That was a nice touch, Hobbes, if I do say so. I fixed it so the plane goes down in a place that isn't accessible until the spring thaw. I fix it so it burns. I fix it so there's a body in it, in case they go to the trouble to fly over and photograph the wreckage. And believe me, the guy who was flying the plane deserved to burn.

"Then I see you get in the car, and I see that you have a cold that makes your nose red and your eyes swollen, so that nobody's going to notice little differences in our appearance and voice, and it clicks! That goddamn cold's got Dooley-Beckman written all over it. . . . Just put the cup on the other side of the table real gentle."

189

Gordon pulled the cup over to his side of the table and directed Hobbes back to the bed with the barrel of the gun.

"I ask myself," Gordon continued, "what is Dooley up to? It's obvious he wants the guys watching the place to think I'm still alive. That means he wants to go through with the deal. But of course, our friend Vern isn't going to give them what I was going to. So what's he going to give them? Why, a phony piece of goods. He's setting them up. I hate the bastard, but you've got to admire the way his mind works."

Gordon took a sip of the coffee. His face had the bruised look that comes with deep fatigue. His eyes burned with the distant light of a man with a fever. He fumbled in his jacket pocket, removed a plastic vial of pills, and managed to get the lid off one-handed. He put one of the small white pills in his mouth and washed it down with coffee.

Hobbes tried to relax. His tension was like a hand clamped at the back of his neck. Gordon was looking at him with curiosity. "You aren't one of Dooley's regulars. I'd know you. What did he do—import you?"

Hobbes didn't answer.

"Never mind," Gordon said easily. "At this point it doesn't matter."

"What do we do now?" Hobbes asked.

"Well," Gordon replied earnestly, leaning toward Hobbes, "we got to figure some things out. Somebody has to make that delivery in Vancouver. Unfortunately it can't be me. The boys watching the place have got me pegged with a bad cold, and if I show up there tomorrow with a miraculous cure, they're going to blow me out of the water. So it kind of narrows it down."

Hobbes said quietly, "Then I go?"

Gordon laughed. "Don't get eager, Hobbsy." His eyes glittered at Hobbes. "You know, I don't think you're a pro at all. You're somebody Dooley dug out of the bushes somewhere, aren't you?"

"Does it matter?"

"It might at some point," Gordon replied. "I'm a very careful man, Hobbes. I like to know all the players."

Gordon finished his coffee, lit another cigarette, and tossed a cigarette and the lighter to Hobbes. "You see, Hobbes," he said, "I've got to make this deal. It's the only chance I've got. So you're right. You're going to do it for me. But we have to figure a few details first."

Gordon fell into a long silence. The gun was balanced on his knee, the muzzle on a line with Hobbes' head. Hobbes smoked his cigarette and waited.

Finally, Gordon sighed and said, "Where is it?"

"What?"

"The microdot. You've got to have it on you. You're leaving in the morning, and Dooley wouldn't risk another meeting before then. Where is it?"

Hobbes shrugged.

Gordon got slowly to his feet. "Stand up." Hobbes did. "Empty your pockets on the bed."

When Hobbes was finished, Gordon said, "Move around to the other side of the bed." Hobbes did.

Gordon aimed the gun carefully at Hobbes before he began sorting through the contents of Hobbes' pockets. When he came to the identity card in the wallet, he grinned and said, "I never did like that picture."

Gordon flicked the car keys aside with his finger and sorted through the change. Suddenly, he picked up the keys and looked at the miniature license plate. Then he broke into a broad smile. "Where is it? One of the corners?"

Hobbes maintained his silence.

"Never mind," Gordon said, "I'll find it."

" Why does it matter—if I'm going to deliver it?"

Gordon went back to sit in the chair, the keys in his

hand, and motioned for Hobbes to pick up the things on the bed. After Hobbes was once again seated across from him, Gordon said, "I'll tell you why it matters, pal. I've got the real goods. The genuine microdot. And that's the one you're going to deliver, see?"

Hobbes felt the blood drain from his face. "I couldn't—"

"Well, now, Hobbes, that's one of our problems. We're going to have to come up with a way that you could."

"I don't see what difference it makes."

"I don't mind explaining it to you, Hobbes. First of all, you are carrying dynamite. If the guys in Vancouver get the slightest whiff of a double cross, they'll bury your body so deep no one will ever find it. And I don't get what I'm after. So, we don't play around, right? We give 'em the real goods.

"The other reason is purely personal." Gordon's mouth made a harsh scar across his face. "I want to stick it to Dooley. That bastard has it coming. And if we pull this off, it ought to ruin him."

Gordon laughed harshly. "Did Dooley give you his famous half-time speech? Did he tell you your country was depending on you? Did he tell you the big bad Russians were going to take over if you fucked up?" The pupils of Gordon's eyes were pinpoints. His upper lip was blistered with sweat. He visibly controlled himself. He wiped his lip with a finger and settled back in the chair. "I've had that speech, pal. It's bullshit all the way through. When it comes down to it, Dooley will leave you hanging in the fire to save his own ass. Because that's all Dooley's concerned about. He has one cause. And that's to make Vernon Dooley Director at Langley."

There was a hesitant knock on the door. Gordon's eyes came up quickly on Hobbes' face. "Expecting someone?"

"No," Hobbes lied.

The knock came again, and Victoria's soft voice. "Thomas?"

192

Gordon stood and motioned Hobbes to his feet.

"She'll go away," Hobbes whispered.

Gordon gave Hobbes a cunning look. Fear clutched at Hobbes.

"Answer it," Gordon whispered. "Remember—" He held the gun up.

Gordon stood beside the door. "Ask her in," he whispered.

Hobbes opened the door. "Thomas?" Victoria said.

Hobbes held a hand beside his leg and made a shoving gesture with it.

Gordon eased around the door. He put the muzzle of the gun against Victoria's temple and took her arm. An animal growl came from Hobbes.

Gordon quickly closed the door and released Victoria. "Easy, Hobbsy," he said. "I'm not going to hurt her unless you make me." He kept the gun trained on Victoria, who was standing, white-faced, staring at Hobbes.

The murderous red cloud that had enveloped Hobbes' mind lifted. He backed warily around Gordon, his eyes fixed on the other man's face.

Gordon grinned. "That's better. Now both of you sit over there on the bed."

Gordon sat in a chair. His movements were jerky; his face was deeply lined. His eyes were alert and fixed on the two across from him.

Slowly Gordon examined Victoria, starting at her ankles and traversing up to her wide, frightened eyes. He chuckled throatily. "I gotta hand it to you, Hobbes—you got taste."

"She's my lawyer."

Gordon threw his head back and laughed. "Some lawyer!"

"You're on the wrong track, Gordon."

Gordon's laugh died. His eyes locked on Hobbes' face. "Tell me about it, Hobbsy."

"I don't care what happens to her."

"Oh!" Gordon said with exaggerated surprise. "That's the way it is, huh?"

"Let her go!" Hobbes said. He locked eyes with Gordon.

"Take it easy." Gordon said in a deadly voice. "You're getting that look again. Remember—if you try it, I blast her first."

Hobbes controlled himself with effort. "Just let her go, I'll do what you want."

"Now, Hobbes," Gordon said in a reasonable tone, "Think about it. You know I can't do that. I mean, this solves our little problem, doesn't it?"

"No!"

"Sure it does, man. You're going to go to Vancouver and bring back what I want, and we make a trade. Now doesn't that simplify things?"

"Look," Hobbes said. "You followed me from your apartment. If you could, the others did, too. They know. They know there're two of us." Hobbes gestured vaguely at the window. "They're probably out there now. There isn't any point in going on—" Gordon's grin cut through his words.

"Nice try, Hobbes. For someone as green as you are, your mind works in devious ways. Nobody saw you slip out. You were goddamn slick, pal. I gotta hand it to you."

"But you did."

"I was in the stairwell on my floor, waiting for you. Through the window, I see the elevator doors open and close, and nobody gets out. I'm trying to figure that one out, when I hear somebody running below on the stairs. I follow. Bingo!" Gordon smiled. "The other guys weren't so lucky. Believe me, Hobbes. They didn't follow. I've got some experience in these things."

Gordon shifted up on one hip in his chair and leaned heavily on his elbow. He passed a hand briefly across his eyes. "The reason I bother to tell you all this, pal, is that I want you to know there is no other way but mine. I want

194

you to quit wasting your energy and my time on wild-ass escape schemes. Somebody could end up getting shot, and believe me she would be first on the list."

Hobbes heard Victoria's breath catch.

Gordon smiled apologetically at Victoria. "I guess we've left you in the dark, haven't we? Let me explain. Hobbes here is going to get on a plane tomorrow morning and go pick up something I need. While he's gone, you and I are going to keep the lonely vigil for his return. When he gets back with my property, which I have every confidence he will, why, you two go off hand in hand, and old Uncle Gordy goes his separate way. Simple, huh?"

Victoria's hand clamped Hobbes'. "What is he talking about?"

"It's okay," Hobbes said.

"Why is he—?" Victoria stammered. "You two—"

Gordon chuckled. "Twins," he said. "That's what the cabdriver called us." He stretched his legs. "It's a little complicated, lady. Hobbsy will tell you all about it when he gets back."

Gordon stood suddenly. "Lie down on the bed." He had them lie side by side, their arms above their heads.

"Any sudden move," Gordon said pleasantly, "will be your last."

By burying his chin in his chest, Hobbes got a blurred vision of Gordon bent over the telephone table. He was facing the bed, the gun at hand on the table. Hobbes closed his eyes tightly and opened them suddenly, and the objects under Gordon's hand came into focus. Gordon was holding a water glass over the miniature license plate, looking through the bottom of the glass as he passed it slowly over the tag. The glass stopped suddenly, and Gordon grunted. He took his wallet out of his pocket and removed a small suede kit from it. From the kit he took tweezers, an eyedropper, and a vial. He worked over the tag with the tweezers. Finally, he held the tweezers up to the light and smiled. He removed his wristwatch, screwed off the back, took something from the inside of the case with the tweezers, and placed it carefully on the tag. He dipped the eyedropper in the vial and transferred one golden bead of liquid to the tag. Then he stood with the key chain in one hand, the gun in the other.

"Okay," he said. "You can sit up."

When they were again sitting on the edge of the bed, Gordon said. "You've got to get going, Hobbes. I leave it to you to get back in the apartment as slickly as you got out. Just remember, you've got a lot riding on success." He indicated Victoria with the gunbarrel.

"No," Hobbes said quietly.

Gordon raised an eyebrow. "Come again, pal?"

"I'm not leaving her alone with you."

Gordon grinned. "My reputation is ruined in this town, I can see that." The grin faded. "I'm not going to do anything to your lady—unless you screw up and don't bring me my property."

"I've got a deal."

"Well, Hobbsy, good for you. But you're not in any position to make deals."

"I won't go otherwise."

"Jesus, you goddamn idiot! I've got nothing to lose, Hobbes."

"But what will you gain?"

Gordon was silent for a moment. "Okay. I'll listen to your deal."

"An old man lives here. Bring him in to stay with you, and I'll go. I think you know him."

"Who?"

"Commander Peevey."

"Horace Peevey!" Gordon stared at Hobbes. "He lives here?"

"Yes."

"Jesus. Old Horace Peevey."

"It's the only way I'll go," Hobbes said.

Gordon grinned suddenly. "Why not? Provided you can get him up here without leaving the room."

196

Hobbes phoned Peevey's room. Hobbes said he had to talk to him. Peevey agreed to come right away. After Hobbes hung up, Gordon said, "Go sit by your girlfriend. I want to tell you the facts of life."

When Hobbes was seated, Gordon said, "If you get some crazy idea of blowing the whistle on me to Dooley, I want to tell you how that would work." He paused to light a cigarette. Hobbes noticed that Gordon's hands were developing a tremor. "Dooley's idea of a subtle approach is to send in a squad of cops with automatic weapons. He hates my guts almost as much as I hate his. If he knew I was alive, there would be no limit to the number of bodies he'd walk over to get me. And before I went, I would take your girlfriend and the old man along for the ride."

"Don't worry," Hobbes said. "I won't tell Dooley."

Gordon got out the pills and took another. Hobbes watched him carefully. His hands were trembling noticeably now. But in a few moments the trembling abated, and Gordon's mouth became fixed in a stiff smile. His eyes were like dark pinholes pierced into his skull.

"I'm not the one that has to worry, Hobbes," Gordon said.

TWENTY-TWO

Commander Peevey stared in turn at Gordon and then at Hobbes. "What the hell is this, Hobbes?"

"Sit down, old man," Gordon said. He motioned toward a chair with the gun.

Peevey seemed not to notice the gun. He gave Gordon a look of contempt. "When you worked for me," he said, "you weren't man enough to give me orders. I can't see that you've changed."

"I've got a gun."

"I can see you've got a gun," Peevey replied. "And if you don't stop pointing it at me, I'm going to feed it to you a piece at a time."

"Hobbes," Gordon said, "this was your idea. You'd better do something, because I haven't got any patience left."

"Please," Hobbes said to Peevey. "Sit down. He's not bluffing."

Peevey sat stiffly in the chair. "Why are you made up to look like him?" he asked Hobbes.

"It's a job."

Peevey's eyes widened. "For Dooley?" Hobbes nodded. "So that's it! That idiot Dooley thought I might blow your cover." Peevey looked at Victoria. "What are you doing here?"

"I don't have much choice."

"This isn't anyplace for you," Peevey said.

"What is this? A goddamn social hour?" Gordon shouted.

Peevey ignored him. "I think you should leave," he said to Victoria.

Gordon leaped to the center of the room and brandished the gun. His eyes were wild, his face was pale. "The first one of you that moves gets blown away."

Peevey studied him calmly. "George, what the hell are you doing? Why don't you put that gun down and let's talk about it?"

"Hobbes!" Gordon growled. He was crouched like an animal, the gun thrust out in both hands.

"Sir," Hobbes said quietly, "I think we'd better do what he says."

"He'd use that thing?"

"I think so."

Peevey shrugged. "What do you want me to do, Hobbes?" Quickly Hobbes told him, while Gordon looked from Peevey to Hobbes, his mouth open, his eyes wide.

"Of course, I'll look after this young woman," Peevey said. "But what in God's name is going on?"

Gordon crouched in front of Peevey and put the barrel of the gun against the old man's cheek. "You ask me the questions. I'm in charge here."

"Very well," Peevey said calmly. "What in God's name is going on, George?"

Gordon laughed wildly. "You arrogant old bastard! *I've* got the gun, goddamn it."

"Of course you do, George," Peevey said soothingly.

Gordon drew a deep breath and let it out with a shudder. He backed carefully away from Peevey, drew a chair from the table, and sat down. "Hobbes is going to run an errand for me," he said. His voice had become emotionless. "You two are going to wait here with me until he gets back."

"And how long will that be?" Peevey asked.

"A couple of days," Gordon said.

"Well, George," Peevey said with a faint smile, "it should be an interesting couple of days."

Gordon stood and moved to the door. "All right, Hobbes." Hobbes joined him at the door.

"I'm going to show you what your friend Dooley was getting you into," Gordon said. He took a pipe and a paper pouch of cheap tobacco from his coat pocket. "You didn't know about the pipe, right?"

Hobbes shook his head. Gordon gave him an evil grin. "If you'd shown up in Vancouver without these, you would've been a dead man." He handed the pipe and tobacco to Hobbes. "They'll give you a pouch of tobacco identical to this one. That's what you bring back to me. You've got a diplomatic passport. You should be able to bring the pouch through with no trouble." Gordon paused. "You know about Tony."

"Yes."

"There was a girl in London," Gordon said. "Zee. Tony and I went with her, off and on. Ask him how she is. He'll expect it."

"All right."

"He's a crazy son of a bitch, Hobbes. You watch it with him."

"Crazy?"

"On the outside he's a slick Englishman. But there are some warped parts in his head."

Gordon handed Hobbes the keys to the Jaguar. Hobbes put them in his pocket. "Don't worry about them crossing you," Gordon said. "Once they get a look at that microdot, you'll get the pouch. Don't screw around with the pouch. I'll know if you've messed with it."

Gordon looked into Hobbes' eyes. "Don't get any ideas,

Hobbes." Gordon's face was a mask of fatigue, the flesh stretched taut. Hobbes for a moment, in the dim light of the hall, imagined he could see plainly the skull beneath the pale flesh. "You're my last chance," Gordon said. "If you fail or if you try to cross me up, I haven't got anything left."

"I understand," Hobbes said.

"I hope so." Gordon bared his teeth in a grimace of tension and desperation. "If I go, pal, I won't go alone."

At seven fifty the next morning Hobbes caught a plane to Montreal. After an hour's wait, he took a direct Air Canada flight to Vancouver. Dooley had booked him first class all the way; it was the style Gordon traveled in. Hobbes tried to relax on the plane. He had spent a sleepless night in Gordon's apartment after leaving the hotel. Finally, an hour before they landed at Vancouver airport, sleep overtook him. When he went through the fluorescent-lit corridors to claim his bag, he felt refreshed, although he knew it was the adrenaline pumping through his body that was giving him a false sense of restoration.

He took a cab to the Prince Edward Hotel on West Twelfth Street, where Dooley had booked him a reservation, another concession to the style in which Gordon lived. It was raining in Vancouver, a cold, misting rain that shrouded the buildings in the distance in a gray curtain that was torn occasionally by a low, gusting wind.

Hobbes had never been in Vancouver. But then neither had Gordon, so he wouldn't be expected to know his way around. The buildings rose on either side of Twelfth in glass and aluminum splendor, punctuated by smaller buildings of an older, more graceful era.

It was only just eleven o'clock Pacific time when Hobbes paid the bellhop at the door of his room. His instructions were to wait for a call from Tony Clawson. He took off his topcoat and lay on the bed fully clothed.

He tried to relax. It didn't work. His body was as taut as a finely stretched cable. He paced the room. He opened

201

the drapes and stared out at the mist-shrouded city. In the distance he could see the flat pewter surface of a body of water and a graceful bridge rising into the mist.

When the phone rang, the noise seemed to burst in his head. He leaped like a startled deer. He went to the phone and answered it in a cautious voice.

"Gordon? Is that you?"

"Yes. Tony?"

"Right! You sound like you're speaking down a tube."

"I've got a cold."

"Oh, yes. Bad luck, old fellow. Take care of yourself. Lay off those nasty American cigarettes you incinerate."

Hobbes paused, then said, "Actually, I've taken up a pipe lately."

"Have you? You should cut quite the dashing figure. Do you know Stanley Park at all?"

"I've never been here before, Tony."

"Oh, right! Well, just ask any cabbie. The green in front of the lion's cages at twelve thirty. Bring your kit."

"Kit?"

"Your gear, Gordy, for a little trip."

"Right," Hobbes said coolly, although he felt anything but cool at the moment.

"Good fellow. See you then." The line went dead.

Hobbes hadn't unpacked. He had only a vague memory of where Stanley Park was from the map he had studied at Langley. It was eleven forty five. He decided to leave immediately. He picked up his suitcase and left the room.

Stanley Park was a green tip of land that jutted out into a narrow inlet, forming a bay on the westerly side. Huge fir trees towered overhead, lining the narrow road into the park.

The lions' cages were within sight of the road. A green sward undulated gently in front of the cages. In its center was a huge tree.

Carrying his suitcase, he walked along the sidewalk in

202

front of the cages. The lions lolled in serene splendor on ledges cut from rock.

Hobbes circled the cages and discovered a parking lot. Along one side was a path that snaked through the trees, disappearing at the crest of a low ridge a hundred yards distant. Behind the crest the misty fog laced the branches of the firs, giving them a ghostly outline. Hobbes went up the path. At the crest he turned off the path into the trees. The ground was spongy and slick under his feet. He circled back toward the cages. He was beginning to sweat under his heavy clothing. He was keeping his eyes in the direction of the sward when he walked into a low branch. Reacting violently, he threw himself back from the sharp sting of the needles, and his feet went out from under him. He landed in a sitting position, his suitcase still in his hand. He swore and was about to pull himself up when he caught sight of the sward and the big tree in its center through an opening in the undergrowth. There was a man standing under the tree. He was wearing a plaid raincoat. His blond hair glistened with moisture. He was standing with his back to Hobbes, motionless, his hands in the pockets of his coat. Hobbes stared at the man's back. Then, suppressing a shudder of apprehension, he got to his feet, brushed off his clothes, retrieved the suitcase, and made his way through the trees to where the man stood waiting.

Victoria's temples pulsed with a dull ache. Since awakening at dawn, she had lain quietly on the bed, feigning sleep. Commander Peevey slumped in the chair by the phone, gently snoring into the pillow that curled around his head. He had refused Gordon's order the night before to lie on the bed beside Victoria. His back, he had said, wouldn't allow it. Gordon had acceded with weary indifference.

Victoria squinted at the pale light filtering in through the window and guessed that it must be approaching seven o'clock. By looking through carefully hooded eyes, she could make out a vague image of Gordon sitting bolt upright in a chair across the room, muttering unintelligibly to himself.

The night before, Gordon had telephoned a delicatessen for sandwiches to be delivered. The cartons and wrappings from the meal still littered the table beside Commander Peevey. Victoria had been able to eat little, and now she felt hunger gnaw at her stomach; but still she waited.

Commander Peevey's snoring was terminated by a groan. Victoria turned her head toward him. His eyes were open. They were inflamed with fatigue. He stretched an arm over his head and groaned again. "Dammit," he rumbled under his breath.

Peevey staggered to his feet, clutching his back with his hands. Gordon leaped out of his chair. Peevey groaned once more and staggered toward the bathroom. "Damn, damn," he said.

Peevey ignored Gordon. He went into the bathroom and banged the door shut. Gordon pivoted, keeping the gun on Peevey, until he stood staring vacantly at the closed door.

Gordon turned and walked jerkily, like a mechanical man, to the sink and ran water in a glass. He took the vial of pills from his pocket and swallowed one. When he turned, his eyes met Victoria's. He motioned with the gun. His movements were exaggerated, giving him an eerily flamboyant air.

"Coffee," he croaked.

Victoria got up, went silently to the sink, and began to prepare the coffee.

"You're a beautiful woman, you know," Gordon said. Victoria froze at the sink. Gordon laughed hollowly. She heard him approach behind her. She felt his hand pass across her shoulders. She shuddered. She could feel his breath on her neck.

"Get away from her!"

204

Gordon spun. Victoria heard the dry snap of the gun's hammer being drawn back. Peevey stood in the doorway of the bathroom.

"I'll kill you, old man," Gordon rasped.

"You'd better do it with the first shot," Peevey said.

Gordon edged to the center of the room. Victoria gripped the coffeepot in her hand and turned. Gordon's eyes flicked between Peevey and Victoria.

Peevey began to advance slowly, steadily toward Gordon. Victoria saw the knuckles of Gordon's hand holding the gun go white. She threw the coffeepot.

Gordon put up his gun arm to protect himself. The coffeepot hit his arm and sprayed water into his face. Peevey covered the distance between himself and the other man in one stiff-legged leap. He rammed his big fist into Gordon's chest. Gordon staggered back. Peevey lowered his head and cocked his fist for another attack. Gordon brought the gun barrel up in a vicious motion and caught Peevey under the ribs with it. The breath whistled from Peevey's open mouth. He bent over, clutching his ribs. Gordon brought the gun up over Peevey's bent head. His face was distorted with a wild fury.

"No!" Victoria screamed. She leaped at Gordon, her fingers seeking his face. Gordon caught her hair and levered her head back. He put the gun barrel under her chin. Peevey had staggered to the bed and was sitting on it, doubled over, his breath rasping through his twisted mouth. Victoria struggled. Gordon pressed the gun barrel deep into her flesh. His breath was hot on her face. She quit struggling and slumped, sobbing, to the floor.

Gordon went to the chair and lowered himself in it. He kept the gun on Peevey, who was sitting up now, glaring red-eyed at Gordon. "Next time," Gordon panted, "I'll put a bullet in her head first and argue with you later. See if you can remember that."

TWENTY-THREE

As Hobbes plodded down the slope, the man turned to face him. His skin was very pale against the green boughs at his back. His hair was yellow and thin, combed straight back from a large, shimmering forehead. The eyes were small, set deeply in his head. They were so pale they seemed to have no color at all. Hobbes recognized him from the photos he'd been shown at Langley.

Hobbes forced himself to smile as he approached. He stopped in front of the man, put the suitcase down, and extended his hand. "Hello, Tony."

Tony Clawson's hand was as delicate as a woman's. "Well, Gordy," he said. His thin mouth curled to reveal tiny, perfect teeth. "Been having a tramp in the woods, have you?"

"I was early."

"Always the cautious one. Ready to get under way?"

Hobbes picked up the suitcase. For the first time he noticed the car parked at the curb. Clawson led him to it. The car was a small Ford of the type cut-rate rental agencies specialized in.

Clawson drove the Ford along the road, deeper into the park. He drove very fast, his small hands resting lightly on the wheel. He negotiated a curve, and a bay came into view. He whipped the car off onto a narrow graveled road that swept down to the bay. Below, Hobbes could see a wooden pier. A small stiletto-shaped boat with a huge inboard engine hulking at the stern was tied up at the pier. A man sat behind the wheel, his torso muffled in a wool jacket. Other boats bobbed at anchor buoys in the bay. A low building with a parking lot in front of it lay fifty yards back from the shore. Clawson wheeled the Ford into the parking lot. The rain was steadier now. As Clawson led the way to the pier, Hobbes turned up the collar of his topcoat.

Clawson got into the rear seat of the boat and reached back for Hobbes' suitcase, which he stowed under the seat beside two white Air Canada flight bags. Hobbes got into the boat beside Clawson. The man at the wheel looked over his shoulder at them. His eyes raked Hobbes with a brooding indifference.

"You remember Leo Fisher," Clawson said

Hobbes nodded at the man behind the wheel. Leo Fisher's expression did not change.

Clawson cast off the lines, and the engine roared into life. Fisher engaged the drive shaft, and the boat knifed away from the pier with a lurch that snapped Hobbes' head back.

Fisher pushed the throttle to the fire wall, and the boat's nose thrust up; then gradually the stern rolled out of the water and the boat leveled on plane.

As they plunged on into the bay, Tony Clawson took a pair of binoculars from a leather case under the seat and turned and carefully swept the shore behind them. Then he elevated the binoculars and swept the sky with the same care. He let the binoculars hang around his neck by their strap. He turned to Hobbes and smiled.

"So, Gordy," he said. "What have you been up to?"

"The usual."

Clawson laughed. "Indeed! Speaking of which, a friend sends her regards. Or I'm sure she would, if she knew I was seeing you."

Hobbes drew a careful breath. "How is Zee?"

"Buoyant. Pneumatic. Kinky." Clawson laughed again. His laugh was high-pitched and brittle. He slapped Hobbes' shoulder. "D'you remember that night at the Mayfair?"

Hobbes grinned ruefully. "The Mayfair? So that's where it was."

Clawson's laugh went up an octave. "I've missed you, old fellow. Life in London seems like Aunt Matilda's garden party when you're not about." He put the binoculars to his eyes and repeated the careful scan of the shore and sky.

When he was finished, he said, "Unless the CIA is into subs now, I'd say we're quite alone out here."

"Do we have far to go?" Hobbes asked casually.

Clawson grinned. "Not far. But then, far enough."

The boat entered a strait. Hobbes knew from the map at Langley that this was the Strait of Georgia. Dead ahead, across thirty miles of open water, was Vancouver Island.

They continued on the same heading for nearly an hour and then entered a harbor clogged with fishing boats. Ahead, through the mist, Hobbes could see the buildings of a village huddled around the rim of the bay.

"Nanaimo," Clawson said, pointing toward the village. "Won't be long now."

They tied up at a public pier. Another rental car was parked in the lot behind the bank on the main street. Leo Fisher drove, and Hobbes and Clawson sat in the back. They drove on a blacktop highway for several miles. Houses gave way to a fir forest. Clawson kept a vigil out the back window.

Fisher took the car carefully off the highway. At first Hobbes couldn't see the road; the entrance was grown over with underbrush. Fisher forced the car through.

The trees created an artificial twilight. Fisher turned on the headlights. The car rocked and scraped along the road for a mile and then came to a small clearing where a cabin stood.

"It's not the Mayfair," Clawson said, grinning at Hobbes, "but try to think of it as home."

Fisher carried the two flight bags, and Hobbes his suitcase, as Clawson unlocked the door of the cabin.

The main room of the cabin was paneled in knotty pine. Against one wall stood a Franklin stove. A shoddy couch slumped in front of it. There were two bedrooms. Clawson directed Hobbes to put his bag in one. When Hobbes came out, he found Clawson in a large square kitchen paneled as the living room was, its floor covered in cracked linoleum. On the massive kitchen table stood a tall naugahyde covered case with chrome lock and hinges.

There was a clatter from the living room, and Hobbes looked through the doorway to see Leo Fisher building a fire in the stove. Hobbes could see Fisher's breath as he labored stoically over the fire.

"Drink or coffee?" Clawson asked. "I'm afraid we didn't stock your favorite booze."

"I'm off Campari," Hobbes said. "This cold makes it taste like kerosene." Hobbes said a silent thanks to Jeanette for that touch of authenticity.

Clawson laughed. "But, dear fellow, that's its natural taste." Clawson held up a bottle of scotch. Hobbes nodded.

When they had their drinks, Clawson led the way into the living room.

Fisher had a fire roaring in the Franklin stove. Clawson and Hobbes removed their coats and stood with their backs to the fire. Fisher went outside.

Clawson drained his glass. "I suppose we might as well get right to it, don't you?"

Hobbes put his drink down, went to his coat, and removed the tobacco pouch.

209

Clawson gave a short laugh. "Now, Gordy, you're getting ahead of yourself. You do trust us, don't you, old fellow? We have no cause to play fast and loose with you—provided, of course, you've brought the goods."

"Where's Leo?" Hobbes asked.

"Leo is the nervous type. Likes to roam around the woods to see if he can find a bear to wrestle."

"He's keeping watch out there?"

"Of course he is, Gordy. You know the drill. What's wrong?" Clawson's eyes narrowed. "You do have the goods, don't you?"

Hobbes took the keys from his pocket and worked the miniature license tag off the ring. He handed it to Clawson. "In the center of the zero," he said.

Clawson's face lit with a smile. "That's better. For a moment there I thought you were going to come up short, and then I'd have to shoot you several times, wouldn't I?"

Clawson started toward the kitchen. "Why don't you watch?"

Hobbes sat at the kitchen table while Clawson unlocked the naugahyde case. He removed the top to reveal a microscope with a boxlike attachment under the object lens. He put the microscope on the center of the table and removed a rubber-sheathed electric cord from a spring clip in the lid of the box. He plugged one end of the cord in the base of the microscope and the other in a wall socket.

"Ever see one of these?" Clawson asked as he peered into the microscope to adjust it.

"Similar ones," Hobbes lied. "Never knew how they worked."

Clawson took a pair of tweezers and two glass slides from the microscope case and then positioned the license tag under the object lens. He put his eye to the microscope again. "Latest thing," he said. "That box below there will give us a readable three-by-five negative in a wink. Ah—" He put the tweezers under the barrel of the

210

microscope and plucked a small dot off the tag. Carefully he put the dot on one slide and pressed the other down over it. Then he put the slide where the tag had been. He peered through the eyepiece. "Looks good, Gordy," he said. "Very authentic." He looked up at Hobbes. "Of course, that's easy to fix up, isn't it? All the right stamps and official-looking signatures?"

"It's authentic," Hobbes said.

"We'll see." Clawson pressed a button on the side of the box under the microscope and slid the bottom half of the box out. It opened like a tray. Inside, Hobbes could see a piece of darkened celluloid.

Clawson picked up the film at its corners. He took a magnifying glass from the case and held the film up to the light. Hobbes waited silently.

Finally, Clawson lowered the film and looked solemnly at Hobbes. "Well, well," he said.

Clawson put the film in a small aluminum container and put the container in the inside pocket of his coat. He put the microscope, slides, and tweezers back in the case, locked the case, and put it on the floor. Hobbes sat with his hands clutched together under the table.

Clawson casually picked up the magnifying glass and dropped it in his coat pocket. "Drink?" he asked. Hobbes nodded.

Clawson refilled their glasses and pulled up a chair opposite Hobbes.

Clawson saluted Hobbes with his glass and tipped it to his lips, never taking his pale eyes from Hobbes' face. He put the glass on the table, reached inside his coat, and brought out a gun. The gun had   long, slender barrel. Clawson placed the muzzle of the gun against the center of Hobbes' forehead. The touch of the cold metal was like a blow. The blood drained from Hobbes' face.

Hobbes tried to swallow. "What is this, Tony?" he whispered.

"Why, dear fellow," Clawson said, "this is the payoff."

TWENTY-FOUR

The sweat ran into Hobbes' eyes, blurring his vision.

"You're getting my gun wet, old fellow," Clawson drawled.

A sudden anger cleared Hobbes mind. A memory floated unformed at the edge of his consciousness. Something he had read. A weapon described in a novel. Then he remembered. The idea was so incredible that he knew it might work.

"Clawson," Hobbes whispered.

"Yes? A last word? Make it brief, please."

Hobbes paused and steadied himself. "Do you know what a deadman trigger is?"

Clawson's eyebrows went up with interest. "No. Can't say that I do."

"It's—it's a reverse trigger. The gun fires when it's released."

"Really? How ingenious. You mean you have to keep the trigger depressed to prevent the gun from firing?"

"Exactly ."

Clawson's eyes flicked down to the table; Hobbes still held his hands clasped under it.

"You aren't trying to tell me you have one of those infernal devices under there, are you?"

"What do you think, Tony?"

"I think you're bluffing," Clawson said. "A deadman trigger!" He laughed, but Hobbes thought he detected a note of uncertainty in the laugh.

"We can both die," Hobbes said. "It's up to you, Tony."

Clawson stared into Hobbes' eyes. Slowly he brought the finger of his free hand to his upper lip and wiped it. "Assuming," he said, "for the sake of argument, that you do have one of those devices under the table, what do we do now?"

"You put your gun on the table."

"If you had a gun under there, you would've used it."

"No," Hobbes said. "I'd get you in the stomach." Clawson's cheek ticked. "You might still pull the trigger."

"I see," Clawson said slowly. A fine line of sweat was beginning to form at his hairline.

"See here, old fellow," Clawson said. "You know I was joking."

"Do I?"

"You know my penchant for this sort of thing, Gordy."

"Do I, Tony?"

"I have your goods, y'know. In my flight bag. I was going to sweat you a little, is all, and then give them to you."

"Put the gun down, Tony."

"See here, Gordy—that's hardly fair. We have equal advantage. It's a standoff."

"I didn't pull a gun on you, Tony."

"Oh, well, if you want to put that fine a line on it." Clawson was now sweating freely.

"Put the gun down, Tony."

Clawson smiled sickly. "And have you blast me?"

"If I shoot, it will bring Fisher."

Clawson looked into Hobbes' eyes. "You bastard," he said. "You have that thing under there, don't you?"

"There are two ways to find out, Tony."

Clawson lowered the gun and put it on the table. Hobbes brought one hand up and took the gun. Then he slowly brought up the other hand, pointed his forefinger at Clawson, and let his thumb fall like a hammer.

Clawson's eyes widened. "You *bloody* bastard," he whispered.

Hobbes pointed the gun at Clawson. "That tobacco pouch had better be in your flight bag, Tony."

"It is! Dammit, Gordy—I was joking!"

"Let's find out."

The pouch was there. Hobbes herded Clawson back to the living room. Hobbes put on his topcoat and the pouch in its pocket. "Put on your coat," he said.

"Why?"

"Put it on. You're taking me back."

"But that's not the drill, Gordy. I'm supposed to report to my superiors and wait while they check out the information. Leo won't let you go."

"You'll have to think of something to tell Leo. If it isn't convincing, I kill you first. Go in the kitchen."

Hobbes followed Clawson into the kitchen. "Put the microscope on the table," he said.

Clawson did.

"Open it and hand me the slide."

"Why?"

"Insurance, Tony. Move!" Hobbes made a gesture with the gun in his pocket.

Clawson handed him the slide.

"You're going to welch on the deal, aren't you?" Clawson said sickly.

"You'll just have to trust me, Tony," Hobbes said. "The way I trusted you."

Hobbes stood behind Clawson while the Englishman

214

spoke to Leo Fisher. They stood in the darkening woods, under dripping trees. Fisher's little eyes darted suspiciously between Clawson and Hobbes.

Fisher's voice was guttural and tinged with a Slavic accent. "Why didn't he bring all the film? I don't like it."

"He didn't quite trust us, Leo," Clawson said. "We have to slip back to his hotel and get the rest. It'll be all right."

Fisher shrugged and tramped off into the woods.

The sun was dying when they reached the harbor. Hobbes sat in the passenger seat while Clawson piloted the boat. He kept the gun on his lap, pointed at Clawson. Clawson switched on the running lights. Out in the strait the water tossed whitecaps up before the wind. The little boat wallowed.

"Rough," Clawson shouted. He advanced the throttle and eased the boat into a wave rushing down on them.

"I've got great confidence in your seamanship," Hobbes shouted back.

"Look," Clawson yelled, throwing the wheel over to point the prow out of the trough the wave had left behind, "you've got what you wanted. The CIA thinks you're dead. You're a rich man. No need to be vindictive."

"Keep your mind on the boat."

The return crossing took twice as long as it had going over. Clawson eased the boat into the pier at Stanley Park. Night had fallen. The rain continued to pelt down. The long ride had given Hobbes time to think.

"How did you get the gun into the country?" he asked Clawson.

"American diplomatic license our artist chaps drew up for me."

"Where is it?"

"Wallet," Clawson replied, rolling his eyes at Hobbes.

"Hand it to me—very slowly now."

The wallet was old and worn through at the seams. Hobbes flipped it open one-handed and saw the diplomatic license and other items of identification. He put the wallet in his coat pocket. He had Clawson hand him the keys to the Ford.

"Now the film, Tony," Hobbes said quietly.

"No! For God's sake, Gordy!" Clawson cringed against the seat.

"The film," Hobbes repeated.

"It's my death warrant, Gordy, if I show up without the pouch or the film."

"You should have thought of that, Tony," Hobbes said, when you got greedy."

"Bloody *bastard*!" Clawson moaned.

Hobbes raised the gun. "Don't make me take it off your body, Tony."

With a whimper, Clawson removed the aluminum container from his pocket and threw it on the seat between them. Hobbes put it in his pocket. He got out of the boat and pushed it away from the pier with his foot. Clawson was slumped over the wheel, staring at the windshield.

"Get going!" Hobbes yelled.

Clawson started the motor, and the boat eased out into the bay. Hobbes stood watching it until it disappeared in the rain.

Hobbes drove the Ford south through Vancouver. On the outskirts he stopped at a roadside phone stanchion. He put the call through collect. Gordon's voice was sleepy.

"Hobbes! Where are you?"

"Vancouver. I've set up the contact with Clawson. They'll be coming for me in a few minutes."

"What's wrong?" Gordon's voice was alert now.

"Nothing. I want to talk to Victoria. I'm not going ahead until I do."

There was a pause. Then the clatter of the phone being put down. In a moment Victoria's voice came over the line.

"Are you all right?"

"Yes. Tired, but we're okay. When will you be here?"

Hobbes had to lie to her. Gordon might be listening. "A couple of days. Can you hold on?"

"Yes. But hurry—"

Gordon came back on the line. "All right, Hobbes. Don't screw up."

"Gordon, when I deliver the pouch to you, what then?"

"What do you mean?"

"What happens?"

"I go my way."

"And we?"

"You go yours."

Hobbes knew he was lying.

Hobbes put another coin in the telephone and dialed the Vancouver number he had memorized.

"Columbia Tool and Die," a woman's bored voice said.

"Patriot," Hobbes replied.

There was a click and then the whir of a phone ringing. It was answered on the first ring.

"Hobbes?"

"Dooley!"

"Hobbes, where are you? Can you talk?"

"Yes. You're—you're in Vancouver?"

"What is it, Hobbes? Are you in trouble?"

"No." Hobbes took a breath. "The delivery didn't come off."

"What! What are you saying!"

Hobbes spoke rapidly. "I got the microdot back. It had the real names. Clawson and Fisher are in a cabin on Vancouver Island—"

"Goddammit, wait a minute! You took the microdot back?"

"It was the real one, don't you see? The real names."

"It couldn't be!" Dooley roared. "What the hell are you talking about?"

217

"I can't explain now," Hobbes said. "I just wanted to let someone know."

"Hobbes! Hobbes!" Dooley panted. "Where are you?"

"Ah—at the hotel."

"Don't move! You got that? We'll be there in five minutes."

"All right."

"Hobbes, don't do anything foolish."

"Mr. Dooley?"

"Yes?"

"I resign. This job, the CIA—everything."

"Wait a minute. You don't quit."

"Yes. I'm afraid I do."

"You're not at the hotel, are you?" Dooley asked in a weary voice. "Now listen to me, Tom. It's not too late. You go back and deliver that microdot."

"But it has the real names."

"You don't know that—not for sure. Listen to me, now. Even if you're right, we lose a few sources behind the curtain. They can be replaced. It's a small price, Tom—a small price for the results we get. You can still do it."

Hobbes was silent.

"If you run, Hobbes, you're a dead man. Do you understand that? And Peevey and that girl. Dead! Do you get that?"

Carefully Hobbes hung up the phone.

A mile from the United States border, Hobbes pulled off into a roadside rest stop. He walked into a stand of young firs. He took the film from the aluminum container and burned it. He threw the container into a drainage ditch. He took the slide from his pocket, pried the glass apart, and touched the tiny dot with the flame from his lighter. The dot disappeared. Then he got back in the Ford, drove to the border, and crossed into the United States.

* * *

It was eleven thirty when Hobbes drove through Seattle and nearly midnight before he arrived at Seattle-Tacoma Airport. He parked in the short-time lot and looked at the contents of Tony Clawson's wallet in the illumination from the dome light. There were credit cards, a New York driver's license, the gun permit, and nearly two hundred dollars. All the identification was made out to Samuel Clark. The only photo, that on the driver's license, was of Tony Clawson. Hobbes burned the driver's license in the ashtray of the Ford.

Hobbes got out of the car. At the United Airlines counter in the terminal he booked a reservation for the direct flight to Washington at seven thirty the next morning in the name of Samuel Clark. He paid for it with a credit card from Clawson's wallet.

He took a cab to the Airporter Inn a mile away from the terminal and got a single room, which he paid for in advance. He left a call for six thirty. He bought a razor and a can of shaving cream at the newsstand and went up to his room.

He removed the contact lenses and flushed them down the toilet. He stripped down to his shorts and, taking Clawson's gun with him, sat on the bed. He had to force his mind to stay alert. He went over the gun, learning how it worked. He discovered how to remove the bullet clip. He found it full of bullets, a shell in the firing chamber. Hobbes shuddered when he discovered it. He practiced firing the gun, clicking the firing pin against the empty chamber. Then he put the gun back the way it had been, with a live round in the chamber. He put on the safety, got up, and put the gun in the pocket of his topcoat.

He got in bed, turned out the light, and stared into the darkness.

Just before he fell into a troubled sleep, Hobbes remembered something Clawson had said in the boat. He had said, "You're a rich man—" Hobbes remembered that he had forgotten to examine the pouch. He promised himself he would do it in the morning. He slept.

TWENTY-FIVE

Halladay found Dooley in an unmarked car outside the Vancouver air terminal, smoking a cigarette. He slipped into the passenger seat.

"Any luck?"

Dooley shook his head. "He slipped us. We may as well go back to Washington. Call in the men."

Halladay took the yellow telex message from his pocket. "You'd better read this, Vern."

Dooley glanced at the paper without touching it. "You reported this to Langley," he said.

"No choice, Vern."

Dooley stared out the windshield. "What does it say?"

"You're pulled off. I'm in charge."

"Permanently?"

"Of course there'll be a hearing before the chief."

Dooley rolled down the window and flipped the cigarette out. "What about Hobbes?"

"He's been put on the list."

"That son of a bitch Peevey should be on the list, too. He's the one that's pumped Hobbes' head full of shit." Dooley's eyes stared wildly; flecks of saliva appeared at the corners of his mouth. "We should get Peevey and that girl and let Hobbes watch." He gripped Halladay's arm. "Listen. One favor. Let me do it—let me get all three of them."

"It's not up to me." Halladay pried Dooley's fingers from his arm. "I'll tell you one thing, though—I don't intend to fuck it up."

"Like I did. That's what you mean, isn't it?"

Halladay turned his head to look at Dooley. His eyes glittered in the red light of a neon sign. Dooley averted his eyes and stared blindly out at the rain falling like steel needles through the light of the arc lamps.

When the seat belt light went out, Hobbes unstrapped and made his way to the plane's rest room. He locked the door and sat on the toilet lid. He took the tobacco pouch from his coat and examined it. It was too heavy to contain only tobacco. The top of the paper pouch was folded over and sealed with a tobacco tax stamp. He turned the pouch upside down. The bottom was sealed with a glued seam. He took the razor he had bought the night before from his pocket and removed the blade. He slipped the blade under the seam and ran it along its length. The glue parted, and the flap gaped. He opened the pouch wide. He caught his breath. The inside of the pouch seemed to burn with a cold blue flame. His hand trembled, and something in the pouch separated from the flame and rolled against the edge of the paper. He picked it up and held it before his eyes. It was the size of the end of his thumb. Hobbes knew nothing about diamonds, but the icy beauty of the stone seared his brain.

Hobbes made a trough of his coat between his legs and dumped the contents of the pouch in it. All the diamonds were approximately the same size as the first. He counted them. There were twenty-five. He put them back in the pouch and folded the flap several times to seal it. Then he put the pouch in his pocket and smoked a cigarette, thinking.

Hobbes walked through the terminal at Dulles expecting any moment to be confronted by one of Dooley's men. He clutched the gun in his coat pocket. He felt the weight of the tobacco pouch against his leg. He made it to the cabstand and got in the first cab. As the cab pulled onto the entrance ramp to Interstate 66, he glanced out the back window. Traffic was heavy; he couldn't tell if he was being followed or not.

He had the cab let him out a block from the Lincoln Hotel. The sky was heavy with clouds. The snow on the streets was frozen in dirty clumps. He went into a café, took a booth at the back, and drank coffee for an hour until dusk had settled over Washington.

He walked to the rear of the Lincoln Hotel. He stood in the doorway of a condemned building and examined the street. A blue pickup with a camper on the bed was across the street in a line of parked vehicles. Hobbes didn't notice it.

Hobbes turned up his coat collar and pushed out of the doorway. He ran across to the service entrance of the hotel and slipped through the door.

In the camper, Halladay turned from the window to the two men behind him. "That's him," he said. One of the men started for the door of the camper.

"Wait," Halladay said. "I'd rather take him on the street. Radio around front, and tell them to let us know if he shows there." One of the men picked up a hand transmitter.

Sophie Crump gave a little cry of fright when Hobbes came through her door without knocking. She was sitting at her table, a bowl of soup in front of her.

"Will you get Mr. Darling and Dr. Marshall? It's urgent."

When the old people were gathered around him, Hobbes told them the situation in his room.

"This man—" Dr. Marshall said nervously. "He's armed?"

"Yes." Hobbes touched his coat pocket. "But so am I."

"Shouldn't we call the police?" Dr. Marshall asked.

"Gordon is desperate. He'd kill both of them."

"We don't need the police," Mr. Darling said. "We'll smoke him out like a bear."

"What ?" Hobbes asked.

"Used to do it in Kentucky when I was a lad, my father and me. Build a big smoke pot, and smoke the old bear right out of his cave."

"Do you remember how to do it?"

"Damn right!"

"It might work," Hobbes said slowly, "if he thought the hotel was on fire."

"By God, it'll work," Mr. Darling avowed. "Fire escape right outside your window. I'll put a couple of smoke pots in garbage cans out in the hall, and we all yell fire. You get on the fire escape and plug him when he comes out. Just the way my daddy and I used to do."

"Are you with us?" Hobbes asked Dr. Marshall and Sophie.

Sophie nodded and clutched her hands.

"Yes," Dr. Marshall said. "And God help us."

Victoria sat trying to read a book. Peevey was nodding in a chair by the window. Victoria looked up to see Gordon watching her.

Peevey's head jerked up, and his eyes opened. He sniffed the air. "I smell smoke."

Gordon sneered. "You're dreaming."

"No," Peevey said, rising and sniffing the air again. "By God, I tell you I smell smoke."

"Sit down, old man."

Victoria's eyes were attracted to a sinuous movement at the bottom of the door. "Look!" Gray tendrils of smoke were curling into the room under the door.

223

Gordon ran to the door and put his ear against it. Now, from the hall, Victoria heard feet pounding along the corridor. "Fire!" someone yelled.

Gordon readied the gun and threw the door open. A cloud of black smoke rolled in. He slammed the door, coughing. "Jesus! The whole fucking place must be going."

"The fire escape!" Peevey cried, pointing to the window.

Victoria felt Peevey slip her coat around her shoulders. Then Gordon was behind her, prodding her with the gun barrel toward the window.

Peevey went out the window onto the fire escape and turned to help Victoria. Victoria stood on the fire escape, breathing in the night air and wiping her streaming eyes with her sleeve. She heard Gordon come onto the fire escape behind her. There was a noise above them, and she turned to see a shadow move toward Gordon from the stairs above. Gordon spun, and the gun gleamed in the light from the window. Then the shadow and Gordon merged. There was a shot, and something sang against the metal stairs and whined off into the night. Peevey brushed past her, his big fist extended. Something clattered at Victoria's feet. She saw two figures running down the fire escape a floor beneath her feet. Peevey urged her toward the stairs.

"I told you he'd be back," Peevey whispered. Victoria looked back and saw a gun lying on the landing.

She broke from Commander Peevey's arm and ran down the stairs.

When Gordon fired, Hobbes recoiled violently against the wall of the building, and the gun spun from his grasp. For one frozen moment he and Gordon stared into each other's eyes. Then Peevey's fist caught Gordon a glancing blow on the head, and he staggered. Hobbes turned and ran down the fire escape. He ran along the street, down the length of the side of the hotel, and into an alley. He

224

could hear Gordon's footsteps pounding on the pavement behind him.

Hobbes remembered a wall at the end of the alley with a gaping hole where a gate once had been. He knew that beyond the wall was the yard of an abandoned warehouse cluttered with rusting machinery and old packing crates. He had a vague plan to hide among the crates and machines and somehow take Gordon by surprise.

Hobbes reached the end of the alley and put his hands out to where the hole in the fence had been. It was covered with a heavy steel mesh anchored with bolts in the concrete of the wall. Hobbes searched vainly about him for something to use as a weapon. A large commercial garbage bin stood on caster wheels beside the wall. Hobbes ran to it and opened the lid. Behind him, Gordon entered the alley at a run. The garbage bin was empty. Hobbes turned to face Gordon.

Gordon pulled up, panting. He held the gun on Hobbes. "God damn you!" he shouted. "Did you get it?"

"Yes."

Gordon raised the gun and pointed it at Hobbes' head. "Give it to me, you son of a bitch, or I'll blow your head off."

Hobbes put his hand in the pocket of his topcoat and closed it around the tobacco pouch.

"Wait," Gordon said. "Give me the coat." Hobbes slipped the pouch through the slit in the pocket of the topcoat and dropped it into the pocket of his suit coat. Then he took off the topcoat and handed it to Gordon. Gordon put it on a sleeve at a time, keeping the gun trained on Hobbes. Then he put his hand in one of the pockets. He frowned and started to transfer the gun to his other hand. Hobbes stepped behind the garbage bin. A bullet sprayed particles of concrete into Hobbes' hair from the wall behind his head. He put his shoulder against the garbage bin and began to roll it forward. He heard a bullet tear into the garbage bin. Then another. He

225

felt the impact transmitted through the metal to his shoulder. He kept pushing forward.

There was a scream of tires somewhere near. Headlights bounced off the wall behind Hobbes. He stopped pushing the garbage bin and listened. He heard a vehicle approach and stop. He heard a door open. A voice said, "Hobbes!" Hobbes knew that voice. It belonged to Halladay.

Hobbes dropped to his knees. He lowered his head and inched forward until his eyes could see around the garbage bin. Gordon stood silhouetted by the headlights, his back to Hobbes. The gun hung in his hand at his side. Halladay crouched beside the fender of a pickup truck. Halladay's gun made no noise. Hobbes saw his arm recoil twice in quick succession. Gordon's body was lifted and thrown back to the floor of the alley as though by the blow of a giant fist. Hobbes pulled his head behind the garbage bin.

He heard footsteps in the alley. He heard doors slam and then the whine of an engine in reverse. The headlights on the wall grew dimmer and disappeared. Silence. Hobbes peered into the alley. It was empty.

He walked to the end of the alley and looked out at the street. The pickup was gone. Across the street Victoria ran through a cone of light from a streetlamp.

She saw Hobbes and stopped, fozen, staring. Hobbes ran toward her. "It's me!" he shouted. He put his arms around her. She was trembling. Peevey rounded the corner behind Victoria and came lumbering to them.

"You two all right?" He peered into their faces. "Where's Gordon?"

"Dead," Hobbes said. He saw that Peevey was carrying a huge old pistol. Peevey stuck the gun in his waistband and buttoned his coat over it.

"I'll explain later," Hobbes said. "We have to get out of here. There are men looking for you two."

"Wait," Peevey said. He pointed at the sky. "The hotel." The sky was splashed with an orange glow. Hobbes became aware of the scream of sirens. They ran back toward the hotel. Long gouts of flame erupted from the windows of the top floors. A fire engine was backing into the curb. Sophie Crump stood with a group of old people, watching the flames. A half block from the hotel, Peevey put up an arm. "You two wait here." He hitched up his pants and strode over to Sophie Crump. He talked to her as firemen hooked up hoses and began to play streams of water on the hotel. When Peevey returned, his face was flushed from the heat. "Everyone got out," he said.

"Thank God!" Victoria breathed.

Peevey shook his head. "That idiot Darling," he said. "Melted the bottoms out of two garbage cans with his smoke fires ."

Through the smoke and crowd of people and fire engines Hobbes thought he glimpsed a truck with a camper round the corner. "Let's get out of here."

"What the hell is going on, Hobbes?" Peevey said.

"We haven't got time," Hobbes replied. He had lost sight of the camper. "Halladay and other men from Langley are around here somewhere. Please—Just trust me."

They walked for five minutes, keeping to side streets, before they found a cab. Hobbes told the driver to take them to the bus terminal.

They got out across the street from the terminal. "Can you tell if anyone's watching?" Hobbes asked Peevey. Victoria hugged her shoulders and shivered.

Peevey peered up and down the street and then across into the lighted waiting room of the terminal. "I can't say for sure. But it looks clean."

"We'll have to risk it," Hobbes said.

In the terminal coffee shop, Hobbes told them what had happened.

"They think they've killed you?" Victoria asked, her eyes wide. Hobbes nodded.

Peevey sipped his coffee, his brow furrowed. "But dammit, Hobbes—if that film had the names of real agents on it, you should get a medal instead of being put on the elimination list."

"I can't prove it. I burned the microdot. And Gordon can't testify."

Victoria was pale. "Why would Dooley want me? Or Commander Peevey?" she asked Hobbes.

Peevey answered. "You have to understand the mentality," he said. "Dooley would think I had something to do with Hobbes' failing to complete the job. I knew both Gordon and him. I haven't made any secret of what I think of Dooley and his kind." He paused and took a cigar from his coat. "As for you, it would be a way of punishing Hobbes. Oh, they'd have their justifications. You helped get me out of the hospital. You contributed to turning Hobbes' head soft. Things like that."

"But if they think I'm dead," Hobbes said, "then they have no reason to want Victoria."

Peevey puffed on his cigar. "You might beat this thing," he said to Victoria. "But it's risky. They're bound to find their mistake when they identify Gordon's body."

"What will you do?" Victoria asked.

"Only one thing to do," Peevey said. "Hobbes and I will go to ground until we can figure out something better." He turned to Hobbes. "How much money do you have?"

"A fortune!"

Peevey stared.

"I've got the payoff Gordon was to get."

"Well," Peevey said as he peered around the terminal, "this is as good a time as any to get out of here."

"I'm going!" Victoria said, her jaw set.

Peevey nodded. "I think that's wise."

"Where?" Hobbes asked.

"South!" Peevey declared. "Let's get the first bus out headed south." He stood. "I'm sick of these Washington winters."

TWENTY-SIX

The next bus south left for Atlanta twenty minutes later. They rode all night and most of the next day. They arrived in Atlanta in the late afternoon. A block from the bus station they found an old but clean hotel that Peevey liked for its anonymity. They gathered in Peevey's room. Hobbes took the tobacco pouch from his coat and dumped the diamonds onto the bed. Victoria let out a little gasp of shock.

Peevey ran a big finger through the diamonds. Hobbes was examining a paper that he had found in the bottom of the pouch. He handed it to Peevey. "What do you make of that?"

Peevey studied the paper for a moment and then said, "A provenance. Proof of ownership. With a blank space for the name of the present owner." He handed the paper back to Hobbes. "I'd say you were a rich man, Hobbes."

"*We're* rich," Hobbes said. "What do you think they're worth?"

Peevey shook his head. "I don't know. It will take an expert to say."

"I'll find one in the morning."

Peevey nodded. "We'll need some money. Most of mine is in a bank in Washington."

"Won't that be dangerous?" Victoria asked.

"Langley doesn't know what the payoff was," Hobbes replied. "Dooley himself told me that."

"So no reason for them to be interested in diamond brokers," Peevey agreed. "While you're doing that, I'll investigate where we go next."

At nine o'clock the next morning Hobbes woke from a dreamless sleep. He dressed and went to see Peevey in his room. They agreed that Victoria should go with Peevey while Hobbes tried to sell the diamonds.

Hobbes bought a pair of cheap sunglasses in the lobby. In a phone booth he looked up jewelers. A firm named Schleimer's attracted him. According to its ad, it had been in business for thirty years and belonged to various international organizations of jewelers, appraisers, and gem brokers.

Schleimer's was on the second floor of an old office building in downtown Atlanta. The floors were covered with a thick red carpet. Display cases lined the walls. The clerk who came to wait on Hobbes was very old, with a halo of fine white hair. Hobbes asked for Mr. Schleimer.

"Old Mr. Schleimer or young Mr. Schleimer?" the man asked.

Hobbes hesitated. "Old."

The old man smiled. "At your service."

"Do you buy diamonds?"

Mr. Schleimer raised an eyebrow. "Buy and sell. That's our business for thirty years."

Hobbes took the tobacco pouch from his pocket. "What do you think these would be worth?"

The old man took the pouch as though customers brought him such packages daily. He opened the pouch and stared into it. He took a diamond from it and held it up to the light. He took a jeweler's loupe from his pocket, fixed it in his eye, and looked at the diamond.

Mr. Schleimer put the diamond back in the pouch, inserted a finger in the pouch, and stirred the diamonds. "Are they all of the same quality?"

"I don't know."

"How many?"

"Twenty-five."

Mr. Schleimer looked at Hobbes as though seeing him for the first time.

"Mr.?"

"Clark. Samuel Clark."

"Well, Mr. Clark, you have a great many diamonds here. It doesn't seem wise to me that you carry them about this way."

"What would you advise?"

"A safety deposit box, by all means."

"Are you interested in buying them?"

Mr. Schleimer gathered up the diamonds. "Follow me, please." He led Hobbes through the store and into a back room. At a bench along one wall a middle-aged man stood working over a diamond brooch. He took the loupe from his eye when they entered.

"My son," the old man said. "Mr. Clark."

Hobbes shook hands with the son. The man had gray, piercing eyes and a narrow, unsmiling mouth.

"Mr. Clark would like us to give him an appraisal on some diamonds," the old man said. He handed the pouch to his son. The son placed a piece of black velvet on the bench and carefully spilled the diamonds onto it. His expression did not change.

The old man gave Hobbes a peculiar look. "If you don't mind my asking, how did you come by these stones?"

Hobbes had an answer prepared. "Inheritance." He pulled the provenance from his pocket. The old man read it and nodded.

The son took nearly an hour to examine all the diamonds. Hobbes watched him. The old man went in and

231

out of the room, waiting on customers at the front of the store. When he was finished, the son handed his father a list he had prepared. The old man led Hobbes to a small office at the rear of the building. The office contained a desk and a chair. Hobbes sat in the chair while the old man examined the list at his desk.

Mr. Schleimer looked up. He handed the pouch to Hobbes. "We can't handle the whole thing ourselves, of course. But we'd be happy to be your brokers, Mr. Clark."

"How much?"

The old man stroked his bald head with his palm. "Here's what I'm prepared to do. I could give you one hundred and fifty thousand dollars immediately."

"That's all they're worth?"

Mr. Schleimer laughed. "No, no, Mr. Clark. My son, who is as good as anyone in the business, appraises the wholesale value at seven hundred and thirty thousand dollars."

Hobbes stared at the old man. "Seven hundred—"

"Here's what we'd do, Mr. Clark: one hundred and fifty thousand now, another hundred and fifty thousand in sixty days, and the balance within six months of that payment. We would, of course, pay you earlier if we sold them earlier."

"I'll take it," Hobbes said.

"I beg your pardon?"

"The deal. I'll take it."

Mr. Schleimer blinked once, bent over the desk, and began to prepare the papers. Afterward he and Hobbes took a cab to the old man's bank. It wasn't quite noon when Hobbes was back on the street with a certified check for one hundred and fifty thousand dollars. Mr. Schleimer solemnly shook his hand. Hobbes promised to let him know where to send the rest of the money.

Hobbes found Peevey and Victoria in the hotel coffee shop with their heads together studying a packet of brochures. Hobbes put the check on the table and sat down.

"And that's only the down payment," he said. He recounted his experience at Schleimer's.

"By damn!" Peevey exclaimed. "With that kind of money we can go to ground in style."

Hobbes picked up a brochure. "The Bahamas?"

Peevey nodded. "Close enough to the States, but not too close. British Crown Colony, so they'd have to extradite us to get us back, and I don't think Langley would want that kind of publicity even if they had a case, which they don't."

"Assuming they bother with legalities," Hobbes said.

"Yes," Peevey said gravely. "There's always that. But we can get into the Bahamas easily. And this island—" he folded out a small map—"Great Inagua, looks like the one. Southernmost of the Bahamas. No CIA station on the island, unless they've put one in since I retired. My idea is this—we leave as soon as possible for Matthew Town, the principal town on Great Inagua, then we go to ground for a couple of weeks and assess our situation. I've still got some contacts I trust."

Hobbes looked at Victoria. "What do you think?"

"I don't see any other choices." She locked eyes with Hobbes. "I feel as if I've invited myself along."

"Don't be ridiculous," Peevey said. "We're all in this together."

Victoria averted her eyes from Hobbes'. "Hobbes has the money."

Hobbes leaned across the table. "Victoria Prentice," he said, "I hereby invite you to accompany us to the Bahamas. Not only are we going to need a lawyer along, but I would enjoy your company."

"Hear! Hear!" Peevey said. He slapped Hobbes on the shoulder. "Hobbes, I'll be damned if you aren't developing a silver tongue."

"That remains to be seen." Hobbes looked expectantly at Victoria.

She sighed. "I accept."

TWENTY-SEVEN

The black property agent with the British accent stood
with them on the coral sand beach shimmering white in
the sun and pointed out to sea. "Cuba," he said. Sixty
miles away the island was a stark green outline against
the pale sky.

The cottage was a mile north of Matthew Town, on a
length of secluded beach, but its best feature, in Peevey's
view, was that it lay a half mile from its nearest neighbor.
They took it for a month, Hobbes paying the rent from
the money belt he wore under his shirt and that he had
bought in Atlanta when he cashed Schleimer's check.

The cottage contained two bedrooms, a bright living
room with a daybed that Hobbes took, a small kitchen,
and a veranda that looked out on the beach. They stocked
the cottage with provisions from Matthew Town, and
Peevey laid down what he called "survival rules": No
one was to leave the general area of the cottage without
his permission; there were to be no contacts with other

people; at the approach of a car along the road behind the cottage they all were to assemble in the living room. Also, at Peevey's instigation, they packed one light suitcase with a change of clothes and extra toilet articles for each of them which he kept on a shelf next to the back door. "We have," Peevey said, "gone to ground." It was his plan to make discreet inquiries of trusted contacts in Washington to find out what Langley was up to. On the first afternoon he sat at a table in the kitchen laboriously drafting and redrafting letters for those contacts. Victoria was in her room. Hobbes mixed up three gin and tonics, put one in front of Peevey, and carried the other two to the door of Victoria's room, where he found her transferring clothes from her suitcase to the drawers of a dresser.

Hobbes held up a glass. "There's a beautiful view from the porch."

Victoria took a blouse from the suitcase and refolded it. "I don't doubt it," she said in a cool tone.

"I'm inviting you to share it with me."

She turned and regarded him with a flat stare. "I don't consider this a vacation."

"We might as well make it as pleasant as possible."

"Look." She threw the blouse on the bed. "I'm scared. Even if I get out of this, my career may be ruined."

"We'll find a way," he said lamely.

Her eyes blazed. "That's easy for you to say. You're rich. You're probably glad—what are you doing?"

He had raised his shirt. He untied the money belt and threw it on top of the blouse. "Now," he said, "you're rich. How about a drink with me on the veranda?"

She stared at him. Then she sighed. She picked up the money belt and handed it to him. "All right."

When they were seated in sling chairs on the veranda, Hobbes said, "I meant what I said about the money. It belongs to all of us equally."

"I'm not worried about the money. I'm worried about the prospect of spending the rest of my life running."

235

He stared out at the green sea. "I wanted to explain about that girl—"

"You don't owe me any explanations," she said angrily.

"She thought I was Gordon."

"I figured that out for myself," she replied coldly.

There was an uncomfortable silence, broken, finally, when Victoria, the words coming as though against her will, said, "I suppose you should be grateful to him for that."

"That?" he said, turning to regard her stern profile. "Nothing happened."

She laughed unpleasantly.

"Frankly, I was scared to death that she would find me out and go screaming to the neighbors that I had done away with her boyfriend."

She sipped her drink in silence.

"But even if I hadn't been scared, you would've gotten in the way."

"I!" She looked at him.

"I should say the you in my mind." He smiled. "An obsession, I guess you could call it."

"You think it matters?"

"Yes. I think it matters."

She looked away.

"Doesn't it?"

"Yes," she said so softly that he very nearly didn't hear it.

Each morning Peevey went into Matthew Town and checked at general delivery for mail addressed to the cover name he had chosen for himself. On the seventh day after their arrival, and six days after posting his inquiry letters, Peevey had a reply. He gathered the other two around the table in the kitchen and read them the letter.

"You mean they still think I'm dead?" Hobbes asked.

Peevey removed his spectacles and tapped the letter

236

with them. "According to my source. I've always found him to be trustworthy."

"How could that be?" Hobbes asked. "Surely they've identified the body—"

"It's a trick," Victoria said. The two men looked at her. "To get us back there—"

"That has crossed my mind," Peevey said. He sighed.

"What do we do?" Victoria asked.

"We wait," Peevey replied.

On the last of a stream of hot and uneventful days that they had begun to imagine as endless they were sitting in a noisy café in Matthew Town, awaiting the delivery of their prelunch drinks, when a strange silence swept over the room. Heads turned toward the street where an open door allowed the strong sunlight to pour in. A man stood in the entrance, his fists on his hips, his face in shadow. He raised his hand and pointed his finger. "Hobbes!" he said. It was Vern Dooley.

Hobbes got up and walked slowly toward Dooley. No one else in the café moved, as if Dooley's finger were holding them transfixed. Dooley dropped his hand. "I'm armed, Hobbes," he said in a voice that only Hobbes heard.

"Yes," Hobbes said.

"Walk out in front of me." Hobbes began to move toward the door.

"No!" Victoria's voice echoed through the silent café.

Hobbes turned. Commander Peevey put his arm around Victoria. "It's all right," Hobbes said. "Wait here for me."

Outside, Dooley paused on the steps of the café. A hundred yards away heat waves danced above the white sand of the beach. "That way," Dooley said.

The beach was deserted in the noon heat. They walked north, away from the town, for ten minutes. Dooley stopped. "This should do it," he said. He sat heavily on a low dune that the night's high tide had thrown along the beach. He looked at his watch and lit a cigarette. His face was pale and deeply lined. "We've got two hours," Dooley said. "You may as well relax."

Hobbes sat on the beach, opposite Dooley. "Two hours for what?"

"The plane back to the States."

"There are laws here," Hobbes said. "Extradition—"

Dooley grinned wolfishly. "I've got all the law I need in my holster."

"I'm not going," Hobbes said.

Dooley leaned toward him. "You can go sitting up or in a casket. But you're going."

"Why?"

Dooley lit another cigarette from the stub of the first. His fingers were yellowed by nicotine. "For three days I've been watching that house, waiting for a chance." His voice quavered from exhaustion. The rims of his eyes were chafed red. "You ran out on me, Hobbes. You fucked me up. Now you're going back and put all that right again."

Hobbes examined Dooley's coat, trying to find the bulge of the gun.

"I knew you were trouble the first time I laid eyes on you," Dooley said. "I should've listened to my instincts."

Hobbes looked at Dooley's thick neck, wondering how much strength his exhaustion had left him. "Those were the real names on that microdot."

"Halladay was a little too eager," Dooley said. His eyes took on a distant, strange cast. "A little too greedy for my chair. They took your body to the morgue at Langley. No relatives to claim you. The bastards thought it would be a nice finishing touch if I made the official identification. I went down to the morgue with a fingerprint kit. They rolled the body out. Something–I don't know what–made me pry an eye up."

Hobbes sighed. "No contacts."

Dooley seemed not to hear him. "Then I knew. The whole thing fell together. I got one of your fingerprint cards out of the files and substituted it for the identification form for the body. They put out their dummied-up story of how you got killed in the line of duty. When we get back, you're going to tell them the kind of traitor you've been. You're going to tell them about the little plot you and Gordon cooked up to get the payoff and double-cross me. Then they're going to give me my job back because they'll know if they don't, I'll blow their story."

"I didn't have any plot with Gordon. He was holding Peevey and Victoria—"

"By the time we get back to the States," Dooley said, "you are going to know every detail of what you have to tell them. You are going to memorize it."

"Why would I do that?" Hobbes asked, but he already knew the answer.

"Because if you don't I will come back here and put a bullet in Peevey's head, and then I'll put a bullet in lover girl's head, and then someday, after you've had time to think all that over, and suffer with it, I'll put one in your head." Dooley's head came erect with a jerk. He stared over Hobbes' shoulder and then got quickly to his feet, the gun now in his hand.

Hobbes turned. Peevey and Victoria stood twenty yards away. "Put the gun away, Vern," Peevey said, "and we'll talk this over."

Hobbes looked up at Dooley. He had the gun trained on Peevey, and a mad light danced in his eyes. Hobbes came up under the gun and caught Dooley's wrist in his hands. He levered Dooley's arm up. The gun fired. Dooley hit him on the ear with his fist. Hobbes' vision blurred. He felt Dooley's wrist slipping from his grasp. Then Peevey was beside him, his big hand enclosing the gun. Peevey smashed his other fist into Dooley's face. Dooley's grip broke from the gun. He fell on his back in the sand.

Hobbes was on his knees, his head sagging. He raised

239

his eyes to look at Dooley, sprawled on the sand. Dooley's mouth was smeared with blood. Hobbes staggered to his feet. Victoria put an arm around him. Peevey was pointing the gun at Dooley.

Dooley wiped his mouth with his hand. He struggled up onto his knees. Peevey and Hobbes exchanged a look. Peevey silently handed the gun to Hobbes. Dooley's eyes were locked on Hobbes' face. Hobbes looked into those mad eyes for a long moment, and then he turned and threw the gun into the sea.

With a strangled cry, Dooley launched himself at Hobbes. He caught Hobbes' knees and toppled him over. Dooley's hands clawed at Hobbes' throat. Peevey kicked Dooley in the temple. With a sigh Dooley rolled off Hobbes and lay on his back, his stunned eyes staring at the cerulean sky.

Peevey put his hands under Hobbes' shoulders and lifted him to his feet. He searched Hobbes' face for a moment and then said, "Have you got the money?" Hobbes nodded. "Lets get out of here," Peevey said.

They began to walk along the beach toward the town and the airport. Victoria slipped her hand into Hobbes' hand. He put his arm around her. The cry came when they had gone a hundred yards. It was a feral, inhuman cry. "*Hahhh*—obbes!"

They stopped and turned. Dooley stood on the beach, his fists raised to the skies, his burning eyes fixed on Hobbes.

Then he collapsed, sobbing, onto the sand, and the three turned and continued on their way.